The House with
the Narrow

Katherine Highland

ISBN: 9798650851127

Profits from the sale of this book in printed and electronic
form go to Autism Initiatives (Scotland) to support their
one stop shop for autistic adults in the Scottish Highlands.

Prologue

December 1981

Time. At once too much of it to bear watching the little girl struggle and too little of it to get her own young mind around how she could reach out to help her without making things worse.

The heavy ticking of the grandfather clock measured out the passing seconds from the hallway, increasingly resonant as the room fell silent. The weight of her empathy swelled the sound with intensity too great for a single sense, giving it colour. It was a dark pewter grey, building like a far-out stormy sea with each tick.

The little girl's knife and fork tapped a fragile silver on the plate; sparked and fragmented into the relentlessly thickening atmosphere. Everyone else had finished eating and was looking at her; the visiting six-year-old cousin overwhelmed and overawed in a world where everything was too big, too small, too loud or too subtle.

Watching from so close by, not practiced yet in how best to intervene, she was powerless in the moment.

With that urgency, her focus and purpose began.

1

April 2019

Spring came tentatively to Inverbrudock; the last damp tendrils of a grey, soggy winter were finally beginning to slacken their grip on the weathered stone of the imposing seafront houses. The North Sea churned a spectrum of monochrome; the lethal slide of mercury, the tumbling crash of steel and slate behind the woman with distinctive dark blue hair as she walked up the short path to the deep maroon coloured door. Fresh paint skimmed the edge of the ornate brass knocker which seemed almost to look down in contempt upon the innocuous white button to the side; the modern doorbell which had taken its role.

She had only seen Christmases here; the family, in general, was not close. It was a relationship of formalities; weddings, funerals, special birthdays and anniversaries at other places where at least nobody had the home advantage. Christmas dinner was the exception. As her generation grew, cousins had connected on social media. She was looking forward to seeing Sharon. In all her memories of those family Christmas meals, the safe, benevolent presence of her oldest cousin brought a still softness to the raw echoing jangle of inner chaos.

The thought came strangely to her that this house knew all four seasons; that its stone walls had been warmed by rare long days of heat under cornflower blue skies and lit salmon pink by the rising sun in the spring and autumn clarity of East Coast light. It was difficult to imagine the house ever having cast off the heavy mantle of midwinter.

Pressing the bell to announce her arrival, at forty-three she felt her adult confidence ebb with the waves dragging themselves back out to sea as memories washed in.

2

December 1982

Red velvet bows and shiny matching baubles adorned the Christmas tree, catching the glow and sparkle of a hundred tiny fairy lights. Seven-year-old Bethany Sawyer watched in fascination as the patterns and reflections changed with the flashing sequence of the bulbs. The spread of warm white over the surface of the baubles and the intermittent ghost of illumination around the bows held her attention even more than the dance of the lights themselves. Dressed in her best clothes, the collar of her dress clawing at her neck as she moved, the little girl cherished the final moments of the good part of Christmas; she stood right on the boundary where it ended and the scary part began. The joy of the end of term; the warm cosy bustle of indoor preparations, helping with baking, decorating and wrapping in the early dusk at three in the afternoon; the cinnamon and clove spiced anticipation of Christmas Eve; the thrill of gifts and smiles and newness on Christmas morning were all past. Looming ahead, beginning with the switching off of the tree lights, was leaving the safety of home and getting into the car to go for Christmas dinner with Aunt Carole and her family in the house with the narrow forks.

"Come on, Bethany; get your coat on, please"; her mother briskly walked through the room switching off the magic as she cast an impatient eye over her daughter. "Don't look so miserable, and you will remember to thank Aunt Carole and Uncle Hector for your presents, won't you? They're kind enough to send them so you have them on Christmas morning even though we'll be seeing them later. After all, you forgot to thank Mrs Macgregor for the colouring book she sent you for your birthday when we saw her in town and I'd told you so many times to remember that next time we saw her. You're not a baby any more; it's time you stopped daydreaming all the time and kept your wits about you."

Raw, familiar frustration burned as Bethany absorbed the stream of criticism. Her birthday had been in September; they had met their former neighbour by chance around a month later, during the October half term. She had meant to remember; she truly had, but right before they encountered Mrs Macgregor she had seen a toddler fall and graze his hands. Her sadness at the little boy's cries of fright and pain, a sadness which she had learned to do her best to hide behind facial expressions which she had to somehow regulate without being constantly in front of a mirror, had indeed distracted her enough to make her forget despite having been warned multiple times not to. She was sad about not having thanked Mrs Macgregor; she liked the kindly old lady and had enjoyed colouring the vibrant pictures. She also knew she could not afford such mistakes; they would, she knew fine well, be stored up and she would be told off for them repeatedly. So why did she keep on making them? She had tried to find the words to explain that forgetting things wasn't like stealing, lying or hitting someone; it wasn't a bad thing she would do deliberately and knowingly. She didn't decide to forget something; it simply wasn't in her head when she needed, and so wanted, it to be. Neither did she decide to bump into things, trip over things, drop, spill or knock things over. It simply kept happening. The responses from adults would be sarcastic ("It's never your fault, is it?"; "Oh, it leapt out in front of you, did it?"), or harshly dismissive ("You need to try harder"; "Stop making excuses"), or comparing her to others ("Funny how so and so never has these problems / didn't keep doing stupid things like that at your age"). Adults were the ones in charge; they always knew best. Oh well, she supposed she must be a bad girl then, even though she enjoyed being good, responded so well when people

3

were pleased with her and being nice to her in between her mistakes and didn't feel the malice that logic told her a bad girl should feel.

Three reminders later, her face carefully composed, Bethany followed her parents into the tiled hallway of the house with the narrow forks. She had called it that once to her mother; another lesson learned. Her struggle to eat with the impractically slender cutlery without making a mess or taking too long had not gone unnoticed; she had embarrassed her parents and she had better not be so hapless again this Christmas. She was seven years old for Heaven's sake. In fact, Emma who was nearly six would probably be trusted with the fine cutlery this year. There was no good reason for Bethany finding those forks so hard to manage. She was so silly for Having A Thing about it. (What did "having a thing" even mean? She was pulled up for it so often, yet it seemed such a senseless expression. A thing was an object incapable of containing any feelings; she got told off for that too, treating things as though they were alive and could think or feel. Yet her feelings were described as "having a thing". Why were the rules so inconsistent?)

Accepting Aunt Carole and Uncle Hector's slightly overbearing hugs, she thanked them enthusiastically for her lovely new pyjamas and word puzzles as the grandfather clock ticked away the seconds and minutes until dinner. Through the arched doorway, she glimpsed the dining table; polished, pristine, challenging her with its vast array of formal settings. Sharon was helping Emma with the finishing touches; Uncle Dave was strapping Joseph into his high chair while Aunt Sandra helped Aunt Carole in the kitchen. Joseph's older brother George was showing a rather bored Louise his latest noisy toy. Sharon's face lit up with a huge smile as she caught sight of Bethany in the doorway and she rushed to greet her cousin.

"Bethany! Hey, it's so good to see you! Come on, hang your coat up and then you'll have to see George's robot. It

4

makes a noise that's supposed to be a machine gun, but he thinks it sounds like a fart and he's absolutely loving showing it off!"

Feeling relaxed at family gatherings was impossible but Bethany glimpsed it now and again when she was around her oldest cousin. Sharon was chatty and efficient, but she spoke to Bethany as an equal; she was one of the few people who could guide and encourage her without making her feel flustered and inadequate. Glad of an audience more interested than Louise, George's peals of laughter over his farting robot set Bethany giggling too and little Joseph joined in, clapping and jiggling up and down in his high chair.

"Don't get Joseph overexcited when he's about to eat, Bethany. How thoughtless of you!"

She had let her guard down and misjudged again; the happy moment passed. Her mother, Sharon and Aunt Sandra were bringing through the first of the serving dishes; chastened and wary, Bethany quietly took her place at the table.

The festive food made Bethany's stomach contract with the combination of rich smell and taste and her nervous tension. Trying to remember not to look worried, she willed her hands to stop trembling. Her eyes followed the scrolled diamond pattern of the wallpaper, counting the shapes up to the ceiling. Her napkin was in place; she checked and checked again, feeling the stitching around its raised edge. She counted the diamond shapes up the wall again, in time with the steady ticking of the clock. Looking again at the food she had to get through with those impossibly narrow forks, she contemplated which things she could eat together to bind the more difficult vegetables from rolling or dropping off the fork without appearing to be playing with her food. Oh, this was most definitely not a game. She glanced across at Emma, eating with the narrow cutlery for the first time as Bethany had done the previous year. She had a small portion, but she was eating as easily as everyone else. One solitary pea had rolled onto the tablecloth and there was a smudge of gravy at the side of her mouth, but she seemed completely at ease; she fit into the festive scene. She looked right. Bethany tried to discreetly mirror her movements; three peas rolled into her napkin, one dropping to the floor. OK, so that didn't work. She returned to focusing on her own plate.

"Bethany! Uncle Hector asked you a question!"

Caught out again. She hadn't heard him; there were at least two other conversations going on besides the turmoil in her mind.

"S-sorry".

Oh great, now she was stammering. Her parents' frowning faces warned of the "Disappointed In You" speech to come when they got her home.

"Ha, she's not in! Wee Bethany away with the fairies again! I asked what else Santa brought you?"

Her cheeks burning with humiliation and rage, the last thing Bethany wanted to think about was what presents she had been given. Surely, she was not worthy of presents, whether they were from 'Santa' or from people! Yet she had to answer, and answer quickly, before her parents could be embarrassed even further by her slowness. She tried to picture the array of gifts under the tree at home; tried to recall how she felt as she opened the various packages, hoping it would break through her frozen mind and help her to sort out the information she needed from the frantic white noise.

"I… er, I got some clothes and some puzzle books…"

"Oh, Bethany, we need to do something about this confidence of yours! The puzzle books were from us, remember? What did you get from other people?"

All other conversations had died away; everyone was looking at her and she hadn't even eaten a quarter of her meal yet. The ticking clock now so strident she could feel the sound; the pattern of the wallpaper hurting her eyes.

"A flat piano!"

The word "keyboard" had eluded her.

"Oh, and a new bag and pencil purse for school."

As had the term "pencil case".

"And the puzzle books weren't all from you; I got some from Mrs Macgregor too!"

"BETHANY! How rude! Oh Hector, Carole, I am so sorry!"

"That's OK, Sheila; I'm sure she'll learn to grow out of this awkwardness eventually."

"I – I only meant…"

She meant she had received more than one gift of puzzle books, from different people, so her first answer had not been as stupid as Uncle Hector suggested. She had been relieved when she remembered the ones he would not have known about, as a result blurting it out and sounding impertinent. She had not intended to sound rude, but she often did, especially under stress. Her seven-year-old mind grasped for the words to explain but it was all beyond her. The conversation had moved on; her embarrassed parents were looking away, disgusted with her and finding pleasure in the innocent brightness of two-year-old Joseph who was watching a foil decoration gently spinning in the draught from the kitchen. As his wide eyes followed the rippling colours, Bethany looked too. The soothing flow of the colours and the knowledge that everyone's attention had shifted away from her calmed her enough to resume eating; losing a few vegetables off that treacherous fork no longer seemed quite so terrible compared to how rude she knew she had been to her uncle. Resigning herself to the storm to come, she smiled gratefully at her baby cousin who had restored a sense of the wonder of Christmas. No-one saw her smile.

3

April 2019

Pushing her hair out of her eyes as the sea breeze picked up, Bethany wished that she could go back in time and explain to everyone, including that bewildered seven-year-old she had been. Such clarification had not been possible before she gained her adult lucidity and knowledge. She wished she could spare that child the snatches of hushed, half heard conversation among the adults as they prepared to leave, about "painfully shy", "not right" and "going to have real problems as she gets older"; the frosty atmosphere in the car going home; the abrupt tidying away of presents which she would be allowed to look at again when she had taken some time to think about how to speak politely to people. As if she didn't think about it to the point of severe anxiety already. For how long, she had begged to know? As long as her parents felt it necessary, her mother had asserted; no, they would not say how long. Oh, and she had probably gotten George into trouble too by encouraging him to make his baby brother laugh himself silly right before a meal. Knowing Sandra and Dave now, her adult self knew this was unlikely; this was no help to the seven-year-old who lay awake torturing herself with the image of her loved little cousin crying for his favourite toys.

The door swung open. Sharon was there alone today; no overwhelming family gathering. Uncle Hector had died three years earlier and Aunt Carole was selling up to move to a smaller house. Louise was a busy single mother living in Edinburgh; Emma was pursuing a career in fashion in London. Bethany had travelled from Perth to help her oldest cousin with the packing up of the house contents. Sharon's warm smile had never changed; with her blonde hair tied back in a ponytail and wearing a casual denim shirt over dark grey leggings, she exuded easy-going welcome and safety as she hugged her.

"Beth! Thank you so much for coming over. Come on in; we've still got a kettle at least. Was the train busy?"

"Not too bad, and it was one of the refurbs! I took some photos for Brandon and Charlene; they still haven't been on one yet!"

ScotRail was in the process of introducing refurbished InterCity 125 trains on their express routes serving the seven Scottish cities, to the excitement of the train loving brother and sister who lived next door to Aunt Carole. Both Sharon and Bethany also enjoyed train travel, thus coming to share their enthusiasm and often correcting people who presumed that Brandon was the authentic railway enthusiast out of the two of them. Although his autism meant that he needed Charlene with him for support, she loved trains like he did and got fed up at times with people assuming she couldn't possibly be into them herself. They had stayed on in the house after their parents took an opportunity to join friends in a business venture in America, keeping Brandon in familiar surroundings and had become close to Sharon who now had a rented flat nearby and would still come to feed their cat while they were away on trips. Bethany had yet to meet them in person but had connected with them on social media via Sharon.

"Yes, I saw them online. Brandon has liked them all. Charlene's so happy he's got people to interact with on there and know it's safe."

Bethany followed Sharon through the dining room, glancing at the table, vast and heavy with memories and now bare beneath the bland anonymity of dust sheets.

4

December 1985

Bethany needed to get away, even if she could only snatch a few minutes. Exhausted and overwhelmed, she put her usual House with the Narrow Forks Escape Plan into action; watching for someone to go to the bathroom so that she could then ask to be similarly excused and have to go up to the guest ensuite on the second floor. Two Christmases ago, she had discovered there was a second bathroom up there when she had needed to go and someone was already in the main bathroom. Sharon had taken her upstairs and upstairs again; this alone had fascinated her. She had never been to a second floor in anyone's house. If she hadn't already come to think of it as the house with the narrow forks, it would have become the house with the extra upstairs. The special kind of quiet which characterised a space not routinely occupied had felt like an additional Christmas gift. It was as though it had been waiting for her; a sanctuary, however fleeting, from the noise and anxiety of these demanding Christmas dinner visits. There were two bedrooms on the second floor; a third had been converted to an ensuite shower and toilet off the larger one which was kept for visitors. Sharon now had the other second floor bedroom so that Louise and Emma could have the privacy of their own room each as they got older; the second floor nevertheless kept that tranquil apple-white stillness, far from the bustle of the rest of the house. Since that first pleasant surprise, Bethany would deliberately wait until she knew someone was already in the main bathroom before asking to be excused. It had become a treasured secret; a chance to both extend and enhance a break from the need to try so hard in front of the whole extended family.

"Aunt Carole, please may I go to the bathroom?"

"Of course dear, but your Uncle Hector's in the main one I think; you remember where the guest bathroom is, don't you? On the second floor?"

"Yes, I do. Thank you."

Appearing suitably nonchalant while the joy of an essential, secret coping ritual bubbled within took all of Bethany's self control as she walked through the hallway and up the wide staircase to the first floor. At the foot of the second staircase, she gave herself permission to stop and wriggle her toes in the way which always soothed away her tension; nobody around to notice the movement in her good black patent leather shoes and ask questions which embarrassed her. She did not know at ten years old how to explain about what she would come to know as stimming, her autism diagnosis itself was still years in the future. Light and free, she became fleet footed as she climbed to that welcoming space of the extra upstairs.

The small bottle of liquid soap on the washbasin released a scent which fit perfectly with that reviving, airy freedom of the second floor; fresh lime with a sparkle of patchouli on the senses. Bethany rubbed her hands over and over in the glide of soap and warm water. The lingering aroma on her hands would comfort her as she faced the return downstairs. Reluctantly turning off the tap, she glanced at her reflection in the mirrored cabinet doors. The distraction of an unguarded moment caught her out in an awkward misjudgement of space and her hand glanced off the almost empty soap bottle, which hit the edge of the basin before clattering hollowly onto the unforgiving tiles.

Not again.

Not another clumsy accident to make people laugh at her or get angry.

The buzz of patchouli and lime faded as the metallic prickle of "In Trouble" adrenalin took over. Bethany turned harshly away from her traitorous reflection, not wanting to look at herself any more. The detached, shiny black nozzle glared the inescapable reality from the stark white floor as Bethany's heart began to pound. She sat down on the closed toilet and tried to think through her panic. The bottle was almost empty. If she quickly washed the dregs of soap down the plughole, nobody would realise it had been broken before it went in the small waste bin. They would merely see a bottle someone had binned because it was finished. When Sharon first showed her up to this bathroom, she had said something about getting another toilet roll from the guest bedroom. So supplies for the ensuite were kept in there. She could maybe even get another bottle of soap and put it in place. Being helpful would make her feel slightly better after her clumsiness and she would much rather tell Aunt Carole that she had put out the spare bottle of soap than admit to having knocked one over and broken it. Finding the replacement would even give her an extra few minutes away up here on her own as well as earning her a bit of gratitude. Bethany's spirits began to rise again as she quickly picked up the bottle, unscrewed the top and poured out the remaining dribble of soap before putting it in the bin, still hiding the broken nozzle as best she could. Rinsing her hands one more time – she could not risk them being slippery with any leftover soap and making her drop things – Bethany reached for the pale aqua hand towel with the embroidered seashells and thankfully patted her hands dry.

The voices took her by surprise. She had been so focused on her own dilemma she had not heard the footsteps on the stairs. Now she heard her middle cousin, Louise. Not kind and gentle like Sharon and right in between them in age, Louise had an impatient urgency about her which always made Bethany become flustered and feel particularly out of her depth. The next mistake always felt imminent when Louise was looking.

"Are you sure it's in your room, Shaz?"

Sharon's voice, closer by; a shield more solid than the locked bathroom door:

"I think so. It must be. I didn't take it back downstairs because I wasn't finished looking at it, but I really want to get it for George today because it's ideal for what he's doing at school and we won't see any of the cousins again until the next family gathering."

"Makes sense. Mind you, as far as Bethany's concerned that's probably a good thing."

Shock and apprehension flooded Bethany as she froze behind the bathroom door. She must not listen in; she should do something to alert her cousins. This was wrong on a way bigger scale than breaking the soap bottle. This was serious. She must do something! Even if she could clear her throat. Her muscles refused to cooperate; the window of time in which to show her presence quickly enough to be doing the right thing closed, silently as a thought, irrevocably as a prison door.

Sharon's voice again; a lifeline Bethany could no longer grasp:

"Come on Lou, why do you have to be so nasty? What's Beth ever done to you?"

"Nothing! It's just… well, she's so… I don't know, she's weird. I don't mean like bad or anything. She's so slow. It seems to take her forever to do things and catch on to things. She's only, what, a couple of years younger than me but you'd think she was even younger than Em. She's not right in the head."

"See, I can't imagine thinking of her that way. I know she seems to have problems sometimes. She seems so scared of the world. But her seeming slower than the rest of us in some ways doesn't mean she's any less of a person. It's more like the rest of the world is too fast for her and it stops her from being who she really is. It's hard to explain, but I can't see her as wrong the way you do. I wish we had

13

more time with her so we could get to know her and maybe help her."

"Speak for yourself, Shaz! If I ever have a kid and it turns out like her, I'll give it away."

"Louise! That's a bloody horrible thing to say! How can you be so cruel? What exactly is your problem? Don't ever say anything like that to me about our cousin or any child again, OK?"

"All right, Saint Sharon! Jeez! Can you just find the geography magazine and we can get back to the party?"

"Fine, but I can't believe you said that, Lou. Bethany doesn't deserve it and neither does any kid you have who might not be perfect enough for you!"

Sharon's bedroom door slammed shut, jarring Bethany's already heightened senses painfully as her chest ached with so many feelings. The sadness and shame of Louise's words; the longing to take the help and friendship Sharon so clearly wanted to give but for which she had no idea how to ask. The helpless frustration of seeing the kind of connection for which she so longed, there for the taking yet not knowing how to reach out to take it. On top of all that, the fear of being caught and the knowledge that she had done something badly wrong by eavesdropping on the conversation. She had now been up here for a lot longer than she could get away with. Still sat on the lid of the toilet, Bethany could see every fine detail of the plush pedestal mat at her feet. Aqua coloured to match the towel, its thick pile subtly and unevenly flattened by recent footsteps. Moments come and gone, everyday, unremarkable. Quick, purposeful visits to this room with no fearful consequences. Fierce envy of those carefree footsteps battered at Bethany's fragile composure and she suddenly realised that her hands hurt from gripping the edge of the toilet lid; her lungs ached from holding her breath. Tentatively, she breathed out. She could hear Sharon in her bedroom, looking for the magazine she wanted to give to their

14

younger cousin. Louise, she presumed, had gone away back downstairs. A fresh wave of anxiety crashed over Bethany as it occurred to her that she would have to face Louise again, however and whenever she managed to get herself out of this room. Deep sadness followed as she realised that it would never feel the same again coming up here to the extra upstairs.

The soap. She still needed to replace the dropped soap bottle. Forcing herself to stand up, Bethany crept silently to the door which led into the guest bedroom. Stealthily, achingly slowly with fumbling hands, she slid the bolt and opened the door. Looking around, trying so hard to concentrate, the shapes and colours of everyday bedroom furniture refused to make sense to her in the urgency of the moment. Cream lace and heather pink slept in poised elegance awaiting the kind of guests who would not knock things over, break things or listen to conversations they shouldn't because they were too gormless to react in time. A door in the farthest wall, at right angles to the wall which held the doors to the ensuite and the landing, captured Bethany's attention. This had to be the cupboard where she would find the soap. Here was a plan; here was something she could do to feel useful again. The little-used carpet drank in her footfall, mercifully absorbing the sound she was not ready right then to imprint on a world which she had now discovered to be even more aware of her failings than she had already thought. She reached the door; turned the handle and pulled.

Nothing.

Nothing happened.

The door did not budge.

In that instant, Bethany's mind refused to accept what was presenting itself to her. She could not afford for the cupboard to be locked. How could she possibly explain having been up here for so long now? Frantically she looked around for a key. There was nothing in sight; not even when she looked a second and third time, remembering how often she looked for things and was incredulously told that they were right in front of her. A search of every drawer in the empty chest of drawers, pristine of course for the nameless parade of comfortable guests, proved equally fruitless.

She returned to the cupboard door, trying it again as if somehow it would be different this time. Frustrated, she pulled and then reflexively pushed.

The door opened inwards.

When was there ever space in a bedroom cupboard for the door to open inwards? Yet another illogical puzzle in this world which seemed to keep on catching her out.

Bethany's eyes adjusted once again. The space into which she was looking was not a cupboard. An empty floor, a blank wall in front of her with a light switch, and to the left…

She was looking at more stairs. Steep, bare wooden stairs. Leading up.

The soap; the length of time she had been away from the others; even the conversation she had overheard were forgotten in the light of this thrilling discovery. The house with the narrow forks had not only an extra upstairs, but an attic on top of that; a proper attic, with proper stairs!

Bethany had to see. The need to explore overruled any qualms she might have had about snooping around a house where she usually felt so intimidated. Somehow, up here in these highest reaches where she had no permission to be, she felt safer than she ever had in this house before.

The stairs smelled of old wood and a concentrated form of the undisturbed peace Bethany associated with the second floor. At the top, another two doors branched off to the left and right. The one on the right was locked with an unyielding certainty which left no room for doubt. With the kind of unexpected clarity of memory which can come to sharpened senses on full alert, Bethany remembered her

16

mother telling her that the house had originally been one big property which was divided into two many years earlier; she realised that this door must at one point have led into what was now a separate dwelling next door. The door to the left opened easily to reveal an attic room, dimly lit by a skylight in the sloping roof. A rug which must once have been a deep green covered the central quarter or so of the floorspace; boxes were stacked in the shadows under the unlit side of the roof. An old-fashioned coat and hat stand fit neatly under the apex of the ceiling against the far wall; a painting in a dusty gilded frame rested against some of the boxes at the side nearest the door. In the half light, Bethany could dimly make out that it appeared to be of a child in a winter coat against some sort of rural background. She thought about taking a closer look, then remembered where and when she was. Panic began to set in again as she hurried back to the stairs. Despite her renewed awareness of the need to get back to where she was supposed to be, Bethany could not resist a compulsion to take one last look around the silent, waiting attic with whatever secrets it held, before closing the door.

It had to be her overwrought mind playing tricks. After all, weren't people constantly telling her that various things were all in her head? Usually this filled Bethany with nameless emotions all too big for her but this time her logical mind would have had to agree, not that she would entertain the thought of telling anybody. It was no more than a fleeting instant, but she was certain in that fraction of time that she saw a girl. She was standing near the far wall, wearing a deep red fitted coat with big black buttons. Her pale blonde hair seemed to draw what little light was available from the skylight and the glow from the bare bulb over the staircase. Her eyes mirrored the wariness and alertness which so often unintentionally showed on Bethany's own face earning her endless exhortations to not look so worried, by everyone from family to complete

17

strangers. Whenever she tried to recall that elusive sliver of a moment, Bethany could never place the colour of the eyes of this child she imagined she saw. The pupils were dark and dilated with some kind of reaching urgency. It wasn't fear; more like a frantic need to connect.

Of course, she had imagined it. All she thought she saw in that moment, she knew had to be a projection of her own self absorption. That must be it. The shadows, the half-seen painting and the hat stand, together with her own state of mind made her think and want to believe that she had seen something which wasn't there. It was because she wanted to be special. She was always being told that too; it made no sense, like so many other things. How could she explain she often felt the exact opposite of special; worthless in fact and was trying hard to make up for it. Bethany's defences were well enough developed by that December day in the attic to know that she must treat this as something she had invented in her mind, keep it strictly to herself and file it away with all of her deliberate imaginings, such as the storybook school she attended in her daydreams where she understood and fit in effortlessly with the clear and unchanging system of values.

She left the attic, closed the door and hurried back downstairs to the family.

"There you are, Bethany! Wherever did you get to?"

"I'm sorry, Aunt Carole! I used the last of the soap in the guest bathroom and I wanted to put the next one ready, but I couldn't find it! I remembered Sharon said the supplies were in the spare room and I looked everywhere…"

"Oh, Bethany! Silly girl! You do overthink things. There's a sliding door in the base of the divan bed in there; the spares for the ensuite are in a box in the under bed storage, but you should have come and told me we needed a new bottle of soap in there instead of disappearing like that. It's not very sociable, you know, dear!"

Bethany shrank once again under the weight of her aunt's sugared criticism, the knowing look she glimpsed in the brief glance she dared cast at Louise and the despairing look she caught on her mother's face. The rest of the visit passed in a blur of apprehension, wondering what would be said to her once she was alone with her parents in the car going home. If only she could understand how she managed to be so wrong without doing anything deliberately bad. Why did she have to pretend and imitate other people in order to try to be good; why wasn't she naturally good? If only she knew how to get it right.

5

April 2019

Sharon turned, noticing Bethany pausing to look at the covered table.

"Those Christmas dinners here were tough for you when you were wee, weren't they?"

"Yes. It feels ungracious to say it, but…"

"No, it's not ungracious. Looking back, I wish I'd done more to try and stop Dad from teasing you the way he did, especially at the table in front of everybody. It's how he was; he didn't mean any harm, but even when I was still in my teens, I could see it was making things worse."

"Oh, I know he was a harmless tease, but I used to end up panicking and blurting things out that sounded rude and I got into trouble so often. I couldn't explain why I was coming across as rude or what I really meant. I was constantly getting things wrong here because I was so nervous, so everyone expected me to and that made it even more likely. Do you remember the year George had that robot with the machine gun noise that sounded like a fart?"

"Oh yes, that robot! That was so funny. George had such an infectious laugh. He still does."

"Well, that Christmas Day he was showing it to me and laughing, so I was in fits too and Joseph was in his high chair at the table; he started giggling and drumming his hands on the tray, then your Mum came in and told me off for getting him overexcited when he was about to eat. As usual, I simply hadn't thought. Then later at home, when I was getting a row because I'd been rude at the table again, my mum threw in as an afterthought that George probably got into trouble because of me encouraging him to get Joseph overexcited."

"What? From Sandra and Dave? Seriously?"

"Oh, I know now that he probably didn't, but I couldn't sleep that night for imagining him upset!"

"Beth, that's awful! Aunt Sheila – your Mum should have known better than that. She would know perfectly well that Sandra and Dave would never punish a five-year-old on Christmas Day for making his baby brother giggle! She must have realised how you'd take that to heart. I'm sorry but that was plain cruel."

"I have to keep reminding myself that none of us knew about me being autistic back then and even if we had, it might not have made a lot of difference when I was so young. I didn't have the words to explain myself properly, but people aren't mind readers; they couldn't be expected to understand without me telling them what was going on with me. I had no point of reference to what was different. I have no experience of my brain every having been wired any other way. I didn't understand these things until I read articles or talked with other autistic people. Things like not realising that I have a reduced ability to filter out distractions; everything I can see, hear, smell and so on. I've never known what it's like to have that filter and I never will. So it looked as though I was slow, or not listening, or not concentrating, or daydreaming. Oh God, daydreaming! If I had a pound for every time I was accused of that! To be fair, sometimes I was. I liked my own world; I was safe there. But I wasn't always daydreaming! Sometimes I was actually trying so hard to catch up! But how could a child with no means of knowing how their brain was 'supposed' to be working explain all that?"

"They couldn't. You couldn't, but that's the whole point of the work you're putting in now, raising understanding and acceptance every chance you get through being open and honest about your own experiences. People are learning a lot from that."

"I hope so. I genuinely want to use them to make things better for other people. I worry that people will think I'm being a 'woe is me' victim when I talk about things that were difficult. I'm not saying I was treated badly. I wasn't. I had a good childhood. I was looked after, fed and clothed, encouraged to be interested in things and enjoy things. I was praised when I did well. I have lots of happy memories. The problem was, I kept on messing up and that exasperated people because they knew I should be doing better. I didn't have the means to justify to myself why I was getting things wrong, never mind defend myself to other people; it came across as excuses, but it wasn't anybody's fault. It would be more accurately described as one big communication breakdown."

"Well, up to a point, that is true. You were a child, though, so there must be more responsibility on the adults around you. Yes, as you rightly say, people cannot be expected to read minds, but they can be expected to listen when children are communicating. Every time you struggled with something, you were communicating. People get so bogged down in milestones and what some arbitrary system dictates should be happening by a certain age and comparing a child to their peers or to what older children were like when they were at the same stage. They take into account everything except for the actual child they're judging. There's not enough of putting aside everybody else and getting to know that child. What works for them; what their natural pace is; everything they're trying to tell us."

"Yes. Oh, that resonates with me! I wish I'd had a bit more scope to explain things. I used to feel as though I were on one of those game shows, you know, where there's a strict time limit then the buzzer goes and you're scored on what you managed to string together in that short time under pressure. Except that the buzzer I was racing against was the inevitable judgements; being told I was making excuses, or that I irrationally Had A Thing about some task or place or lesson or whatever. Once it was put into one of those categories, the subject was closed; there was no point in trying to explain any more. Those categories were all the knowledge the adults around us had at that time; they weren't being deliberately cruel. I know my parents genuinely were doing the best they could in terms of bringing me up and preparing me for adulthood; they saw me not trying or being difficult and they corrected that accordingly so that I would grow up to do better and have more opportunities to fulfil my potential. They were doing the right job, but with the wrong specifications. Sometimes I did behave badly or thoughtlessly; all children do. It wasn't all autism. And sometimes they did say things they shouldn't have, like when Mum said that about me getting George into trouble. Parents make mistakes. I used to feel that they wanted things to be my fault because they were fed up with me; I can see now that they were well aware I was incompatible with the 'normal' world in some unknown way and it made them terrified for me, so because I was the one aspect they could control, they wanted to be able to find things they could get me to change. Hence all the criticism."

"It's pretty amazing that you can look at it like that, you know. You should give yourself more credit, Beth. Come on, let's get a cup of tea and make a start on packing up these boxes."

The cousins worked in companionable quiet for a while, Sharon directing Bethany to what she wanted boxed up.

"Hey, Shaz, I found some of your school reports!"

"Right enough! Let's see. Oh wow, Mr Duncan! Now, he was one for teasing people. He used to insist on calling me Rose. I had no idea why. It didn't particularly bother me; I assumed I reminded him of somebody called that, or that maybe he thought it was my middle name even though that's actually Ruth. I corrected him the first couple of times then gave up. I did ask him once, 'Why do you call me Rose? It's nothing like Sharon!', but he just smiled and looked away. I was a bit irritated at the time, but it wasn't a big deal; he wasn't important to me. It wasn't until I was looking in a gardening magazine for some ideas for Mother's Day, the year my mum had a phase of replanting the flower beds when I was sixteen, that I realised: of course. Rose of Sharon! It was a complete lightbulb moment. You know, the funny thing was, although I never let on to him that I'd worked out why he called me Rose, soon after that he stopped doing it. I guess there was some change in my response that he picked up on and the joke had run its course."

"See, that would have driven me up the wall, a teacher or anybody calling me something that had nothing to do with my name and not telling me why. I'm not saying I'd have felt 'picked on' by it, but not knowing why would have done my head in! I'd have played into his hands keeping on at him to tell me why he called me that. I've so often asked somebody why they said something, what they meant, or why they found something funny, and they've laughed and looked away like you described. Or shaken their heads, said 'Oh, Bethany'; sometimes even patted me like a dog. There's already loads going on that I don't pick up on; these unwritten rules and non-verbal cues. Like how Mr Duncan instinctively knew that the power dynamics of him calling you another name and you not knowing why had shifted. I wish I could read people!"

"It makes me furious that people do that to you, or to anybody! Why do they think that's OK? Especially touching someone in such a condescending way! As for reading people, you do, more than you realise. It's mainly yourself you can't read."

"You think? Then how come a few years ago at Elaine Macdonald's leaving do at work, I hung around chatting to Crevan and Dana after everyone else had realised they'd clicked and wanted to sneak away together? Why did Stacey have to pointedly steer me away and give me a lecture about taking a hint? I can still see her; head tilted to one side, smugly singing my name at me. 'Beth-a-neeeeee!' I've gone over that conversation – not with her, with Crevan and Dana – in my head so many times and even now with hindsight I cannot find any hints, in anything they said or did. Even my hindsight isn't twenty-twenty!"

"Beth! Oh honey, I wish I could take these memories away from you, but nobody can. Maybe there were no hints. Maybe Crevan and Dana were looking forward to spending some time on their own but still enjoying having a conversation with you! Or maybe you did miss some subtle cue; I wish you could allow yourself a bit of a margin for error. It's making you so unhappy and every mistake, real or imagined, seems to stick with you for such a long time whereas the good things you do melt away. Look, here's one example. The Christmas when you were, you would have been twelve, I think. You were the one who thought to suggest moving the china Westie to the back of the cabinet before Sandra and Dave and the boys got here, because it was the image of their wee Peggy who had been put to sleep a few weeks before. When I went to do it, you helped me rearrange the shelf so that there wasn't a big obvious gap. Five people lived in this house and saw that cabinet every day; you hadn't been here since the Christmas before, yet not one of us thought of that. You did, and you made a difference. You did a good thing, and Uncle Dave did notice. He mentioned it on their way out to my mum, who I am sorry to say took the credit, but I actually told Dave and Sandra when I went to see them one time shortly after you got your autism diagnosis. They weren't even slightly surprised when I told them it was you who had the foresight to get me to move that ornament. Sandra had been on edge anyway in case she got upset in front of the whole

25

family; she was devastated about that dog. You really helped her."

"I never knew that! Oh, I'd been reminded several times throughout December not to mention Peggy of course. I was terrified of slipping up; of being so desperate to think of something to say that I would end up leading myself to that subject because it was in my mind. For once, I didn't."

"Of course you didn't! You need to stop being so surprised when you get things right or don't get things wrong! It would help with how other people relate to you, I'm sure. I'm not having a go; these patterns are extremely hard to break, but you're directing people to hold low expectations of you. Which leads to more of these pre-emptive strikes; the 'don't mention's and 'now remember's and 'be careful's that frustrate you and feed into your low self esteem. It's a vicious circle."

"They frustrate me because I never get the chance to prove that I wouldn't have made the mistake. The credit goes straight to the other person. It changes it from 'Bethany was clued up enough not to mention her aunt's dog who had died' to 'Smart third party was on the ball enough to stop useless Bethany from making a faux pas'. OK, that's using an example from when I was a child and children do need more guidance, but I'm in my forties now and it still happens! It's like psychological mugging; ambushing me and stealing my opportunities for establishing credibility. Take our last staff meeting at work for example. We'd been discussing a possible event which right now is confidential to us, as in the Perth branch. So Anita came out with 'Bethany, don't say anything to Rhona yet'. In front of everybody, because she knows I'm friendly with a colleague at the Inverness branch. Stacey's brother works in one of the Glasgow branches, but nothing was said to her! How am I ever supposed to move on if I never get the chance to show that I have developed skills and judgement? It's not even a matter of stereotyping because

I've been getting it all my life since before my diagnosis and I still get it from people who don't know I'm autistic. You're one of the precious few people who has ever let me get the words out as far as this to explain why it hurts the way it does."

"See, this is the cycle you're trapped in, Beth. It's not enough for you to know that you wouldn't have made the mistake. Or if there's even a chance that you might have, it's another thing to beat yourself up about. So you focus on your demons and that's what you project. I do understand why, though. I understand how the process works. I'm not dismissing your experiences at all. It was unfair of Anita to say that to you in front of other people; she may have already said something to Stacey when you weren't around for all you know, but she should have kept it to a general reminder to everybody not to discuss whatever it was with anyone in other branches. She didn't need to single anybody out to get the point across. We need to figure out how to get you out of this rut and projecting more positively, then you'll find it will happen a lot less and when it does, it won't matter to you so strongly. And it will always happen, because people do say things as a precaution when they're focused not on the person they're warning or what they think of them but on the consequences if something goes wrong. If something gets said out of turn or missed, or an accident happens or whatever potential problem they're trying to avoid. We need to get your reserves of self belief built up so that they can withstand these pitfalls with room to spare instead of you constantly running on empty. It's making you sabotage yourself by projecting this preoccupation with everybody, including yourself, seeing nothing but impairment in you."

"I see what you're saying; I do get called out for focusing on the negative all the time, but it stands out so much more!"

27

"I wonder if that's because the negative things, the mistakes, glitches or whatever you want to call them, have often been a product of something you and the people around you couldn't understand. When you did good things and were praised, you knew you were doing good; you understood exactly what you were being praised for and why. You knew how that worked because you are a good person! So there was no mystery there; nothing to have to try to work out. You were in control of it; you were making a conscious, clear headed choice. When things were going wrong, though, often you didn't know how or why or what to do to change it. Or explain it, as we were talking about before. To have a powerful fear response like that and be essentially dealing with it on your own from such a young age is bound to have an effect on any child; of course that's going to stick in your mind more than the good interactions and responses where you knew exactly what was what! Anyone who pulls you up for focusing on the negative, if they're doing it in a critical way as opposed to a constructive way, would do well to think about that!"

"Gosh! You know, I'd never thought of it like that before but that makes absolute sense! That's the last of the papers from the drawer; are we going to seal this box up now?"

"Yes, I think we should, so we can mark it clearly to make sure it goes straight to the new house and not into storage. Mum will want to go through it. Meanwhile, I think we should start another box in the kitchen and have another cup of tea."

"That definitely sounds like a plan!"

It was Bethany's turn to make the tea. As Sharon checked her phone which was charging in the sitting room, she refilled the kettle, meticulously wiping drops of water off the side and washed out their mugs as it boiled. The slightly dented round tin with the faded scene of red and white sailed yachts was a far cry from the formality of the Christmas dinner table. Savouring the way the tannic bloom of the tea blended with the tang of airtight metal to her nose as she eased off the lid, she dropped a bag from the tin into each cup: poppies on Sharon's; sunflowers, Bethany's favourite flower, on the one her cousin had thoughtfully set aside for her visit. Waiting for the tea to brew, she glanced into the half filled box on the breakfast bar. There they were, prongs glinting from the end of a loose wrapping of kitchen roll; those dreaded dinner forks. She had not had to eat with one of those for over thirty years. Wondering if they would feel any different in her fully grown hands, she carefully unwrapped the kitchen roll and lifted out one of the forks.

"Hey Beth, thanks for doing that; I'm gasping for a cup of... oh, you found the dinner cutlery! I bet that takes you back!"

"You could say that. I used to dread having to try to balance my vegetables on these forks and keep up with everybody."

"Oh, wow! Now that you say it, I can imagine how difficult that must have been for you especially when you were first given them!"

"I took so long the first time! I was only six. Everybody else finished way before me. By the next Christmas, I... oh, this is a bit embarrassing, you're going to think this is so silly. I had come to call this house, 'the house with the narrow forks'. I still think of it as that now!"

"Really? It affected you that badly? Oh hon, I am so sorry there's such a lot we didn't know. I knew you were always on edge about my dad teasing you, but I never even thought about that cutlery!"

"Honestly, Uncle Hector wasn't that bad; it wasn't his teasing so much as the fact I often didn't realise when someone had spoken to me if there were other conversations going on and I was trying to focus on getting the food into my mouth without making a mess. I couldn't process quickly enough, and I would make myself sound

29

either completely slow or abrupt and rude! I've always had problems figuring out when people are joking too, particularly if their humour is quite dry and deadpan. I do understand sarcasm; I'm not ashamed to say I enjoy using it when the situation merits it, but even now as an adult I still get caught out by people's humour sometimes. Then comes the condescending look, the shake of the head and the clarifying in that speaking to the simple wee soul tone: 'Oh, Bethany, It Was A Joke!'. Yes, I have to say, the narrow forks on top of all that when I was a kid made up quite a minefield."

"Beth, that's so sad to hear; it could have been so easily fixed if we'd known. Did Aunt Sheila and Uncle Gerry know?"

"Not sure about Dad, but Mum did. I said something once about were we going to the house with the narrow forks again at Christmas and I got a row for being silly and Having A Thing about something I should be able to manage perfectly well at my age. Remember autism wasn't even remotely on the radar in those days in this family!"

"That's true. If I'm honest my mum would more than likely have said the same thing if they'd asked if you could use the everyday cutlery, and I don't suppose you'd have wanted to stand out either."

"Definitely not. Especially when Emma was using them too by the next year and managing fine!"

"Emma had smaller portions, which was right for her age. Of course she lived here, and I guess Mum would have been averse to the idea of giving a guest a smaller portion. We could so easily have waited a few years before setting that cutlery for any of the younger children in the family. Nobody would have been any worse off for that. I'm truly so sorry you weren't heard when you needed to be."

Sharon got up and walked around the breakfast bar, picking up one of the forks.

"Good Lord, it must have been a nightmare trying to eat with these when you were so young, not in your own house, coping with your anxiety and all the noise and sensory overload of Christmas... Obviously I don't in any way see you as clumsy but knowing what I do now from reading about autism and how it can affect manual dexterity, it's a wonder you were able to manage your Christmas dinner here at all!"

"Well, I'm glad to be able to say I did, because your Mum always did cook such a delicious feast. I massively enjoyed the actual food and seeing all my cousins and finding out what gifts we'd all had. It was so kind of your Mum and Dad to send my presents – I presume George and Joseph's too – before Christmas even though we'd be here on the day, so that we'd have them to open on Christmas morning. I would hate to give any of you the idea that my memories were all bad."

"It means a lot that you should say that. Right, you know what I think we should do? We need to give you some closure on this. Let's finish these cups of tea then we'll go and get some chips from Vinnie's chippy; paper wrapping, sachets of sauce and all, and eat them with those blasted forks!"

"That sounds so good! I love it! Yes, we certainly need to do that."

The sea wind had calmed into the blunt glare of what Bethany called greylight; that harsh full daylight with no visible sun, spread through a uniformly off-white sky and harder on the eyes than it had any logical right to be. It so often abundantly followed the putting forward of the clocks, starting off British Summer Time with an unwelcome encroachment into streetlamp-spangled dusk. Vinnie's seafront chip shop, a few minutes' walk along towards the pier, held extra appeal with its promise of warm parcels of mouth-wateringly fat chips and the appetising aroma of golden batter. Sharon linked her arm through her

31

cousin's as they walked along the promenade, the ever-present seagulls wheeling and calling overhead. Bethany watched as one alighted on the weathered blue railings.

"I wonder if the seagulls are all asking each other, 'How are you? What are you up to for the rest of the day? Do you have any holidays planned for this year?'"

"Seagull small talk! Interesting concept."

"Yeah. Theirs is maybe more along the lines of 'Have you stolen anyone's chips today?' 'No, but I shat on a line of washing.' 'What are you up to this weekend?' 'Stealing people's chips!'"

"Haha, quite possibly. One actually did that last time Louise was staying here with Lucy. The washing part, that is, not the chips. Louise was so annoyed with Lucy because she'd asked her to bring the washing in and she got distracted by something on her phone and forgot. I don't think she was distracted in a good way either."

"I take it she's still being bullied?"

"I gather so. She's not friends with any of them on social media but there's a group to do with the school. Oh, they don't post her name or anything they could be reported for; they're too clever for that. I gather Mrs Maynard, who taught them all for Modern Studies, was particularly unsympathetic and had no interest in learning about autism and how she could make things more accessible to Lucy or tackle the bullying. Of course they're sly and sneaky but Lucy retaliates every so often; she's thirteen, too young to be coping with all this plus teenage hormones kicking in, and she invariably gets caught, so she's seen as the difficult one causing trouble. Add to that the complete lack of discretion when she struggles, and the bullies have it made. Apparently, Mrs Maynard made some throwaway comment one day when Lucy was taking a bit longer to process something she'd been asked; she said something about her being like a limp lettuce leaf. So that's been the theme for months. Suddenly that nasty wee clique is so interested in salad whenever Lucy's around, or saying things like 'Lettuce pray', 'Lettuce see what happens', 'Leaf it alone'; you can imagine the gist. So I think there'd been something posted on the group page, supposedly about healthy eating but with a comment Lucy would know was aimed at her. That vicious Roseanne one, the worst of the gang, squirted salad cream on her once. Of course Louise was angry because she had to wash Lucy's uniform again which had been clean on that morning and she'd put herself in the position to be a target for all this by not paying attention and not fitting in."

"Oh, poor Lucy! I can't bear to think of her going through that. Picked on at school and blamed at home! I wish all teachers knew better than to say things like that in front of bullies who will use it! That was so irresponsible of Mrs Maynard. Doesn't she get how bullies will latch on to a comment like that? She shouldn't be calling Lucy names anyway, especially knowing she's autistic! It doesn't have to take an actual insult word to cause harm when there are bullies hungry for things to use! And as for Louise, I know she's your sister, but her attitude is so wrong."

"Oh, I know. You don't have to excuse yourself to me for saying that. I could shake her at times for the pressure she puts on Lucy."

"Still, I suppose at least she didn't give her up like she told you she would if she had a child with problems!"

The bitter words were out before Bethany could stop them. Sharon stopped walking; her blue eyes in the moment unreadable to her cousin but every other one of her non-verbal cues as clear as the plainest of words. Her intake of breath; the draining of the colour from her face; a stillness which seemed to reach even to the wisps of hair around her ears as realisation hit.

"You heard that? Oh Beth!"

"Sharon, I'm so sorry; I shouldn't have brought that up. This is about Lucy, not me. But yes, I was in the second floor bathroom and you'd come up to your room to look for a magazine for George. I honestly didn't mean to listen. I tried to cough to let you know I was up there, but I froze instead; my throat wouldn't work!"

"That geography magazine! Yes, he'd quite recently started school, but he was so interested in something the teacher had mentioned. I remember now that you weren't in the room with everybody else when I went upstairs with Louise! Oh Bethany, I was so angry with her for saying what she did. If I'd had the slightest idea that you'd actually heard it…"

"I should have made you aware I was up there as soon as she first mentioned my name. She'd said something about it being a good thing I wasn't at your house often. You were talking about there not being many opportunities to give the magazine to George because the cousins were only here now and again. I… the thing is, I was already in a panic because I'd knocked the soap off the ledge with my clumsy hands and the nozzle had broken. It was nearly empty as it happened, so I'd rinsed out the dregs and was about to go into the guest room to look for the replacement as I knew that's where the stuff for the ensuite was kept. I was just thinking I'd managed to get out of having to confess to your Mum that I'd broken something and was going to look useful instead by replacing something that had run out, when I heard your voices. I guess I'd used up my processing credits for the time being so I kind of shut down instead."

"Oh God, Beth. Please don't feel bad about having listened; I completely understand how that happened. I wish… You were up there for quite a while too. Oh no, were you upset?"

"No! I mean, not hiding away up there crying or anything. Things like that tended to make me go cold inside and sort of file them away. The truth is, once I'd gone past the point where I could have let you know I was there, I was trying not to get caught! So I waited and then tiptoed into the guest room to look for that soap. Which of course I couldn't find. However, I might as well confess now that I've admitted to eavesdropping, I did have a bit of a mini-adventure. I opened what I thought was a cupboard in that spare room and, well, I ended up having a bit of a snoop around your attic. That's why I was away for so long; I couldn't discover stairs I hadn't known about before and not go up to have a look."

"No way! That's a pretty cool story. I remember how fascinated you were that you could go upstairs and then upstairs again in our house. Of course I don't blame you for having a look! Not that there was much up there."

"No, I didn't look in any boxes or anything. I vaguely noticed the hat and coat stand and there was an old painting up there. I was too stressed out and excited at the same time to take anything in. In fact my imagination got the better of me for a second; this is going to sound fanciful, but I thought I saw a girl standing in front of me. It was no more than an instant. She had fair hair and dark eyes with an intense expression, almost as if she wanted to communicate, and she was wearing an old-fashioned red fitted coat with dark buttons. Your house isn't haunted by any chance, is it?"

"Not that I know of! I don't know whether that would add to the value or reduce it! Mind you, I have an open mind about that sort of thing, and it is an old house; who knows? Come to think of it, I've occasionally caught a snatch of a female voice singing when the house has been quiet. I always assumed it was Charlene; she sings around the house quite a bit."

"It probably was. I'm open minded about ghosts too, but I'm sure that day it was my imagination. I think there was a child in that painting up there; the coat stand would have made me think of old-fashioned clothes. If it was a ghost and if we encountered her now, Goodness knows what she'd make of my blue hair!"

"I love it; it certainly suits you. Brandon's been calling it GNER blue ever since he first saw it in one of your photos."

"Yeah, I remember the London trains being that colour. They were so smart. Although I genuinely love the colour, it's a kind of defence. I'm always being told I stand out in ways I don't necessarily want to; for instance, apparently, I have a distinctive walk. Which makes me feel as if I'm going around like some sort of novelty act when I'm simply putting one foot in front of the other and it shouldn't be anything remarkable. It's not that people are saying anything negative; it's uncomfortable to hear because it's not something I'm choosing, any more than I choose to bump table edges and door frames and catch my feet on thresholds. That's because proprioception gets messed up and my brain gives me the wrong information about distance and how much space I've got between myself and the things around me. I hate it and I don't want it to be my 'signature'. So if the first unusual thing people register when they see me is that I've got dark blue hair, at least that is something positive that I'm choosing and controlling."

"I wish you didn't have to feel so hyperalert; it must be exhausting, but good on you for finding ways to deal with it that work well for you. I've learned things from you that could help Lucy. I even feel I understand Louise a bit better for what you said about Aunt Sheila – your Mum – being hard on you because it was the only way she could feel in control of influencing a future that made her scared for you. There's quite possibly an element of that in Louise. Here we are; let's get those chips."

Vinnie's pride in cleanliness showed in every gleaming white tile, every inch of the spotless countertop and the newly washed rustle of his immaculate apron as he waved a greeting to Sharon.

"Hey, favourite customer!"

"All right, Vinnie, how's it going? This is my cousin Bethany, the one who lives in Perth. She's come to give me a hand packing up the house."

"Hi, Vinnie! Sharon's been telling me how good these chips are; I'm looking forward to them."

"It's a pleasure to meet you, Bethany. Love the hair."

"Thanks! It's my natural colour, of course."

Vinnie and Sharon laughed good-naturedly.

"How's your Mum doing, Shaz?"

"She's good; mixed feelings of course, but she'll be better off in a smaller place. I'll still be around to see Charlene and Brandon of course, and I'm not that far away so I'll still be coming in for my fish suppers."

"I should hope so! Are those two still on their travels right now?"

"Yes, they're doing the Far North line. They'll be back in a couple of days. I'll be popping in later to feed the cat."

The doorbell buzzed as more customers walked in.

"So what can I do for you this time?"

"Two large portions of chips and a couple of sachets each of ketchup, please. Only salt on my chips. Beth?"

"Yes, just salt for me too please."

The chips rustled on the scoop as Vinnie efficiently heaped them onto the paper, wrapping them into firmly secured packages as Sharon handed over the cash.

"Could you pop the change into the lifeboat donation box, please, Vinnie?"

"Thank you very much. Here's a wee bit of fish for Charlene's cat as well."

"Oh, cheers mate! See you soon."

There was always something special about walking along a seafront holding hot parcels of chips. Bethany guarded them closely from the marauding seagulls as they headed back to the house, feeling as though she were on holiday. There was a certain poignancy to the house having finally become such a relaxed and friendly place as she was visiting it for probably the last time.

"It will be so strange for you coming back here to Charlene and Brandon's but having no access to the house you grew up in, seeing new people in there. How are you feeling about it?"

"You're right; it will be strange, but I'll get used to it. Even if we get to know the new owners when it's sold, I don't think I'd want to go in."

"No, neither would I. Anyway, you've got such a lovely flat judging by your photos. I'm lucky with mine too. Home is where your stuff is, that's for certain."

Sharon got out her keys as they walked up to the front door; the sky was beginning to darken and the breeze take on the keener edge of night air. Something stirred and a bush rustled at the side of the house.

"Mrrrrrrriaow!"

The big marmalade tabby cat came running, already purring in anticipation of the fish treat he could smell. He rubbed against Bethany's ankles, vivid ginger-and-paprika stripes vibrating with purrs all the way to the twitching tip of his long tail.

"Hey, Cheminot! I thought you might appear when you smelled what your Uncle Vinnie gave us for you!"

"Is it OK to let him in?"

"Oh, yes, he'll be fine. I've put aside a chipped old plate that won't be kept when Mum moves, and I often give him a bit of fish on that when I'm here."

Sharon unlocked the door, taking the chips from Bethany and leading the way through to the kitchen. Bethany stroked the cat as he jumped up on a chair looking for his treat.

"He's so gorgeous! How long have Charlene and Brandon had him now?"

"It must be about five years now. Gosh, is it that long since their Eurostar trip? You know, Louise still insists on telling Lucy that he's Brandon's, because of his name being the French word for 'railwayman'. Don't get me wrong; Brandon loves him, but he's primarily Charlene's and she named him! 'Now Lucy, don't pester Brandon's cat.' Honestly, I have to bite my tongue sometimes. I've told Louise all about how he appeared around the doors here right after they got back from that trip; how Charlene had him checked for a microchip, did everything she could to find out if he belonged to somebody and then adopted him. She's still in touch with Flora at the cat rescue. Flora worked in France for a while and travelled a lot on TGVs, so she highly approved of his name."

"I bet! So Lucy's getting the pre-emptive strikes too then. Does she merely have to glance in Cheminot's direction to be told not to pester him?"

"Pretty much. Oh, she ran up to him a couple of times at first, but she did soon learn to wait and let him come to her."

Bethany washed her hands as Sharon set out the chips, then unwrapped the bundle of dining forks, holding two of them up as Sharon cleared a space on the varnished pine breakfast bar and pulled out the matching tall stools.

"Are we really going to do this?!"

"Of course!"

Sitting across from one another, the cousins clinked the narrow forks together like champagne flutes. Looking at each other's expressions sent them both off into fits of laughter as they dug the elegant cutlery into the glorious informality of ketchup-laden chips; the close presence of several sheets of kitchen roll on standby was the sole concession to the ceremony and rigid etiquette of olden days.

"Cheers!"

"Cheers! This is so surreal."

39

"Oh, there's nothing like Vinnie's chips. We must get together more often, Beth."

"Absolutely. It's not even as though I'm that far away. Fifty minutes on the train. I'm always tired after work and I tend to need the weekends to catch up, but it would give me such a lift to spend time like this more often."

"Me too. I've enjoyed today very much. If anyone had told me this morning that I'd be eating chips tonight with my Mum's good dinner forks, I'd never have believed them!"

"Ha! If anyone had told me this morning that I'd ever eat anything again with your Mum's good dinner forks, I'd have left the country!"

"I daresay you would have and who would blame you? Oh, talking of leaving the country, if anybody has reason to be thinking of doing that at the moment it's Barry."

"Barry? What, Joseph's husband?"

"Yes, that Barry. Poor guy seriously needs to get into the habit of checking things before he sends or posts them. He was on his work email account…"

"Don't you always love it when a story about something dodgy online starts with those words?"

"Precisely. Well, he was asked to share a link for people to do some program security improvements. Cleaning up junk files to speed up the system and reduce the chances of malware and viruses, that sort of thing. So Barry prepares the post with a comment: 'Sharing throughout the company. Please open Doorways, run and wait until system purge is complete.' Except that he must have caught the T as well as the R on his keyboard at the beginning of the message. So every one of his colleagues got an email saying 'Sharting throughout the company. Please open Doorways, run and wait until system purge is complete.'"

"NO WAY! Oh, poor Barry! I feel for him, but that's hilarious! The more you think about it…"

"I know! Oh, I wish I had a screenshot!"

All the released tension and emotion of the day tipped both women into hysterical laughter. Waving their forks with the last few chips eaten in between fresh bouts of mirth, they didn't even hear the front door opening.

"What on Earth?!"

Carole Penhaligon stood in the kitchen doorway, crisply efficient in a steel grey trouser suit with her blonde hair pinned in a stylish up-do. Her neatly pencilled eyebrows raised as she took in the spectacle of her eldest daughter and niece sitting at the breakfast bar, surrounded by boxes, chip papers spread out in front of them and a contented Cheminot purring on a pile of dust sheets.

"Are those the dinner forks? Why are you using those to eat chips?"

"Mum! Oh, we were packing up the cutlery when we decided to take a break, so these were the nearest to hand. We were talking about Christmas dinner as we were packing them, and it made us realise we were hungry!"

Bethany wistfully admired Sharon's quick thinking as she hurriedly swallowed her food, praying she would manage not to choke as her mouth went dry.

"Hi, Aunt Carole! Er, yes, we were talking about Christmas dinner. I... I don't think I ever properly thanked you for cooking all those lovely dinners when we were children. I didn't realise how much hard work it must be. I was always kind of preoccupied with, well, I was a bit overawed here..."

"I know, dear. You were such a scared little rabbit in the headlights. You were never confident using the dinner cutlery, were you. I did wonder if we started you with it a bit too young. Now that we know that, well..."

Carole tailed off; her turn to be uncomfortable as the tricky subject of autism loomed large.

"It's OK, you can say it! That I'm autistic. It's not offensive to call it what it is. In fact it's important to talk about it as something there's no need to be afraid of."

"Yes, Quite right, dear. I suppose we did ask too much of you giving you those to eat with when you were, about how old?"

"Six. The first time, I was six."

"Gosh, such a precise little memory. Yes, we wouldn't have expected Lucy to manage with such formal cutlery at that age. We know what's wrong with her and that does make such a difference."

Bethany flinched at "wrong with her"; Sharon cast a warning glance at her mother.

"Aunt Carole, Lucy's brain and my brain are just differently wired from non-autistic people's. We find some things difficult because of it and some things take us longer, but we're not less or broken. I'm lucky because I'm old enough and have sufficient good support to get that now, but Lucy's still so young. We should be building her self esteem as a family, not saying there's something wrong with her. I don't want to have a go, especially when it's such a sad time for you selling the house. I just hate to think of Lucy being made to feel bad about herself."

"Well! Quiet, shy little Bethany has certainly come on, hasn't she!"

"MUM! That's so rude! Beth's right here in the room, she's been working her socks off helping me all day and she's got a completely valid point about Lucy!"

Whatever barbed comment Carole may have been about to make about Sharon's lifelong fierce protectiveness of her cousin was for once filtered out; a driven and highly conventional but reasonable woman, something in her niece's bold, measured words had hit home.

"You're right, Sharon; that was impolite of me. Bethany, I apologise, and I appreciate your thoughtfulness. I suppose we fear our children and grandchildren having... disadvantages, because we know the world is not a kind and fair place, so we can come over as critical and that adds to the problem. You've turned out well for not having had the

42

kind of self knowledge that's available to Lucy. Autism wasn't known about in girls when you were a child."

"I know, and there are still so many women and girls who can't get a diagnosis or even get a professional to take them seriously. Especially non-white women. Yet it's always been around. There've been autistic people as long as there've been people. Even in the Bible when they thought some people had demons. There would have been medical explanations like epilepsy, schizophrenia and autism. So many people have lived and died never knowing the facts about why they had the difficulties they did. We can't help them, but we can honour them now by making things better for people like Lucy and all the autistic children still to be born."

"I've never thought of it that way, but that does make sense. You know, I wonder if that was what was wrong… Sorry. If that was the case, with wee Harriet."

"Who?"

Carole's immaculately shadowed eyes were looking far away into a past which she was seeing in a new light. Instinctively giving her space to adjust, Sharon began tidying up the chip papers as Bethany stroked Cheminot, whose sleepy purring ramped up several notches as he stretched towards her hand with a silent miaow.

"She was a wee girl who lived in the other half of this house, where Charlene and Brandon are now, about… gosh, it must be around a hundred years ago now. It was soon after the house was divided into the two separate properties. She was the youngest of a big family, by a few years. When the house was divided, the connecting door in the hallway between the two attic rooms was put in; Mrs Sutherland had a terrible fear of fire and of being trapped upstairs, so the two families agreed that there could be a door there as an alternative escape route into the other property on the understanding that it was strictly for emergency use. All the children knew the rules, but wee

Harriet took to using the half of the attic that belonged to this side as her own hideaway. Your great-grandparents had a fair idea she had made herself a den up there but they never minded; they knew she would never intrude into their living space and at that time the stairs to the attic didn't go straight up from a door in one of the bedrooms. That side of the spare room used to be part of the top landing; that room was remodelled when the ensuite was put in. So they saw no harm in it. She would sing to herself, chatter away; amuse herself for hours in her own wee world. She needed her routines and her place to be on her own; she never seemed to have a lot in common with most of her siblings. They weren't cruel to her or anything, they were simply older and liked to do the usual things, running around together playing noisy games. Anyway, one day, inevitably she got caught. Oh, her father was so angry. He dragged her out of there and shouted at her that from now on the door would be locked and the key kept in the master bedroom since she couldn't be trusted and that she was forbidden even to go up to their side of the attic again."

Bethany's horrified gasp pulled Carole back to the present.

"Poor girl! How old was she?"

"She was only ten. Such a sad thing."

"How would she have coped with losing that sanctuary, that routine, so suddenly and completely?"

"Well, Bethany dear, that's the terrible thing. She never got the chance to cope with it. She was so upset, while her father was locking the key away and telling her mother to march her round here to apologise to your great-grandparents, she ran away outside and straight into the road. She was hit by the fishmonger's cart and didn't stand a chance. She froze right in front of the horse; it bolted in fright, she fell and went under the wheels."

"Oh no! That's awful!"

44

"Your great-grandmother rarely spoke of it; it devastated her. She had rushed out to see if there was anything she could do but it was obvious the poor wee soul was gone. She told your grandparents how she would never forget seeing her lying there in her wee fitted coat. She was so attached to that coat; she was hardly ever seen without it. Deep red, it was, with big black buttons. The poor child lying there lifeless. Absolutely tragic…"

Bethany's eyes widened as she looked at her equally stunned cousin. The shock was clear on Sharon's face, knowing that there was no way Harriet had ever been mentioned in front of Bethany even if Sharon could possibly have any long-buried memories of hearing about her. Nothing earthly could explain what Bethany had described having thought she saw in that fleeting moment in the attic over thirty years ago.

Carole excused herself to look for some photo albums, leaving Sharon and Bethany staring at one another as they absorbed what they had found out.

"It wasn't my imagination that day I told you about, was it? I saw her! I must have!"

"Oh, definitely. How could you have known about her coat? Even if you had been influenced by that painting up there, it didn't have anything bright red in it. I remember, it was all muted, sepia type colours."

"I was ten that Christmas too; the same age she was when she died!"

"So you were! I bet Mum's right about her probably being autistic too. I believe Harriet was reaching out to you. It makes total sense, especially after what you'd unfortunately heard that sister of mine saying. I still can't believe you've been carrying that all these years, Beth!"

"Remember though, Shaz, I heard what you said as well and I've been carrying that too, in a way more positive sense. You were years ahead of your time in terms of how we think about accessibility; what you described there was

45

the social model of disability as opposed to the medical model. You said that it wasn't a case of me being too slow for the world but the world being too fast for the way my brain works. Which makes society the place where adjustment is needed, not the people who happen to need to do things a bit differently. Or a lot differently. Autism Rights Group Highland do a lot of advocating for this sort of attitude shift; I've been following their work. It's all about advocating that the autistic brain is as valid as anyone else's brain because we are equal; that is part of our human rights. I've mentioned what you said that day to a lot of people since I was diagnosed, and people are blown away that a sixteen-year-old came out with that in 1985. I think that's a lot of the reason why Harriet connected with me. She never got the chance to get past the injustices we had as children and make something better from them. I have been given that chance, and it was what you said that started that process by reframing my autism."

"That means a lot, Bethany."

Sharon reached across to squeeze her cousin's hand.

"Do you think Harriet's at peace now?"

"I don't know, Beth. Such a shocking and violent way to go, and right after a huge upheaval to her routine and coping strategies."

"Yeah. No time to have processed it and the last thing she knew was her parents being angry with her for something that was so precious to her. Poor Harriet. I'd like to think she's aware on some level of things getting better now, bit by bit, for autistic children and for the autistic adults we get to grow up to be."

"Me too. It's pretty cool to think of her watching over you, and now Lucy, like a guardian angel."

"I've often wondered, you know, in a purely scientific sense about ghosts as electrical impulses which are left over from somebody's lifetime. Whether it's as a recording, an apparition of somebody following a former routine, or

46

unfinished business, or something powerfully resonating with the traces of the person they were. After all, nobody fully understands how our brains work; we knowingly use a mere fraction of what's there. Those electrical impulses could work in all sorts of ways. Not just telekinesis and all that dramatic stuff you see in films. It could be nudging a random play function so that a meaningful song comes on at a significant moment, or tweaking an algorithm on a social networking site so that a post or advert gets boosted or appears where and when a specific person particularly needs to see it. Or suppressed if it's cyberbullying like what's happening to Lucy. There are all sorts of ways in which a spirit could intervene in the modern world and the quirk of fate never be known for what it really was."

"That's an incredibly interesting idea. I wonder if Harriet's listening to us now; in fact, I'm sure she is. Maybe she'll give us a sign. I think if she can, she will..."

Carole was back in the kitchen doorway, a bemused look on her face.

"I found one of these on the second floor landing! How in the world did it get up there?!"

Bethany and Sharon both turned to look. The house itself seemed to hold its breath in that moment; in Carole's hand was one of the narrow forks.

It was Bethany's turn to think on her feet.

"Oh! Yes, I took one of the boxes up there as it was half full with various bits of kitchen stuff rattling around so I thought some of the guest towels would help pad it up and stop them getting scratched. One of the forks must have fallen out without me noticing; sorry about that!"

Irritation flickered briefly on Carole's face before her expression relaxed and she let out an unexpected chuckle.

"Really, Bethany, what is it with you and my dining forks?! They are quite valuable, you know. Thank you, though, for coming to help Sharon today. You've both done an excellent job."

The front door closed behind Bethany for the final time as Sharon walked with her to the station.

"You didn't actually take the box of kitchen utensils up there, did you; that was quick thinking! I had no idea what to say."

"Maybe Harriet inspired me! I never usually think of anything under pressure until it's far too late. Talk about a sign; if that wasn't one, I don't know what would be!"

"I know! Way to go, Harriet! I feel kind of proud of her."

"So do I. Mind you, as far as signs go, if it was going to be a fork in a place it shouldn't be then leaving it lying on the upper landing was relatively mild. We might find the rest of them sticking out of Mrs Maynard's tyres."

Sharon broke into loud laughter.

"Oh here, don't give Harriet ideas! Can you imagine Mum's face? 'The etiquette!'"

"Yes: 'Don't poltergeists go to finishing school any more? Surely you know it's salad forks in the front tyres and dessert forks in the rear ones?'"

"Shame Mrs Maynard doesn't drive an 18-wheeler; you could have the full formal dinner place setting then!"

Their hilarity echoed beyond the moment; beyond the glint of watery evening sun on the attic skylights where a century ago a little girl's sanctuary was abruptly lost. Quietness settled over the street where her shock and rage had passed outside of time; too intense and too soon, a multidimensional web of neural reactions seared into the fabric of eternity.

6

May 2019

Brian Calder stood back to cast an appraising eye over the smooth new plaster where there had previously been a doorway. These older houses, built before drywall had even been invented, always posed a challenge when he and his mate took on remodelling jobs in them but it was one he enjoyed. He especially enjoyed showing Hollie, their apprentice, how these old buildings had been painstakingly put together when it was even more of a craft than today with the need to construct from scratch using materials in the raw. Taking out the connecting door up here in the attic which dated back to when this house and the one next door were one big property, then building up the new unbroken wall with lath and plaster had been laborious but necessary. The same two families had lived in the adjoining properties ever since the house was first divided up; grandsons and granddaughters had raised families of their own. Now that Mrs Penhaligon had sold to a buy to let landlord, the connecting door between the attic rooms, kept up to now as an alternative fire escape route from the upper floors, had to go. Stretching his back and brushing a calloused hand through his greying hair, Brian allowed himself a moment of admiration for a job well done. Turning to pack up his tools, he noticed a floorboard sticking up at the corner. How had he not seen that before? The light up here wasn't ideal; he had often needed his torch to supplement the single bulb over the stairs and single grimy skylight in the attic room behind him, but he was surprised not to have seen this loose board before. Taking out his phone, he quickly called his mate who was loading spare wood back into the van.

"Jim! I've got a floorboard sticking up here; can't think how I haven't seen it before, but I want to take a look at it. It's near the top of the stairs so somebody could take a nasty fall. I'm going to check if it's sound enough to nail down or if it will need a new one; I can't leave it like this. If it needs a new one, we can do that tomorrow before we start downstairs."

"Righto, Brian; no bother. I've let Hollie finish for the day and she's away home, so I'll wait until you're ready."

"OK, cheers Jim. Five minutes."

Brian lifted the board, quickly satisfied that it was in good condition and all that was needed were some new nails. As he leaned over to set it back in place, he glimpsed something small and dark in the dusty space underneath. Lifting it out, he was astonished to find himself holding an old book. Bound with creased black leather, its pages brittle and yellowed, it was clearly old; possibly around a hundred years. He wondered at first if it was a Bible, but the cover was entirely plain. Very cautiously, anxious not to damage the delicate surfaces, he opened it. In neat old-fashioned handwriting, childlike in its meticulous precision, was written on the first page:

"This is the private property of Harriet Eleanor Sutherland, 1923."

It was a kid's diary. Brian felt the hairs on the back of his neck stand up at the thought of it having been hidden under that floorboard for almost a hundred years; a hiding place he had only found because he noticed so suddenly and so late in the job that the floorboard was sticking up. Taking out his torch and looking into the cavity again, he discovered a fountain pen and a long dried up pot of ink. Whoever this girl had been, she had obviously created a secret hideaway for herself up in the attic; he wondered if she had forgotten about the diary as she grew up and other more mundane concerns took over. Sutherland. Wasn't that the name of the neighbours in the other half of the property?

She must have been one of their ancestors. He would hand it over to them; it felt wrong to read any of it. Tucking the book safely into his pocket and setting the pen and ancient ink to one side, he set about securing the floorboard before tidying up and returning downstairs to the van.

"That fixed then? I was just about to phone and check on you."

"Aye, sorry Jim, I got a bit distracted. I found something up there. A wee lassie's diary. It was hidden under the loose floorboard. I didn't read any of it; didn't seem right to. I was wondering why she left it up there all this time. Her name was Sutherland, same as the neighbours so I'm thinking she was one of their family from around the time the house was divided. It's dated 1923! I think we should give it to them. I'll take it now; I don't feel right keeping it even overnight."

"No, I agree with you there. Best go and chap their door now, then we'll head off."

Brian loaded his tools into the van then picked up the pen and ink pot; it felt right to give those the same respect as the diary itself. Charlene Sutherland smiled at him as she answered the door; her red hair tied back, hands and light checked shirt dusted with flour from a baking session.

"Hey there, Brian; are you wanting to drop off the keys to next door now? It's fine if you want to keep them until you've finished the main job."

"Actually, it's not the keys. I found something when I was working up on the top floor and I think it might be to do with your family. I think you should have a look at it."

He showed the diary to her.

"Oh! Goodness, that looks extremely old. Please, come in for a minute; I'd better wash my hands before I touch it."

Brian gently set the fountain pen and ink pot on the kitchen table as Charlene dried her hands.

"I'll save some of these cookies for you and – it's Jim isn't it, and Hollie? – when you come back tomorrow. Now, let's see what you've got there."

She took the book, opening it with great care. She gasped when she saw the name inside, her eyes misting over.

"Oh, my Lord. It's poor wee Harriet's diary!"

Brian's heart sank at the words 'poor wee Harriet', as the most likely explanation for the diary having been abandoned in its hiding place occurred to him. He resolved there and then to call to find out when his daughter was free for a visit as soon as Jim dropped him off home in the van, even before going in to shower and change out of his overalls. Making time for playing ball games with Taylor and Madison, revelling in being Granddad suddenly seemed like the most important thing in the world he could possibly do.

"You said you found this up in our attic?"

"Well, the other side actually; what was Mrs Penhaligon's attic. There was a floorboard sticking up and I wanted to secure it properly with it being near the top of the stairs. I lifted it to check it was sound underneath and that's where I found it. So, she was what, a great-aunt?"

"Great-great-aunt. She died young, in an accident with a horse and cart. In fact, this diary is from the year she died. Thank you so much for finding it and bringing it to us, Brian."

"That's OK, and I'm sorry the wee lassie met such a tragic end. Even though it was so long ago, it's horrible to think of. You take care now, and we'll see you tomorrow. Regards to your brother too. The job we're doing tomorrow is downstairs and will be a bit noisy; will he manage OK?"

"Sure, I'll remind him, and I'll have those cookies ready for you. I really appreciate you having let him know what to expect. Take care, Brian."

The timer buzzed on the oven; Charlene set the diary safely on the bookshelf in the living room before lifting out

52

her batch of cookies. Vanilla and pecan aromas surfed the wave of hot air from the open door as she slipped her hands into the padded softness of the Black Watch tartan oven gloves, retrieved the baking sheet with its golden bounty and slid the gently rounded biscuits onto a cooling rack. Closing the door, she set the baking sheet aside to allow it to cool enough to wipe clean; checking that Cheminot was not around to take an interest in the fruits of her labours, she poured herself a glass of wine and sat down in her favourite dark chocolate coloured leather armchair to examine the diary.

Brandon was occupied with their model railway layout, which took up most of the bigger of the two bedrooms on the second floor; he had been up there since she called up to tell him about an email she received, an update on the expected release of the ScotRail Inter7City model. As she so often did, Charlene silently gave thanks that she and Brandon were able to enjoy their comfortable life and interests in this big, familiar house. Well aware of their fortune and privilege compared to so many, she never begrudged juggling her home-based proofreading work and the extra housework with two of them in a place this size. Space and quietness were so essential to Brandon's wellbeing, ever since she learned more about Harriet including her possible autism, she had wondered how the little girl had coped as the youngest of eight children. Bethany's visit to help Sharon clear the house next door had been a revelation; Charlene and Brandon had been away but after they got back, Sharon had come over with a bottle of wine and told her an astonishing tale. Bethany turned out to have seen, many years earlier, what all indications suggested had been an apparition of Harriet in their attic where she used to hole up as a child before her untimely death. Carole Penhaligon had known more about the exact circumstances of Harriet's fatal accident than Charlene or Brandon had ever been told; Carole's grandparents, though obviously distressed by it, had not had the deep grief specific to the Sutherlands' circumstances. To lose a child by her running outside into the road as a direct result of their anger and punishment, for a transgression which when put in perspective by the loss of her young life seemed like nothing at all, was simply unimaginable. No wonder they could never bring themselves to tell subsequent generations of the family anything more than the bare fact, harsh enough in itself, that Harriet died in a road accident at the age of ten.

Taking a sip of Pinot Grigio, Charlene set the glass on one of several train themed coasters on the mahogany coffee table, safely out of range; living with a cat tended to teach people not to take anything for granted when it came to the risk of anything being knocked onto something valuable or fragile. Cheminot had been kept inside for most of the day so that he did not end up locked in next door when the builders were working; he must be still sleeping in a patch of sunlight somewhere, possibly his favourite spot on the padded seat in the big bay window on the first floor landing. She would know about it when he woke up as his focus would be on being fed; listening out for the soft thud of his paws on the stairs, Charlene opened the diary.

Harriet's handwriting carried a sense of a well behaved, people pleasing child down the years. Her name, the date and the touchingly innocent, earnest declaration of privacy communicated her conscientious practices of the childhood skills so valued a hundred years ago in neatly formed letters. Her penmanship conveyed an aura of enduring patience; a voice overshadowed in its day even before the untimely silence of a life blotted out, finally getting its long-deserved chance to be heard.

7

1923

Saturday, August 25th

Today is my tenth birthday! I am supposed to feel all grown up with my age into double figures, but I feel no different. Why would I? I am, after all, merely a day older than yesterday. Though I do feel like a real lady using this beautiful fountain pen. My sisters and brothers have been so kind buying me this book to write in and a proper fountain pen and ink. Mother said that it will encourage me to be a dreamer and spend too much time on my own! How could she be so unkind to Amelia, she was so happy that I loved my gift! She looked sad when Mother said that. I am sure this present was her idea. She knows I enjoy writing so; lots more than embroidery. Oh, it is so tiresome to get the thread through those tiny needles! My hands do not want to do as they ought. I look at Martha and Barbara's samplers and they are worked so prettily with their fine colours. I would so love to be able to stitch like they do. Perhaps when I am older like them. What I would really like to be able to do is go fishing like my brothers. I could sit by a still loch or a rushing river for hours. Boys get to do such carefree things. Now I must put this away as Father will be home soon and I must be at the table on time for my birthday tea. After all, I am a big girl now.

Wednesday, August 29th

I have decided I am not going to write in my book every single day. I want it to last for years and years. I do hope that nobody asks to see it or what I write in it. Oh, what a horrid thought, having to show it to Mother and Father! Tis well that they are so busy with the excitement of Alexander being soon to marry and both Martha and Barbara engaged. Amelia says that they will soon be expecting her to think about finding a husband and in a few more years it will be my turn. I hope I get to live in a house where there is always somewhere peaceful to go. It is so frantic here. It makes my head tired. I do so love coming up here to my secret room! I would be in such dreadful trouble if Father found out, because in truth this is part of Mr and Mrs Fraser's house, not our house. We are only allowed to go through the door in the attic if there is a fire and we cannot get downstairs in our own house! Our attic is peaceful too, but this feels as though it is all mine. I can think and sing and write; all of the things that make me feel quiet and rested inside.

Sunday, September 2nd

I am so happy that it is September once more! Tis my favourite month of all, I fancy. The air is fresh after the exhausting heat of summer and there will soon be crunchy leaves to walk on. It will be dark earlier and I will be able to watch the moonlight on the sea before I have to go to sleep. The moon throws silver on the water and when the waves are crashing, the bits of silver are scattered further apart as though the moon knows people out in boats and ships will be frightened and need more light, so it wants to make sure everybody gets their share. I said a special prayer of thanks in church today. Not out loud but God would still have heard it. So many people are wringing their hands over the summer having passed, I know I should not say to them that I welcome the autumn because they do not like it and it makes them sad and cross when I show my excitement. I am sure God would not mind me being happy about the new season when He created them all.

Thursday, September 6th

I did some extra practice on the piano today. I love to play when I am feeling quiet inside and do not falter. Mother cannot understand why I can play well one day and then be all thumbs the next. On the days when I cannot make it flow, she thinks I am being wilful. It makes me so sad as I try so hard and it confounds me when it simply does not work. Some mornings in the winter, when the frost has set overnight, the latch on our gate sticks fast. All of the working parts are still there, but it takes such strength to move them. Sometimes my whole mind feels like that; stuck fast and however hard I scrunch up my forehead and try to make my thoughts move so that I know what to do next, nothing will happen. It frightens me and it makes me feel as though I want to hit something, though I know that is terribly wicked. I wish I knew why it happens.

Monday, September 10th

I am so vexed and bothered! Mother says it will soon be too cold for my summer dresses and I will have to wear serge and wool again. It is utterly horrid! It feels as though a thousand tiny elves are scrubbing my skin with horsehair brushes. The one nice thing about winter clothes is being allowed to wear my favourite coat without anyone saying it is odd. It feels so right and safe, like a cloak protecting me from anything that could hurt me. It is finely made and does not scratch me. Stockings make my legs feel as though they are suffocating. I know that is foolish because we breathe through our mouths and noses, not our legs! I know not how else to describe it. Mother says it is not ladylike to speak about how my legs feel. I expect that writing down how they feel is a much bigger wrong. Oh, I pray they never find this book!

Friday, September 14th

Alexander is to be wed tomorrow. I will have a new sister in law! Mary is so lovely and kind. She will look most beautiful in her white dress. I will sing with all my heart in church. I so enjoy singing, more than I enjoy talking. Except to myself or one nice person. Singing has a pattern to follow but talking is like being blindfolded in a dance hall. There are so many intricacies to think about, and one cannot predict what will come next. Singing is like having that blindfold taken off and being able to see where I am going again. There will be many people at the wedding. I am glad they will be looking at Mary, not at me. I would enjoy meeting new people more if I could meet them one at a time.

Tuesday, September 18th

The wedding was beautiful, and Mary looked radiant. My second oldest brother, who it seems was climbing trees and teasing me only yesterday, is now the master of a house of his own. I will have nieces and nephews one day! That is such a joyful thought. Mary said that my singing voice was like an angel's and she showed me how to dance a foxtrot. I felt like a film star! Oh, I am so looking forward to Martha's wedding and Barbara's. It is a peculiar feeling when we are all doing something so different from usual on a Saturday and afterwards I know I will become tired but I must not let that thought trouble me.

Friday, September 21st

James and Ernest are in disgrace! They let off some firecrackers on the promenade and William was sorely perturbed by the noise. We must all be so circumspect with him since he returned from the war. Loud noises upset him dreadfully! Amelia and I were playing a game of Snakes and Ladders when it all happened and Father shouted at us to leave the board and hasten upstairs at the double. The adults do not like to speak of William's attacks in our presence. I know merely that he saw and heard horrifying things and that it has altered him. Father once said that William has something called shellshock. I asked him what it meant and he would not speak of it to me. He told me that I am too young to understand about it and that all I must know is to behave gently to William. I surmised that shellshock may be something I had too, though not so grievously as William, because sudden loud noises or too great a tumult of raised voices frighten me a lot and it feels as though something is striking the inside of my ears. When I asked Mother about it, she rounded on me and chastised me most severely! She said that it was wicked, vain and self indulgent of me to say such a thing as I have never endured the horrors William has. I asked how I could know it was such a wrong thing to ask when nobody will tell me anything about it! Mother told me that I must never speak of such things again and that I must go to my room and think about how fortunate I am not to have had to be a soldier and go away to war. Thus I understand that it cannot be shellshock I have as one must have been away to war to catch it. Perhaps I truly am merely lacking in grit and character. I fear James and Ernest will be punished most harshly for upsetting William as they are older and ought to know about shellshock and what things they must not do. Oh, I hope I never have to go far away. There are so many dangers which nobody will explain to Amelia and me because we are too young and we are girls. Perhaps if we were given the chance to understand these things, they would not seem so frightful. Amelia says she will never sail on a ship because she remembers when she was very little, before I was even born, being pulled away out of our sitting room in great haste as tragic news came of our aunt and uncle in Ireland. They were going to an exciting new life in America on a mighty new ship which everyone said was unsinkable. It struck an iceberg and foundered. Our aunt and uncle were lost with many others. It was some years before Amelia properly understood the terrible thing that happened. She still fears ships and the sea. It is a pity as we live right beside the sea and the sight and sound of it is so beautiful, I wish that Amelia could love it as I do.

Monday, September 24th

School was horrid today. Hugh was picking on Frederick again because he is slow. He did not hear Hugh speak to him so Hugh said he was stupid and glaikit and called him some other names I would not wish or dare to write down. Frederick struggles with his lessons because he cannot hear well and he also walks with a limp. I urged Hugh to leave him alone but he merely laughed. Alice was quite taken in fright! "Oh Hattie, you are so brave! Weren't you afraid that Hugh would torment you as he does Frederick?" I told her I did not believe that Hugh would strike a girl, though in truth I am not so certain of that. Yet how could I have stood by and not tried to help poor Frederick? Does he not have enough troubles as it is? It makes me heartsick that he appears so alone! He is so much smaller than Hugh and has never provoked him. Why must Hugh be so mean?

Friday, September 28th

I can now look at a list of all the wireless programmes in a magazine! The first issue came out today. I love the smell of the paper and the shushing sound as I turn the pages. It is a little bit like the whisper of the sea at night when the air carries sound more clearly and there are fewer sounds to hear so that they stand out more. I often lie awake listening to the waves long after Amelia has fallen asleep. The rain on the skylight in this attic room is another sound I adore. I get lost in time watching the raindrops weaving their way down the glass. Sometimes they seem to be drawn to one another, reaching the bottom as one. I wish I could fashion a quilt from the different skies on different days in that square of glass. It would be such a merry patchwork of blues, whites and greys sprinkled with a few reds, oranges and pinks from the sunrises we get on those rare most colourful days scattered across the year.

Wednesday, October 3rd

Well, what a day! I fear I have brought down many tribulations upon myself. My class took a nature walk to the Brudock Burn after lunch. Hugh deliberately kicked Frederick on his poorly leg and I pushed him in the burn! (Hugh, not Frederick.) He truly deserved it, being so beastly to that poor boy. Of course, Miss Tranter simply saw me push Hugh, not Hugh kicking Fred. There was such a commotion! Alice screamed, "HATTIE!" Her hands were clamped over her mouth and her eyes were like saucers! But then both she and Frederick were so brave. They took my part fully with Miss Tranter, promising her most emphatically that I was telling the truth and Hugh had kicked Frederick's bad leg. Miss Tranter said she cared not who started this disgraceful skirmish and that I am in serious trouble! I had to go to see Mr Kennedy and neither Alice nor Frederick was allowed to accompany me. Mr Kennedy was as severe as Miss Tranter. "Two wrongs do not make a right, young lady! Children who cannot keep their tempers will be kept in check; no excuses are acceptable!" I said to him, "Did not Jesus himself teach that we must help and protect those less fortunate than ourselves and did he not overturn the tables of the money lenders in a rage because they harmed the less fortunate and brought badness into what ought to be a sanctuary?" I thought steam would surely blast from Mr Kennedy's ears like an overfilled kettle! He called me an impudent little madam and went to his special cupboard. I knew what was about to happen to me but I was so angry that Hugh hurt Fred and the teachers seemed not to be troubled by that, I barely even felt the tawse on my bottom. It pains me greatly now though. I asked Mr Kennedy if Hugh would also get the tawse for kicking Frederick on his bad leg and he said it was none of my concern. Poor Alice looked so afraid for me when I returned to class. She and Frederick had both cried and pleaded with Miss Tranter not to allow me to be given the tawse. She had bid them both be quiet and said it was for Mr Kennedy to decide. I told them that the punishment had not hurt me; that Mr Kennedy had stayed his hand somewhat because I am a girl. It was an untruth, but I told it to spare them sorrow. I thought I would be severely reproved again at home but the tale had travelled ahead of me. Mrs Fraser had heard of what happened from none other than Frederick's mother, who said that I was a brave soul and my parents should be proud that I helped her son when adults failed to. It appears that Hugh has been tormenting Fred for many months and because he knows how to do it secretively, he has never before met with a challenge to his cruelty. James and Ernest shook my hands and said they were proud of my mettle! Mother was tight lipped and urged me to stay out of trouble in future but she said no more and neither shall I!

Friday, October 5th

Hugh is avoiding me at school. I fear he may yet seek revenge; he is not of a character and disposition to allow a girl to make a fool of him. Frederick follows me everywhere, which vexes Alice as he is always there when we wish to chatter together. We both helped him with some arithmetic at break today and then began talking of politics in hope that he would tire of the subject and pursue his own interests! I like having him as a friend and especially seeing him plucking up courage to speak in class because he feels revived, but I wish to talk alone with Alice sometimes! Alice says that her father thinks there will be another general election called soon. There was one last year, but Mr Baldwin wants to be extra sure because he has been doing business with many important men from other countries. Only some ladies over the age of thirty may vote whereas almost all men over twenty-one may, and it was merely a few years ago that women were first allowed to vote at all. I find that so unfair as whoever is in charge makes the rules for all of us. I do so hope that by the time I am twenty-one, I will be able to vote too!

Sunday, October 7th

My secret hideaway almost got discovered yesterday! I am writing this to remind myself to remain more alert. I was singing one of my favourite hymns, feeling so happy as it is the weekend and I have more time to be still. I had not a care in the world and I did not hear Martha come up to our attic to look in Mother's trunk for a pattern for her trousseau! I heard her call out, "Harriet? Is that you?" I stayed very still and quiet until she went downstairs; I feared she must have heard my heart thumping! Then I crept down to my bedroom and began singing the same hymn again. When Martha came out of her and Barbara's room, I called out to her, "Did you call me a little while ago? I thought I heard you but when I came out of my room, I could not see you." Of course she said she had been in the attic and thought she heard me singing, so now she thinks I was in my room the whole time and the sound travelled up the water pipes as mine and Amelia's room is next to the bathroom! I must be more wary. Martha is so excited about her wedding; I must hope that she will soon forget all about the whole episode and not grow suspicious! I do not think she would carry tales, but this is my secret and it would be so dreadful to have it discovered.

Saturday, October 13th

This has been a busy week helping Mother and practicing my music. I have had little chance to spend precious time up here. Today has been one of those days which for no particular reason felt wonderful in every way. It has been a crisp, brilliant autumn day with frost and berries and clear blue skies. I walked to the shop with Mother and Amelia and the air felt like the fizz of lemonade. Mother was in a happy mood and we got barley sugar drops as a special treat. Amelia and I played in the fallen leaves later on, kicking them at one another and laughing until it was getting dusk and we had to come in. As I write, the square of sky above me is a deep blue green like the sea on a calm day as the sun goes down. If I ever really could make a quilt of all the skies I have seen through this skylight, this would be the one I would put right in the centre. I almost feel I could swim up into the sky and float in it like water, gazing down on all the pools of light from the streetlamps and the warm glow from the windows of the houses. I so love days like these and wish I could keep them to take out and have over and over again!

8

May 2019

An insistent miaow brought Charlene back to the present as she closed the diary, its pages so poignantly blank after that final entry. Cheminot jumped into her lap, purring with that special enthusiasm cats convey when they have woken from a long sleep and are making up for lost time. Charlene hugged him, burying her face in his fur; abruptly aware that she was crying. Wiping her eyes on her sleeve, she stood on trembling legs to go through the motions of feeding the hungry cat as her mind processed the impact of everything she had read. That ordinary, happy day when everything came together; that deepening dusk almost a century ago which must have been one of the last Harriet ever saw. The sad but detached bare facts of family history; a young girl tragically dying in an accident, a name on the family tree with dates of birth and death poignantly closer together than they ought to have been, now had so much more depth and meaning. The people other than her parents who must have been devastated; all that loss no longer blurred by distance in time and lack of personal knowledge. The bullied disabled boy, Frederick, hero-worshipping the girl who had stepped up to become his champion. The school friend, Alice, so afraid of the potential harms which may befall Harriet; a punishment from the headmaster, retribution by a lout. How traumatised she must have been by news of the harm that actually came. Her sisters; two planning their weddings, the other evidently a close companion. A brother already psychologically scarred by war, who had to go through it all again less than two decades later. A sister in law – Charlene and Brandon's great-grandmother – who had taught her a new dance and compared her singing to an angel's. Harriet had been looking forward to so many things, now so heartbreakingly palpable. Attending her sisters' weddings; becoming an aunt; having a home and maybe a marriage of her own one day; even becoming eligible to vote, so aware of her potential to be active in society. She would have been such a valuable advocate and helped many people. Charlene was in no doubt whatsoever about that. There was also a lot to support the possibility of her having been autistic in even these few snippets, the sole first-hand account of Harriet's life. The sensory discomfort she described with her winter clothing; her heightened response to loud noises; her unreliable dexterity threading needles and playing the piano; her experiences of mental fatigue and brain freeze; all added to her already known enhanced need for solitude. The lifelong background awareness of relatives lost on the Titanic had gained a new dimension too, through Harriet's relating Amelia's painful memories of the family receiving the news. Charlene splashed cold water on her face, not wanting Brandon to see her upset; sitting down to finish her wine as the still purring Cheminot climbed back onto her lap, she raised her glass in salute and silently promised Harriet that her legacy would no longer be hidden away. Reaching for her iPad, she opened a chat with Sharon and Bethany.

Charlene: Hey, I have some incredible news. The builders have just finished blocking off the connecting door between the attic rooms and one of them found an old diary under the floorboards on the Penhaligon side. You won't believe whose it was. It was Harriet's. She got it for her tenth birthday and she only got to write in it for a couple of months before she died. I don't mind telling you both I've had a bit of a cry after reading it. All these years she was merely a name in our family history; a sad footnote, taken so young but no real detail except that she used to spend a lot of time on her own. Oh, there was a lot more to her than that. I'd say she was definitely autistic; she described feelings and difficulties which were identifiably sensory overload and executive functioning issues. She had such a strong sense of justice. There was a boy in her class who had a hearing problem and walked with a limp. Another boy was picking on him and Harriet pushed the bully into the Brudock Burn, then when she got into trouble for it she pointed out that Jesus advocated for protecting the vulnerable and overturned tables when people were disrespecting the sanctuary of the temple! To the headmaster, no less! OK, I suppose there is a chance she may have embellished a bit in her diary, but I do vaguely recall there was some story about her fighting a boy and getting the tawse at school a few weeks before she passed. She was taking an interest in politics and in more women getting the vote. At ten years old! I know children were often shaped to be like miniature adults back then, but she was writing with genuine excitement about how she hoped to be allowed to vote by the time she was twenty-one! That is one of the parts that sets me off, seeing her making plans for a future she never got. The little details too. Her friends, at least one anyway, called her Hattie. I never knew that anyone called her anything other than Harriet. Her best friend was called Alice. Harriet loved to sing, and my great-grandmother taught her to do the foxtrot at her wedding. She loved the sound of the sea and the colours of the sky. The way she described things reminded me of your writing style, Bethany. She dreamed of making a patchwork quilt of all the different colours and patterns of sky she watched through the skylight when she was hiding out in the attic. The last entry – I'm nearly crying again here – she described the deep blue-green twilight as the square she would put right in the middle if she could have made that quilt. She described the moonlight on the sea being scattered further when the waves were violent as if the moon knew people out at sea would be frightened and it wanted to make sure everybody got some light. All that character and insight may never have been found if Brian who was doing the plastering hadn't noticed a loose floorboard on that side! I'm blown away here!

Sharon: OMG!!! This is so exciting, and so sad. You know, as I said to Bethany, I used to hear snatches of a girl's voice singing every so often when I was upstairs and the house was quiet. I thought it must be you until I found out about Bethany having seen her. Now that you mention she loved singing, I am sure it was her spirit I heard. I am so glad she seems to have had some happy times. And pushing a bully into the burn! That is fabulous! Oh, you must be feeling so many mixed emotions after reading that! Have you told Brandon?

Charlene: Not yet. He's been busy all day; I'll be making us something to eat soon. Just fed Cheminot. He's been in all day too because I didn't want him to end up locked in your old house or stowing away in the builders' van!

Sharon: Of course, best to keep him in while the work is being done. How are the builders getting on anyway?

Charlene: They're good. A couple more days and they'll be finished for now, then they'll come back in a few weeks to prime the new wall where the connecting door used to be once the plaster has set and dried. They've kept us informed the whole time about what they would be doing, in which parts of the house, when they would need access in here and when it would be noisy. They even played Brandon recordings of some of the power tools so that he would know what noises to expect. I cannot praise them highly enough. They have a female apprentice too. Harriet would be proud!

Bethany: Oooooooooooomg! I'm just catching up with this chat now! I am so excited to know more about Harriet. I'm sorry that some of it must have been so upsetting for you. At the same time, it seems so right that we have the chance to get to know her a bit better; the finer details, as you say. It doesn't do her justice to know her as simply a tragic wraith floating around the attic. She was this amazing, complex, spirited, caring person; she was Hattie Sutherland, who took on bully boys and strict teachers to defend somebody else. All of this at a time when as you say, women and girls had so much less autonomy to give them the foundation on which to build a personality like that! I remember one thing so vividly from that day I saw her; she didn't seem afraid or cowed or whatever you might expect from the spirit of someone who passed so suddenly and traumatically as she did and so young. She rather seemed to want to reach out; to connect and tell me something. Maybe she wanted me to find her diary! I hope I didn't let her down!

Charlene: No, I don't think it was that. Brian said that he had noticed the floorboard sticking up and couldn't believe he hadn't seen it before. He actually seemed quite disturbed by it. From where he said it was, if it were sticking up enough to concern him, somebody would have noticed it before now. I think she led him to find the diary to give to me.

Sharon: Yes, Charlene's right. Those floorboards were completely smooth; we were all keenly aware of our footing when we were taking things out of the attic down that steep staircase. I still believe Harriet was quite simply reaching out to you at a moment when you needed it; not with any particular message other than solidarity and certainly not to ask anything of you, only to connect.

Charlene: I'm going to go now and sort our dinner. We should get together some time soon though; the four of us. Brandon's so enjoying being in company; he needs to pace his socialising so that he can recover his energy afterwards but people who include him whilst also letting him be are so good for him. I know you both have that balance right and it would be so lovely to meet you in person, Bethany.

Bethany: Awww, thanks Charlene. I'm definitely up for that.

Sharon: Absolutely, me too. Speak soon!

After the usual end of group chat goodnights, Charlene closed the chat window and locked Harriet's diary safely away in the polished rosewood bureau where all their important papers were kept. Things were coming together so well for Brandon, she hoped that the new tenants next door would not do anything to disrupt the peace and stability which was helping him to grow in confidence. Once that unknown was resolved, she told herself, she could relax.

9

July 2019

Perth's large Victorian railway station with its vast platforms, network of brown and cream latticed footbridges under a soaring roof and hints of a magnificent past in its preserved stonework had always inspired Bethany to push herself to travel. The building, though in need of a sensitive refurbishment and larger than its twenty first century service needed, combined a deep serenity with a sense of its complex structure having absorbed traces of the excitement felt by over a hundred and fifty years' worth of passengers on their journeys. It was an evocative base from which to travel and to which to return home; one of many reasons Bethany loved Perth and had jumped at the chance to move there when she saw the job at the city's branch of Mackenzie Books advertised. The station's café had been modernised several times but still felt part of that subtly reassuring, infused welcome which builds gradually over considerable time in a fundamentally unchanged setting. Bethany settled at a corner table with her mug of tea, watching people come and go with varying amounts of luggage swishing through the double doors as Sharon's train from Inverbrudock moved towards the top of the information screen. Their days off during the week coinciding was an event worth making the most of in itself; Charlene and Brandon being due to travel back from Inverness in the evening at the end of a round trip on the West Highland Line then through Skye and the line from Kyle of Lochalsh had decided their plans. The cousins would spend a few hours in the Highland Capital before meeting up with Charlene and Brandon to travel back together; the other three changing trains again at Perth to return to Inverbrudock. The introduction of ticket barriers had made it more complicated to meet up with people at the station; Sharon would meet Bethany on the platform for their train to Inverness once she made her way over the bridges and walkways from the opposite side of the station where the train from Inverbrudock, which started in Aberdeen, came in. Bethany understood the need for the ticket barriers, but they were an unwelcome source of stress as they were unreliable at accepting tickets. Even in a station as familiar and beloved as this, Bethany would be glad to get away from the compact, harshly lit modern concourse and into the main body of the station where wood and weathered stone softened and smoothed the cutting edges of light and sound. Finishing off her tea, Bethany got her ticket out ready then set the tall off-white mug down on the varnished table and put her napkin in the bin, calling out a thankyou to the friendly girl behind the counter as she made her way to the ticket barriers. Safely through without incident this time, she smiled at the kindly blonde staff member on duty who had come to her rescue on more than one occasion when the barrier failed to read her ticket.

"Yay! It worked this time!"

"Good stuff! Are you off to Glasgow today then?"

"No, Inverness; a day out with my cousin. She's on the Glasgow train from Inverbrudock. I'm meeting her over on Platform 7."

"Oh, that'll be nice for you both then; it's a lovely day for it. The Glasgow train's on time and so's your Inverness train. Enjoy!"

"Thanks! Have a good day."

Platform 7 was beginning to look busy, though most people tended to stand in one small area where the space widened out for people coming through from the rest of the station. Bethany watched the spot where the upstairs walkway from the Aberdeen and Glasgow platforms joined the bridge she had walked over from the hub of the station as she heard the distant murmur of Sharon's train arriving and departing. She soon made out her cousin's light hair and favourite blue leather look jacket in the knot of people coming through. The tension of being out and about in an unpredictable, sensory tiring world was undoubtedly eased by travelling with a trusted companion; for all Bethany enjoyed and needed her space and alone time, she felt a huge rush of relief at the sight of her cousin. Sharon's face broke into a smile and she waved excitedly back at Bethany. The cousins squealed and hugged, not having seen one another in person since the day they worked together packing up in Carole's house.

The three-carriage train seemed lost alongside the endless sweep of a platform which shortly before six o'clock every evening easily accommodated the nine-carriage Highland Chieftain from London with room to spare. Local knowledge impelled Bethany to ensure they stood a little further along than the bulk of the crowd but not too far in the hope of finding suitable seats. Although not a railway enthusiast in the sense that Brandon and Charlene were, she enjoyed travelling enough to want to pay attention to anything which could ease her anxiety and make it feasible to keep doing it including travelling alone. Today, she had a welcome break from that level of demand on her coping resources. Finding one of the last remaining free double seats, she and Sharon settled in for the scenic journey up through the mountains of the Druimuachdar Pass; the summit sign for the highest point on the British mainline railway network having been restored to the Gaelic spelling from the anglicised "Drumochter". Safely seated together, the background unease slid away as gently and unobtrusively as the train's northward glide began.

Outside of the urban edges of Perth, tall evergreens soon began to dominate the lineside scenery; their steady permanence a contrast to the bright yellow, blue and white streak of the train passing through. Their tickets were

73

checked as they slowed slightly to pass through Dunkeld and Birnam; a tiny rural station which always made Bethany think of school and studying Macbeth. English and Scottish literature were among the few subjects she enjoyed; they gave her a sense of a world beyond the school gates where she would have more freedom and control over her own schedule. The fatigue of secretly working hard at fitting in alongside the mandatory academic workload was clear in retrospect. Young people were not supposed to be tired out by everyday routine; even being out of energy by home time had to be bottled up and concealed. The structure of Shakespeare, unfamiliar enough to be interesting but recognisable and accessible to her enquiring mind once she got used to the language and rhythms, had energised her in a way she still could not quite explain. Perhaps it had to do with opening up a world into which she could escape in her imagination, but in an accepted and approved context of study as opposed to the endless rebukes for daydreaming. A summer holiday trip to Pitlochry, the next station up the line, during her teenage years had brought unexpected reality for her to the Birnam Wood so famed through the prophecies which tricked Macbeth: The train that day had stopped at Dunkeld and Birnam; recognising the name, she had rushed to the door and pushed down the window as was still possible on the local trains on this route at that time, breathing in the scent of the surrounding woodland. Over the years she had come to surmise that the particular resonance Shakespeare, Macbeth and seeing Birnam Wood held for her came of learning to deal with a world where words were so often used to say one thing and mean another. Happy memories of or associated with school were few and far between; those which endured now carried an additional poignancy as Bethany contemplated the pitfalls and trials she knew were now facing Lucy.

Sharon bought them cups of tea from the trolley. They each stirred in the contents of the milk sachets and replaced the lids securely.

"How's Lucy; have you been in touch with her lately?"

"She's dreading going back to school, Beth. She messaged me last night really upset. Louise still tells her to tough it out; that everybody has problems, mostly worse than hers and school isn't supposed to be easy or fun and she needs to ignore the bullies and apply herself!"

"Ugh, the perennial 'just ignore them'! The go-to cliché for people who haven't been through it and haven't a clue what it's like! I don't get this concept of problems being a competitive event either; that support is dictated by comparison to other people's lives instead of what the individual's limits and needs are and what help they need!"

"I think Louise is closing her mind to it because she doesn't know what to do, so she's minimising it in the hope it will go away. It gravely concerns me that she can't see what that's doing to Lucy at the age and stage she's at; undermining and isolating her. She'd be far better being honest with Lucy that she doesn't have the answers, but making it absolutely clear she's on her side and willing to listen to her."

"Do you think she actually is on her side though, Shaz? I mean, she's made it clear over the years that she has some specific ideas about what a child of hers should and should not be like. I'm not talking about what I heard her saying about me that time. She was still a child herself then. I mean things she's said to and about Lucy. When she got her autism diagnosis, she was told to treat it as highly confidential, by which Louise meant shameful. She asked my mum not to tell anybody except my dad. Lucy has told me Louise has discouraged her from having contact with me; she hasn't been stopped from messaging me, but she's never been allowed to add me on social networking sites. I suspect it's because I share autism positive posts as well as stuff about how other people's attitudes and lack of understanding are the real problem. Lucy even overheard Louise saying to Aunt Sandra that she didn't want me to know about her diagnosis because she thought I would encourage Lucy to think of herself as disabled and special. She said she would rather encourage her to keep thinking of herself as 'normal' and having 'normal' people as her role models!"

"What? She actually said that to Sandra? What on Earth did Sandra say to that?"

"It was on the phone, so I don't know exactly but apparently Louise came off the call in a pretty foul mood."

"That figures. Sandra wouldn't have held back. She'd have been disgusted by that attitude and she thinks the world of you too. She admires you so much for being so honest and balanced about your autism; being positive without pretending it's all roses. The things you write about noticing details and getting pleasure from them as well as the practical advantages of being thorough and meticulous about things. How you describe the routines and environment that help you work in a bookshop and enjoy it. Your approach is so important for helping young people and newly diagnosed people come to terms with it. I think in her misguided way Louise is on Lucy's side the only way she knows how to be, but she desperately needs to stop seeing her or her autism as the problem. Otherwise that kid is going to get completely messed up and it will take years to undo the damage done to her now."

"I agree. I've tried to reach out to Louise; I've told her that we need to move forward and work together to use my experiences to help Lucy but she insists that Lucy is nothing like I was at her age and she's not going to be defined by autism and it's none of my concern."

"Oh gosh. How rude of her, and Lucy is in many ways exactly like you were at that age. My sister is completely in denial. I think you're right about her having a set image in her mind of what her child should be like. You know I will keep the lines of communication open as best I can in terms of passing on the autism advice you put out there until Lucy is old enough to decide for herself about what and where she reads up on autism, at which point I'm certain she will want to have more direct input from you."

"I know. I appreciate it, Sharon."

Pitlochry passed in a colourful whirl of tourists getting on and off the train. Looking out from the station, which was right at the end of a bridge and elevated above the town centre, Bethany recalled navigating through crowds on narrow footpaths to be rewarded by interesting shops full of crafted gifts and Scottish novelties from the cheerfully kitsch to high end clan crest, tartan, tweed, history and music speciality items. She recalled the best sweet potato soup she had ever tasted on a later visit as an adult; free to order it and take her own chances after having been restricted for years in what she was allowed to order. One spectacular reaction on an extra tiring day out at five years old to some orange juice unexpectedly having bits in it had brought lasting repercussions. Though that sweet potato soup did happen to be almost completely smooth with barely discernible flecks of red pepper, she had never had an issue with bits in soup; most kinds of soup were supposed to have them and they belonged there. Nobody had ever asked her as a child and it was the kind of thing she knew attempting to tell adults in charge of her carried a high risk of coming over as rude. Whenever she was told not to order something because "it might have bits in it and we do not want a repeat of the orange juice episode", she had accepted it and played safe; trying her hardest to be good. That soup, savoured at leisure in the quiet early winter mid afternoon on her own at a table with a muted red and white checked vinyl cover that was cheery but not too shiny, had refuelled her after a long walk through the quieter wooded pathways near the river and the salmon ladder. She could still taste its velvety, almost smoky richness and feel the pleasant warm fullness lingering throughout her journey home.

The trees were gradually replaced by moorland as the train climbed towards the Druimuachdar Pass; the close cling of heather gave a shimmer of subtle colour to the primal landscape as streams danced alongside the fences escorting the railway track through this wild and evocative place. Even on this small commuter type train, Bethany and Sharon felt a sense of what Brandon called "the Druimuachdar Hush". Particularly noticeable on the much bigger Highland Chieftain, the combined effect of the altitude and the train seeming to coast, almost float along as the line flattened out after the long stretch of upward gradient created a feeling of ethereal timelessness where everything went quiet and still. The small, homely sounds of cups and personal effects on the tables gently rattling and instinctively lowered voices became suddenly clearer and the rest of the world felt comfortably far away, packed in cotton wool to lessen the impact of returning to it.

After Dalwhinnie, the trees began to reclaim their role as sentinels over the line and soon the train was pulling into Kingussie, then Aviemore nearly a quarter of an hour later. Aviemore was a place which Bethany often felt she would like to explore; famous though it was for winter sports, she had travelled this line enough to know there was more to it than that. The mountain skyline on both sides of the long, linear town suggested a compelling seasonal cycle of light and shadow with the clarity of the mountain air. The brief minute or so when the train stopped there was enough to give a sense of a deep, abiding earth energy; of connecting mindfully with nature and history by walking along the tree-lined roads which ran alongside to the east and meandered tantalisingly off to the west of the station. The entirely aesthetically fitting presence of the Strathspey Steam Railway to the east added to the feeling of a magical place, though Bethany could appreciate the real hard graft which must go in to keeping it running so successfully. Charlene had told her it was almost entirely run by volunteers with a small, dedicated full time staff who devoted their energies to it with a passion. Aviemore had an aura of intensity which beckoned and promised to capture the heart; a beautiful place to live but a move there would need an assurance of being permanent, she thought to herself as the train resumed its journey.

Inverness Station had less soul than its counterpart in Perth but the sparkle of the Highland town which was now officially a city infused itself effortlessly into the hard, spartan surfaces and turned the light from harsh to invigorating. The ticket gates were mercifully open; Bethany and Sharon made their way seamlessly out of the side gate onto Falcon Square. Seagulls swooped and pecked at carelessly discarded litter. Nestled into the innermost reach of the Moray Firth with mountains nearby and a wide, cleanly sparkling river running through its heart, Inverness air vibrated with a heady mix of crisp inland purity shot through with raw seams of coastal texture like a frosted pattern swirled into clear crystal. The Eastgate Shopping Centre with its high-ceilinged galleries and glass dome evoked that translucent clarity; despite the lack of independent local shops which both Bethany and Sharon would have wished to see there, somehow it still felt specifically and distinctively Inverness. The High Street fared little better in terms of unique shops but the glimpse of mountains beyond the bridge over the River Ness which formed a direct continuation from the High Street helped to keep alive the sense of being somewhere special. Bridge Street, the short stretch between the High Street and the actual bridge, held more regional Highland themed shops as did parts of nearby Church Street. The Whisky Shop on Bridge Street, though still part of a chain, exuded Highland hospitality. Bethany wanted to buy a bottle for Crevan and

Dana as a gift for their upcoming wedding; though she was not a habitual drinker of spirits, she knew that the couple enjoyed it and their wedding deserved something special. Crevan had faced a lot of prejudice as a transgender man and despite her deep embarrassment, shame and regret over not having picked up on their wish to get away alone at Elaine's leaving do until Stacey ostentatiously steered her away pointing out her mistake with great relish, Bethany felt first and foremost a warm glow every time she thought of the happiness they had found. Somehow in Inverness it felt perfectly natural to accept the taster samples she and Sharon were offered by the friendly staff at half past noon; the warm honeyed glow with exactly the right floral notes for the time of year caressed Bethany's senses and she even managed to swallow without it catching her throat and making her cough. Highland air truly did seem to change things! As her carefully selected bottle was slid into the orange carrier bag, Sharon's suggestion of a walk along the riverside followed by lunch sounded idyllic.

There were a lot of tourists around but the riverside walks still afforded plenty of space. The wide River Ness ran so clear, every detail of the pebbles on its bed could be seen; baskets of flowers hung from the lamp posts along with colourful banners advertising the many reasons for coming to visit the city. Music, history, theatre, fine dining on locally sourced produce and a whole programme of events were reinventing Inverness as a tourist destination. Passing the dignified St Andrew's Cathedral, shaded and peaceful even on a warm and busy July day, then the eclectic grey and white sprawl of the Eden Court theatre complex they walked onwards to the bridge leading to the Ness Islands.

"Charlene and Brandon will have been making the most of their time away in quiet places like this. I'm so disappointed that the family renting our old house are so noisy."

"Yes, Charlene did mention a couple of times in messages about loud music. She said the whole building was shaking. That will be a nightmare for Brandon. Obviously, they'll be wanting to forget about it for as long as possible; they won't be wanting to think about it on the journey home."

"No, I daresay they won't."

"Thanks for not doing a 'Don't Mention'. It means a lot that you trust me! Anyway, have they actually spoken with the new neighbours?"

"Charlene took them some of her home baked cookies when they moved in. They thanked her but clearly thought it was funny. Which marked them as ignorant from the off. They've got four of a family; I gather they're from early twenties down to mid teens. The girl is the youngest. Tegan, I think. Then there's Gordy, Stu and Daz. The oldest one, I think that's Daz, seems a complete arse to be perfectly honest. He's shouted 'Train spotter' and made 'whoohoo' noises out of the window at Brandon. I guess he'd seen him at the station, or one of the others had and told him. Charlene was dreading that sort of thing. Then the Tegan one said to them in the street, 'So you like choo choos then?', in a put-on babyish voice."

"Oh, no. That's the last thing he needs. This could really set him back. She actually used the term 'choo choos'?"

"She did. Charlene said, coldly and politely, 'Well, we both do, but we usually call them trains'. Then she and Brandon walked away with their heads held high, but she could tell it had bothered him. They don't like to let Cheminot outside any more either; they suspect these people are probably not animal lovers and they're worried about him getting into the house since he's been used to it from when we lived there."

"Oh, poor Brandon and Charlene. If the lads are older, we can hope they'll start to move out one by one. Are they the ones playing the loud music?"

"I think it's all of them, including the parents. It's not every day and doesn't always go on late; I think a couple of them work shifts, so the noise tends to come and go but in some ways that's even worse; the unpredictability."

"Absolutely. They won't be able to relax. Aww, the poor souls. They so don't deserve that."

"As you say, let's hope some of them move out. Especially that Daz."

Bethany felt somewhat deflated at the news of how stressful life had become for Brandon and Charlene. They walked on in silence for a while, stopping to take in the soothing sight and sound of the river before going to a pub on Church Street for a late lunch on their return to the city centre. Thankfully securing themselves seats in a booth, they studied the menus and Bethany went up to the bar to order. The house Pinot Grigio refreshed them after having been outside in the sun, though there had been enough shade on the tree-lined Ness Islands. Their sandwiches and side order of coleslaw were brought to them after ten minutes and they gratefully tucked in, discovering how hungry they were after the journey and exercise. After their lunch, they still had a couple of hours before they were due to meet Brandon and Charlene to catch the train back south together.

Passing the Inverness branch of Mackenzie Books, Bethany glanced through the door and noticed Rhona, the colleague with whom she had become friendly through emails and training courses, working behind the till near the door with no customers nearby. Glad of the chance to at least see if it was quiet enough to introduce her cousin and show Rhona the whisky she had bought for Crevan and Dana, she steered Sharon through the glass doors into the cool restfulness of the shop with its soft hum of air conditioning and the fuzzy-edged smell of books.

"Hey, Rhona! Are you busy right now?"

"Bethany! I didn't know you were coming up; it's good to see you! How's Perth?"

"Good, thanks! This is my cousin Sharon, she lives in Inverbrudock. We've come up for a day out because our days off coincided for once. Rhona does the same job here that I do in Perth."

"Nice to meet you, Sharon. Days off at the same time and good weather is definitely something to take advantage of! Where is it you work?"

"I'm a receptionist at the Maritime Hotel, near where I live in Inverbrudock. This is a lovely shop; so welcoming. I love the atmosphere in bookshops. I'm a big reader, same as Beth."

"Thanks! Do you have a favourite author? I know who Bethany's is!"

Bethany and Sharon exchanged smiles as they both chorused "Peter May!"

"Good choice! It's the way he describes things; he has a way of bringing the characters' experiences to life."

"I think it's because he pays attention to all the senses, not simply what the characters are seeing and hearing."

"Yes, that's a good point, Sharon. I'm still hoping we'll get him to speak at an event at one of our branches."

"Oh, me too!", agreed Bethany. "Mind you, I'm glad we also encourage independent authors whose work is more niche and who won't get the publicity breaks the well-established mainstream writers have but have an equally important message to put across. There's an author in Northern Ireland called Keelan LaForge; I came across her work by chance but quite frankly everybody should know about it. She wrote a trilogy called 'His Mighty Hand', about a psychologically abusive relationship and it's the best account I've ever seen of how these situations can arise in the first place and why they end up continuing in plain sight with the abused partner completely trapped and dependent."

"Oh, that is interesting! I'll need to look her up." Rhona made a note of the name. "We've got a few community type events coming up in the autumn, I believe. Frank's been talking to some of the schools about having sessions to bring together initiatives for kids who love reading; creative writing, volunteering to read to elderly people, mentoring other kids who need a bit of help with literacy, setting up online book clubs to encourage refugees to read more to learn English, that sort of thing. All under proper guidance and controls when children are involved obviously, but there's plenty that bookshops can be doing."

"That's exciting, Rhona. I know Anita's interested in expanding that aspect of our work too. It helps keep us current when more and more is being done online. Oh, did you hear that Crevan and Dana are getting married in October?"

"No! That's lovely news! Do give them all our congratulations, won't you? Oh hey, Frank; Crevan and Dana from Perth are getting married!"

Rhona's boss came over from the display he had been checking.

"You remember Bethany, don't you?"

"Of course; how could I forget that hair! Good to see you."

"Hi, Frank! I'm up for the day with my cousin Sharon here."

"Hi Sharon; thanks for popping in on your family day out. So, Crevan and Dana are getting married? That's so good to hear."

"I know; I'm so happy for them. I've just bought their wedding present in fact!"

Bethany showed the whisky to her colleagues. "I'm not a frequent whisky drinker myself but the staff in the Whisky Shop were so good; they helped me choose without putting any pressure on. We got a cheeky wee taster as well! Real Highland hospitality."

"Yes, that's an excellent dram. Very thoughtful of you. There isn't a Whisky Shop in Perth, is there. I always thought that was odd", remarked Frank.

"True, though we do have Exel Wines on South Street; they have a proper specialist whisky and gin section too, with unusual lines, more range than you'd get in a supermarket. I've bought gifts for some of my relatives in there. Not exclusively the men either; our Aunt Sandra likes a dram."

"Yes, I can testify that she does!", Sharon put in with a chuckle. "In fact, so does Charlene – that's a friend of ours, used to be my next door neighbour until our family home was sold. Charlene's mostly a wine drinker like us but she does enjoy a dram on a special occasion."

"In fact, we're off to meet her and her brother soon; they've been doing the round trip on the West Highland Line, through Skye and back here on the Kyle Line. We're all catching the same train back down to Perth then Sharon, Charlene and Brandon, her brother, will all head back to Inverbrudock."

"Lucky them! I haven't done the West Highland for years", said Frank. Rhona had gone to assist a customer while the others were talking; she returned with the customer to ring through a purchase.

"Right, we'll leave you to it; it was lovely to catch up."

"You too! Safe journey home."

Bethany and Sharon made their way to the station. The streets were becoming busier; the rapid and complex movement of people at their differing speeds in all directions with unpredictable changes of course or stopping in the middle of the street becoming disorientating for Bethany to process. Out of nowhere a clipboard wielding researcher swooped into their path. Bellowing overfamiliar greetings, he exhorted Bethany, or "pretty blue-haired lady" in his saccharine volcano of patter, to smile as he wasn't that bad; he was a nice guy really. Sharon's protective hackles immediately sprang to attention; with considerable self control, she held back to allow her cousin the chance to assert her autonomy in the time she needed.

"Could you step out of my personal space, please, and this is my normal face; how can you expect people to engage if you open by complaining about their appearance? We are meeting friends and catching a train; we don't have time for this."

"Aaaawwwww, come on, don't be like that! I'm sure you can spare two minutes."

"I said no. Not. Interested! I know you're doing your job, but you need to learn to respect people's choices!"

Sharon squeezed her arm as they walked away. "That was amazing! Well done; I'm so proud of you!"

"It worked out this time; mostly because you're here. When I'm on my own, the hyperfocus is even more tiring and I don't have that moral support. I so often lose my words, or swear at them which isn't at all what I want to be doing; sure, I swear in conversation in the right company, but when I have to deal with an unexpected hostile interaction I'd rather keep the high ground and make my point. They make me so angry! If they can't even accept my answer about whether I'm available to talk, then why would anything else I tell them be credible? I have these, I suppose you could call them social scripts for various situations which I try to remember to rehearse every so often. It's so hit and miss as to whether it helps; it depends how tired I am, how the rest of the day has gone, how noisy and busy it is; so many factors. On the plus side, it gives me a boost when it works out; it does make it even more frustrating when it doesn't. Or when I get it wrong. That guy today actually was crossing boundaries, but for instance there was the time three years ago when I snapped at a poor guy in the local shop when he looked in my basket and asked if that was all I was buying, because I was picking up a couple of bottles of wine for a Bank Holiday weekend and I thought he was judging me for buying nothing but alcohol. It turned out he meant I could go ahead of him as he had a full basket. I wanted to crawl under a rock and never come out again. I relived a whole string of occasions when I've been told I bring all my problems on myself and I'm a bad person with a bad attitude and my own worst enemy and so on. I could never face opening those bottles of wine; I ended up donating them as a raffle prize."

"Oh, Beth, that's so harsh! OK, you misinterpreted that guy in the shop's intentions and reacted hastily; on that occasion you made a mistake, but there are reasons for that happening and it honestly doesn't take away from how good a person you are!"

"It's not even just that. When things like that happen, I can't apologise. I know I should, but I'm already so exposed and vulnerable, I cannot give people that power. I end up changing the subject, babbling on about something irrelevant. Or the weather. It makes me thankful to be British; weather chat doesn't irritate me at all. It's a safe retreat; the social equivalent of the refuge hut on a tidal causeway. I cannot afford to be wrong because it vindicates everyone who's ever had a go at me. Oh, let's change the subject before we see Charlene and Brandon. We've had such a lovely day; I didn't make a mistake this time. I should stay with that."

Sharon's heart ached as she squeezed her cousin's arm again. She wished she could ease the constant burden from which she seemed to get so little respite, but she knew no words would help. Bethany was right; the best thing to do was to stay in the present on a day which was going so well and to help her get back out of the shadow of the remembered misjudgement years earlier of which her handling a situation well today had cruelly reminded her.

The train home was one of the busier services. Sharon suggested joining the queue at the barriers early so that

Brandon and Charlene could join them and they would have a better chance of getting a table together. Reserving seats had not been feasible as Bethany and Sharon's plans had come together at relatively short notice. The train from Kyle of Lochalsh appeared around the long curve which took the line out towards the river and the Far North beyond; Charlene's red hair and tall Brandon's long dark ponytail stood out among the assortment of people getting off. He stopped to take a photograph of the train which they had gotten off and exchanged a few words with the guard as Charlene rushed to hug Sharon, who introduced her to Bethany although they all already recognised one another from photographs. Their trip had been a success; Brandon had found the crowds in Glasgow Queen Street station a bit too intense for him and become agitated but a friendly, calm gentleman working on the gateline had allowed them through early and brought them some water. Glancing around to make sure her brother was still occupied with his camera, Charlene's eyes sparkled as she enthused about what a difference such a simple, common sense gesture had made. The respectful way the staff member had spoken to both of them, taken an interest in their trip, made sure they were confident about getting on the right section of the train as the Oban and Fort William / Mallaig sections went their separate ways at Crianlarich, and wished them well on their travels had given their journey a positive and healthy start. The world-famous scenery had shone in the sunshine with enough interludes of cloud and showers to rest their eyes and provide variety. The excitement of children on board when they went over the Glenfinnan Viaduct, well known for its appearance in popular fantasy films, had been infectious; loudly excited children in a confined space could be problematic at times but these had been well behaved with attentive parents who kept them entertained and gently but firmly in check. The ferry to Skye had sailed smoothly; they had been mistakenly allocated a double room at their accommodation on the island but the bed had been the sort which could be bolted together as a double or separated to form two singles so the owner had gotten that organised and given them complimentary drinks and snacks while they waited. Brandon had been a little panicked at the delay and withdrawn socially as he was tired and out of routine; not wanting him to be misunderstood, Charlene had explained that he was autistic and the owner had understood, offering any extra help needed to make sure he was comfortable. Brandon came over, nodding and waving to Sharon and Bethany; he stood at his comfortable distance minding the luggage, relaxed in their easy going, empathic company.

There was a table free as far as Perth, which was all they needed; the connection to Inverbrudock would be a different train. Brandon needed to be facing the direction of travel and in the aisle seat so that he could go to the doorway if he felt too confined. Not being able to open the windows on modern trains could be a disadvantage for him; regulating his body temperature was often difficult and this added to his anxiety but being free to move around helped. He showed his photographs to Bethany and Sharon as the train began its journey; Charlene set out their tickets and Brandon's Railcard ready for inspection.

Travelling with an invisible disability had its own specific challenges, including meeting acquaintances one would rather not encounter. The immaculately made-up woman walking through the carriage caught Brandon's eye and he nudged Charlene: "Incoming. Set ableism detectors to Def Con Three!" Charlene rolled her eyes; not now, after such a lovely holiday and in front of Sharon and Bethany.

"We dread seeing this woman when we go to do our food shopping in Inverbrudock. She's one of the supervisors, often hanging around the tills and she speaks to Brandon as though he were five years old. Most of the time she only speaks to me, as though he weren't even there. She manages to come across as speaking to me over his head even though he's taller than both of us."

"Oh Brandon, what a pain for you!"

Charlene smiled gratefully at Bethany, thankful for her understanding that just because she generally did the talking and Brandon preferred this didn't mean that he should not still be directly addressed when appropriate and included in the conversation.

True to Brandon's prediction, the elaborately coiffed and made-up woman stopped at their table.

"Oh, so you're taking your brother on a trip. That's so sweet! Does he manage?"

"Why don't you ask him and give him the dignity of answering for himself?"

Leaning over Brandon, the woman slowed down her speech, raising the volume proportionally.

"Do you manage all right on the train?"

Brandon cringed away from her, blurting out "I'm a train enthusiast; what do you think?!" Bethany and Sharon exchanged disgusted and sympathetic looks at this infantilising and intrusive encounter; Charlene intervened to back up her brother before things could turn nasty.

"My brother is autistic. He can hear you perfectly well, as can most of the people in this carriage right now. He may need an extra moment or two to answer a question and he may appear abrupt when someone needlessly gets far too close to him. You do not need to speak to him like a child."

Bethany had never actually seen someone's nostrils flare before; she had always thought that was merely an expression.

"Well, I was merely trying to be public spirited! Disability is no excuse for rudeness!"

"As I explained, my brother, like many autistic people can seem abrupt when someone invades his personal space. Speaking loudly at close quarters like that is actually painful as well as stressful to autistic people. His reaction

90

to that, in the context of his disability, was not rudeness. The problem is communication, and it is discrimination when you judge him for something that is a factor of his condition. We both had a most pleasant and constructive conversation for a good twenty minutes with a member of station staff in Glasgow yesterday when he was distressed by the crowds, noise and being too hot. The gentleman spoke slowly, but with respect and in a natural tone at an appropriate distance. If you want to know how to approach my brother and others with similar difficulties, I'm happy to help you out with that example from this excellent train company!"

"Hmmm. Well, people cannot be expected to read minds."

"Which is why I'm happy to clarify his reaction for you and offer a bit of insight."

The woman huffed, tossing her perfectly styled hair over her shoulder before stalking off down the carriage.

"Perhaps travelling in the school holidays in the height of summer isn't the best environment for people like that and they'd be better off keeping to themselves at home."

The unabashedly loud, condescending voice came from across the aisle where a woman in her sixties, mouth pursed disapprovingly and handbag clutched in the lap of her zigzag print dress, had pointedly addressed her embarrassed-looking husband. For a few moments, even Charlene was speechless. Bethany could not hold back.

"Excuse me? 'People like that'? Did this train just go back in time to the Victorian age; are we going to be surrounded by a cloud of steam when we get off in Perth? My friend here has as much right to enjoy a tour around this country in which we are so privileged to live as anybody else has. You should be ashamed making such a callous and bigoted remark."

The lady gaped at her, spots of colour coming out on her cheeks.

"Highly commendable sentiments I'm sure, my dear, but I'm a lot older than you and I don't expect you've got the life experience yet to decide what's best for someone with your friend's, ah, affliction."

Sharon's quiet "Oooooooh" held warm anticipation combined with disgust.

"Oh, is that a fact? For a start, the kind of ignorant hate speech you're currently spewing out is my friend's 'affliction', not his autism. Oh, and by the way, I'm autistic too, so I think you'll find that counts as relevant life experience. I'm also older than I look; not that it matters, just another assumption on your part. Should I be hiding myself away too because some aspects of the season might make things more difficult for me? How would you feel if somebody said that people with arthritis should hibernate all winter because they'd get in the way if they stiffened up and had to walk more slowly?"

"Absolute nonsense. Girls don't get autism and arthritis is a completely different thing."

"Are you for real? Nobody 'gets' autism. It's not a cold or a new pair of shoes. It's a neurological difference and girls most certainly can be autistic. We may show it differently, which is why so many of us have not been diagnosed earlier in life, but I guarantee you will have met autistic women in your life. You simply won't have known they were, and they probably didn't either. And you're right; arthritis is a different thing. It's purely physical; it's something people talk about without getting squeamish. That was the whole point of the analogy. Not that people with physical disabilities don't face discrimination. They absolutely do, and it's important to point that out. What I'm saying is, not to put too fine a point on it, cut the crap and back off being so vile to my friends."

The gentle applause took Bethany completely by surprise. The other passenger turned away, muttering something about how could anyone who dyes their hair that ridiculous colour expect to be taken seriously as her husband apparently found something in his rambling magazine utterly riveting. The couple who had applauded were sitting at the next table up from the older couple; the lady, a compassionate-looking soul around Sharon's age with short chestnut hair and laughter lines worn with pride, got up and came to speak to her.

"Thank you. We have two autistic foster children: a son and a daughter. Hearing people like you speak out gives us hope for them. You too, explaining to that lady who recognised you earlier about how things should be. I hope we didn't hurt your ears clapping; I know that noise can be uncomfortable!"

"Oh no, two people clapping gently isn't a problem! I do appreciate what you said; I'm glad your foster children have you."

Returning to her smiling husband, a handsome Asian man with greying hair framing a kindly face, the lady gave the now thoroughly silenced hostile passenger a look of contempt. Charlene leant across the table with tears in her eyes. "Thank you so much, Beth. You've no idea what it means to have somebody back us up like that", she whispered. Brandon's unperturbed doodling in his notebook as he watched the scenery, his body language relaxed as the security of knowing that ignorant and prejudiced people were in the minority here allowed him to unwind, spoke volumes.

At Perth, Bethany said her goodbyes, making Charlene promise to give Cheminot a big cuddle for her. Walking through the enfolding, sensory soothing embrace of the station after waving her friends off to Inverbrudock on the Aberdeen train, she reflected on a day which would stay with her for a long time. One final celebratory glass of wine in the bar of the Station Hotel felt like the perfect way to round it off; a small glass, acknowledging the fatigue which would soon catch up with and overtake the adrenalin currently in pole position. She loved this unique old hotel with its rich reds and creams, dark wood panelling, stained glass and contrasting homely touches of plants. Although Perth was easily in reach of where she had grown up a short distance outside Falkirk, she had treated herself to a night here more than once after being taken to a wedding function there as a child. She had found the loud music, socialising and unfamiliar food unexpectedly easier to cope with in this building, which had the same feeling of wrapping itself around her in a comforting cocoon as did the station. The wide corridors, quiet corners and grand staircase curving high out of view had provided her with breakout space at that wedding before she even knew such a concept existed, let alone that she had a good reason to need it. She could not remember the people who had been getting married; they were relatives on her father's side, but she had no recollection of any other contact with them except for their names on Christmas cards. All she remembered of that wedding reception was the hotel. Now it was part of her home city; a place to call in for a drink on the way home from a trip. She could entirely understand why, according to what she had read on a website, Queen Victoria had a private walkway built from the station straight into the hotel. How she must have cherished those times in her extraordinary, pressured life! Thinking of relaxing here after the pressure of duties as she sipped her wine sent Bethany's thoughts back to the conversation she and Sharon had with Rhona in Inverness. Perhaps she could plan an event at her branch, along the social and community lines Rhona had mentioned.

An anti-bullying initiative! The thought came to her as warming and golden as the July evening sunlight pouring through the tall windows of the Garden Bar. Her conversations today about Lucy and about Brandon and Charlene's new neighbours, as well as the intimidating behaviour of the passenger on the train making her demeaning remarks intended for Brandon to hear, had sparked an increased urgency in her ever present need to do something to make a real difference. She must do something tangible to help; something which would be entirely down to her. The weight of her empathy crushed her soul when she witnessed or heard about bullying incidents, even when bullying may not have been the intention. Her vivid imagining of the pain, fear and frustration others must be feeling took over her thoughts to the point where their burdens became hers to bear; she felt as though she were contributing to the bullying by not being able to stop it. She knew enough to be well aware she could not stop all bullying; no individual could, but if only she could do something which would remain set in stone as her contribution; even if it helped a small number of people, it would be better than nothing. Her mind rushed ahead to a day when she would be celebrating here, looking back on this idyllic day out as where it all began. Aglow with renewed purpose, she finished her wine, thanked the barman as she placed her empty glass on the bar and set out into the balmy evening to walk back to her flat.

In Inverbrudock, Brandon took the luggage into the house leaving Sharon and Charlene to walk to Vinnie's chip shop. The breeze coming off the sea seemed to blow a fine layer of dust and sweat off the heat of the day, freshening the still mild evening.

"Bethany was an absolute star on the train! I will never get tired of advocating for Brandon, but it was such a treat to have another person take on an issue for once. An autistic person too; it does carry extra weight when the person speaking out has personal experience which I can never have despite being so close to my brother."

"I know; I was so proud of her! She put one of the clipboard mafia in his place in Inverness too. He leapt out in front of us, blocked our way which they're not actually allowed to do and started straight in on her because she instinctively flinched away. All the usual 'smile, it's not that bad' rubbish. So, she told him to please step back and that he couldn't expect people to engage if he had a go at their appearance and that we had a train to catch. He wasn't for accepting that, so she told him to learn to respect people's choices. She said to me afterwards that she was able to put together what she wanted to say in time because I was there and it boosted her morale; she finds it easier not feeling the focus is on her all the time when she's out with somebody else. Then she immediately remembered a time when she misjudged something, and it brought her right down again. She simply cannot let herself retain a feeling of achievement. It's like, I don't know, she thinks she'll jinx herself or something."

"I cannot imagine living under that sort of pressure. Brandon does that too; beating himself up over mistakes, but he's generally quite contented as long as he's in his comfort zone. Bethany seems to have a much greater need for approval; for acceptance by the world beyond her own immediate circle."

"Yes, she does. She seems to need to constantly insure herself against the next perceived failure by getting everything perfect. She's at her best when she's defending somebody else, like she did on the train. If that lady had started out making remarks about her, the response would have been markedly different. She'd have either completely withdrawn then tormented herself about 'having no personality' or been more brash and less constructive in her defensive reaction."

"How could Bethany ever think she had no personality? Even if she has times when she becomes less verbal or nonverbal, there's so much more to her personality, to anybody's personality, than speech! Society badly needs to stop confusing personality with social energy or the amount of words someone speaks. Some people are entirely nonverbal; are we supposed to write them off altogether personality-wise? Of course not."

"I think a lot of it comes from when she was a child and she did struggle a lot more visibly and more often with getting her words to come together. She's told me it's OK to talk about it with you. She had it drummed into her repeatedly about being shy and quiet as a result and it frustrates her because she simply needs a bit more time; it doesn't mean she doesn't want to speak with people or that she has any less to say. It's given her a tendency to panic if she feels she's gone too long without speaking in company or if she's struggling to respond in real time to someone with more social energy; the 'oh no, I'm going to get called shy or quiet or a mouse yet again; I can't cope with how that makes me feel so I need to stop that happening' inner monologue kicks in. Then she gets barbed or pitying comments about not making enough eye contact; assumptions that it means she's timid. Again, making her feel that she's completely misrepresented herself. Eye contact is simply one thing too many for her to have to remember; it tires her and distracts her from processing and forming responses. She feels shamed by people for having to visibly concentrate to keep up with them, and humiliated when they give a running commentary on every fleeting facial expression and every little thing she does a bit differently. People seem to have this air of congratulating themselves, right in front of her, on how many subtle idiosyncracies they've observed about her. To her, it's like being on display in a zoo and not performing as the keepers expect or want. She's given me examples of things people have commented on, like how she holds something or how she walks, or probing questions about why she looked amused or anxious for a fraction of an instant, as though she cannot have any mental privacy. It is not, as is often dismissively said to her, all in her head! She told me once that she often feels like a mobile Brownie points charging station for everybody else, at the cost of that charging up by others draining her own self worth. Nobody should feel like that! As she says, if she made the same kind of comments about other people's mannerisms or expressions or ways of doing things, it would be pathologised as an autistic lack of awareness of etiquette and boundaries yet it's somehow acceptable for anyone to make intrusive personal remarks about her and other autistic people! She's told me how scared she is of the intense emotional anguish it makes her feel when she gets labelled and minutely analysed, to the extent that she worries she'll harm herself. It terrifies me, but that emotional intensity is seen by so many non-autistic people as being something an adult should be able to conquer, so that's something else she's learned to repress at potentially an extremely high cost. She has described herself to me before as 'emotionally ambitious'; she has this craving for living intensely. and approval from people in authority or people she perceives as being above her for whatever reason is a big part of that. It's like a drug for her, something she has to strive for, almost like a psychological extreme sport. Unfortunately, those people tend to be the types most likely to dismiss her as shy and quiet. At the same time, she still gets told a lot, including by professionals, that she's sounded abrupt or rude and that any social difficulties she has as a result are her own fault, so she's become conditioned to believe that firstly she's a bad person and secondly in order to get any support she may need, she has to be perfect."

"That's really worrying. So essentially being perfect means completely hiding her autism and making sure it never shows. If professionals are imposing that sort of conditionality on her getting support, that's actually quite serious discrimination."

"I do think that sometimes the support is still there but doesn't feel that way to her, because guidance and looking at the facts of a situation which may include her having

98

gotten it wrong feels like complete rejection. A lot of the problem is people talking to her, or at her, leaping in with opinions and advice when they should be listening to her; bearing in mind that it can take longer for her to get to the truth of what she's trying to say. She may need to backtrack a time or two in order to get there. It's all about giving her space; adapting to the timescale she needs. Unfortunately, that's not always compatible with overstretched resources."

"That's true, and I can see what you mean. Here we are; I'm so looking forward to my fish supper after all the travelling! Brandon and Cheminot will manage an extra fish between them, no doubt. Thanks again for feeding him. Cheminot, that is!"

The two friends laughed as they walked into the chip shop. Vinnie was as unperturbed as always by working in the heat; he smiled brightly as he shovelled freshly cooked fish in puffy mounds of golden batter into polystyrene trays, loading them up with chips before wrapping them up with practiced efficiency. He served up an absolute monster of a cod so that there would be plenty left over for the cat; he knew that Charlene would remove all the batter and check his portion for bones before setting it down for her pet. Calling out their thanks and waving goodbye, the two women hurried back along the promenade.

The windows of what had been Sharon's family home were open wide and loud music could be both heard and felt vibrating through the erstwhile peace of the late evening. Charlene rolled her eyes, hoping that Brandon was not becoming stressed out in their own home. Daz, the oldest son, was leaning out of the window of what had been Emma's room smoking what may or may not have been a plain roll-up. The breeze lifted a few dark strands of his lank hair before dropping them again as though in distaste. Abruptly the music stopped; Daz turned around in surprise then called out something they could not quite make out though the meaning was clear. He was berating either

Gordy or Stu, judging by the male anatomy specific insults they did catch, for having unplugged the boom box. A fainter answering voice carried indignant denial in its tone as Sharon and Charlene gladly took advantage of getting to the door unnoticed and unmolested; Daz's response was clearly audible from that close by.

"You must have, you rocket! Gordy's still at his work and Tegan's round at Hayley's."

Stu was the mystery unplugger, then, though his mumbled response begged to differ.

"Well, it wasn't me; I was having a tab out the window."

This, to be fair, was indeed the case.

"Sake man, just plug it back in, yeah?"

Stu evidently complied as the noise and vibration started up again; Charlene sighed as Sharon gave her a sympathetic look. Taking their much-anticipated fish suppers into the house to the delight of a ravenous ginger cat, they resigned themselves to the unwelcome soundtrack; not for long, as the racket was mercifully cut short once again.

"Another harmonious family evening by the fireside next door, then!", chuckled Charlene as she and Sharon plated up their food. They ate in hungry, companionable silence to Cheminot's purring and the distant heartbeat of the waves.

Meanwhile, Darren Slaughter reeled off most of his extensive repertoire of swear words except for a few of the ones he reserved for women, as he examined the unaccountably silenced boom box. He couldn't blame Stu this time; the plug was still firmly in the socket. It had to be a fuse. He had only bought the thing a month ago! His Dad had mentioned that the electrics had tripped a couple of times, though the landlord had assured him they had been tested and approved as part of the home report from the sale of the house. Checking the trip switches, he found nothing out of place. Grumbling to himself, he turned up the TV and opened a can of lager. He didn't think to ask his brother if he wanted one.

It was getting dark by the time Sharon left. Depositing the fish and chip wrappings in the bin as she closed the gate behind her, she waved to a couple she recognised walking their dog along the seafront. She checked her phone; Bethany had texted her to say that she was home safely, going on to enthuse about getting ideas from the conversation they had with her colleague Rhona in Inverness. Sharon knew better than to ask any more than Bethany chose at that point to tell her; she had always guarded her plans closely for fear of them not working out. Bethany had been through her share of disappointments because she ran out of energy or could not find enough reliable input and backing from her peers and colleagues to make the ideas gain traction. Often, she would try to do things on her own and find that her guardedness worked against her; she would push people away or simply not reach out enough to give a scheme the chance to catch on. Sharon hoped that Bethany would not open herself to any more damage to her self belief by trying too hard or being too reticent to share the load. She would support her in whatever she chose to do; she would listen and advise as and when it was invited from her. There were always lessons still to be learned in life; everyone, including the people about whom she cared most, needed to find their own way.

10

August 2019

Less than a week to go. The final days wherein it was far enough away to cushion the stab and slither of fear inside had passed with the high, carefree sun of July. Now the painful, crushing din of Edinburgh's Fringe Festival season in full swing was carrying its dread transition to Lucy's world. Everything became louder, more garish; people rushed and pushed and squashed, cramming their daily lives into a city suddenly too small to accommodate them. The air itself smelled and tasted different, bearing the bitter tang of a primal threat; by this time next week, Lucy would be back at school.

The Festival itself never quite reached Marydean; its turbulence was carried on the waves of stress and frustration as residents emerged from each day's fraught, extended commute. Lucy's mother was one of them; her tolerance of her daughter's needs diminished at this time every year, precisely when those needs became more acute.

The last days wherein she could look forward to the same day the following week had come and gone. Next Wednesday, she would be back in the other routine. The routine which began every weekday morning with a struggle to open her eyes after a fitful night of either nightmares or dreams of freedom which left her aching with loss as she awoke to reality. Weekends were a blink of an eye compared to the respite of the long summer break; it would be some time before even they felt like any sort of oasis again.

She had tried everything she could to fit in. She smiled and said hello to people; had tried asking them about their holidays, their interests, their classes. Most of the time they would simply look at her as if to question why she was speaking to them at all; sometimes she would be accused of butting in, or of having been listening to their conversations. More often than not, they would tell her to go away or turn away laughing amongst themselves. She had all but given up on that technique now. She still smiled and said hello; most of her peers ignored her and left it at that. Except for Roseanne Bell and her clique.

Roseanne and her friends were the ones who had started the whole "limp lettuce leaf" business. Well, that wasn't strictly true; it was Mrs Maynard who originally started it. Lucy doubted that the teacher would even remember her impatient remark that day almost a year ago when she had caught Lucy out in one of her zoned-out moments. Her mother despaired of telling her that she merely needed to concentrate; that there was no excuse for her letting her attention wander the way it did. It wasn't something she chose to do; she didn't feel it coming on or even realise she was doing it until something, usually a mocking reprimand, shook her out of it. The best way she could describe it was that her mind simply stopped. She was not thinking about anything; not aware of time passing. She was somewhere out of it; not asleep, not awake, just stopped. She had never quite understood how it had made Mrs Maynard think of a limp lettuce leaf. After all, lettuce wasn't any more inert than any other food and it wasn't bad for being so; it wasn't supposed to be doing anything! Besides, it was green; a fresh, lively, healthy colour. Why did Mrs Maynard have to say something so silly in front of the whole class including Roseanne and her mates? Teachers weren't supposed to behave like children! Why did she join in with them laughing after she said it? Lucy's face burned with fury as she relived that day in her mind yet again. It was by no means the worst thing she had ever been called in school, but she had known with a sickening certainty from the raucously enthused reaction that she was never going to hear the end of it. How could the bullies be expected not to make the most of a whole new theme gifted to them by a teacher? And how could she expect any protection and help from the teachers if they were going to actually encourage people to pick on her? People they knew were already doing so? She had so often been told "Well, don't give people a reason to pick on you and then they won't." Yet Mrs Maynard had given her bullies a whole new arsenal of ammunition; how was that right? When she asked adults to explain to her what she was doing that was so terrible it gave people carte blanche to pick on her, they could never give her a straight answer. All she could glean from the various responses was that she needed to be anything at all other than her natural, authentic self.

Catching herself holding her breath and grinding her teeth, Lucy hurriedly made herself breathe deeply and fix her facial expression. She really must practice not letting her face show what she was feeling. It made her cheeks turn red far too easily and people would make fun of her or ask too many questions. Sometimes she wished that the bullies would beat her up, then at least she would get a bit of support; surely her mother and teachers would not agree with violence. They would be able to see the harm and they would have to take it seriously; take her seriously.

Her mother called her to come and have her tea. Lucy hurriedly checked her reflection in the mirror to make sure she was not still wearing a wrong expression then went to sit at the table.

"I hope you're going to be more positive about school this year, Lucy", Louise Penhaligon said as she set plates of pasta Bolognese on the table. "You would be so much happier if you decided you wanted to be."

Lucy had tried that. She had studied so many bullied characters in the school stories she read so voraciously, clinging to every detail of the ones who turned things around to become popular girls. The problem was that none of the girls they had to win round were anything like Roseanne Bell. In fact, girls who acted the way Roseanne did were more likely to be the unpopular ones; ostracised for being mean! They would sometimes have a sudden epiphany leading to a complete character change overnight or else turn out to have a tragic reason behind it, making their actions forgivable equally quickly so long as they said sorry and shook hands. There was no point trying to tell her mother that; she would undoubtedly say that Lucy was making excuses again and accuse her of blaming everyone but herself.

"This pasta is delicious, Mum. Thank you."

A justified compliment, delivered with a bright smile, to her mother's cooking was the safest way to proceed. The meal continued in a brittle truce; Lucy loaded the dishwasher then returned to her bedroom to read some more. "Jane Eyre" had struck a chord with her when she read it during the summer for next year's reading list; encouraged by her interest, her mother had bought her a copy of "Villette" which she saw in a second hand shop. Lucy was rather wishing that Charlotte Bronte had swapped her chosen names for the main characters; Jane Eyre appealed to her a lot more strongly than her own namesake Lucy Snowe. Although Lucy Snowe was more resourceful and independent in her work and travels, Jane Eyre owned her emotional intensity in a far more exciting way. Lucy had cried when she read of Jane drawing an unflattering portrait of herself then making one of her love rival Blanche Ingram which was the Victorian equivalent of airbrushed, keeping them to look at and remind herself that Mr Rochester was out of her league. Knowing instinctively to conceal her overly involved reaction from her mother, she had curled up with that empathy; she was of course fully aware that Jane Eyre was not a real person, but that incident in the book was real for the fact that someone's mind had been inspired to invent it. Her heightened response to pain

105

in others saw her imagining herself going back in time to ask Charlotte Bronte who or what hurt her so badly that she came up with that idea.

Louise took the clean dishes out of the dishwasher and put them away, wiped down the kitchen surfaces then made herself a decaffeinated cappuccino. Anne Boleyn cappuccino, as Lucy called it; a head with no body. Lucy was newly discovering a taste for coffee and could not see the point of decaf; she loved the buzz regular coffee gave her. Louise sighed as she wondered once again why her daughter had to be so difficult. Why did she constantly seek reward or some sort of crutch to cope with life, whether praise and thanks, the energy rush of a cup of coffee or the next break from school? Every time she connected with her, such as the genuine joy Lucy showed when she gave her the copy of "Villette" or the times they laughed together about Anne Boleyn cappuccino and other themes arising from her fascination with Henry VIII and his wives, she allowed herself to feel hope that Lucy was learning to relate naturally to people. Then every time, she would soon find herself once again wondering if she would ever understand her; if Lucy would ever let her in.

"Surely it should be a body with no head?", she had teased, playing along on a rare good day.

"Everybody thinks that, Mum", Lucy had replied earnestly, "but actually we experience everything with our brains. Even if you stub your toe, it's your brain that tells you to feel it. So logically, her head lost her body, not the other way around."

Louise could hardly disagree. However brutal a cad Henry VIII had been, she found herself silently thanking him for not having gone with the other method sanctioned by the courts of the time to choose at his pleasure for executing either of his allegedly unfaithful wives. Lucy's intensity and instinct to empathise could not have coped with the details of that.

106

"And why not Katherine Howard cappuccino? She had her head chopped off too!"

It was a gamble; fortunately, Lucy had laughed, albeit awkwardly. She had then immediately gone into a diatribe way beyond her years about how that simply wouldn't be funny because Katherine Howard was not strong and cunning like Anne Boleyn; how she was merely a frightened, unhappy girl who was used by men and probably groomed as a child. Although Louise had impressed upon Lucy what the world could be like when teaching her about stranger danger then about online safety, making it no surprise that she knew about things like grooming from a young age, to hear a thirteen-year-old relate that to a figure from history made her wonder whatever happened to her childhood. She had always anticipated that these pivotal mother and daughter bonding conversations would be less rare and be about make-up and pop music and American sitcoms, not people being beheaded. Would she ever find the happy, confident, vivacious daughter she had thought the newborn infant she was holding in her arms fourteen years ago would be, a future of playdates, friends, boyfriends (or girlfriends; one never knew these days) and achievements all stretched out in a glittering gold ribbon of how she imagined her life would unfold? Instead, her child was so out of step she was being called autistic by the doctors. She could relate to and empathise with a queen consort from five hundred years ago about whom comparatively little was known. In fact she had astonished her History teacher, who had set an assignment to write creatively about the Tudor court, by crafting a story of a parallel universe wherein the firstborn son of Henry VIII and Catherine of Aragon in fact survived to become Henry IX, so that Henry and Catherine never split up because she had given him the son he wanted. In the story, Henry IX was the one to marry Katherine Howard and he treated her properly and kindly, giving them a long and happy life together. How could her child produce a story like that yet completely fail to fit in with her own classmates? Louise still lived in hope that the autism diagnosis would turn out to be wrong; that Lucy was merely going through a difficult phase. Phases were grown out of; autism was not. Lucy was nothing like Bethany, the desperately awkward, socially inept little cousin she remembered! She had not seen or had much contact with Bethany for years; there was no specific falling out, she simply had nothing in common with her, though she appreciated her admittedly consistent and thoughtful birthday and Christmas gifts to Lucy and ensured that her daughter thanked her properly. She understood from Sharon that Bethany was working and had a rented flat; perhaps she had improved, but Louise felt cold inside at the thought of seeing her or of Lucy having any ongoing contact with her. She could not justify banning her from any contact at all, but she had drawn the line at Lucy being exposed to the things Bethany shared on social media, often quoted to her by Sharon. Lucy was not going to become someone who disadvantaged herself by advertising being autistic! Especially as Louise still harboured hopes that the diagnosis was wrong. No; Lucy just needed to get a grip and try harder to align herself with the real world. She would thank her mother one day for pushing her instead of coddling her. Resolute, Louise rinsed away the dregs of the Anne Boleyn cappuccino and put the mug in the dishwasher.

The dreaded morning came creeping into Lucy's consciousness like smoke under a door, curling up into the peace of her dreams, insinuating itself under her closed eyelids and forcing them open with the merciless hard line of the alarm. No starting this day gently; no going at her own pace. Pushing off the safety of her duvet, Lucy padded across the room to kill the unwelcome screech. Keeping the alarm where she had to physically leave her bed to switch it off was the best way she could avoid giving in to the temptation to go back to sleep. Fighting to wake up enough to perform her getting ready tasks quickly was the next stage of the battle. Pretending to be one of the lively, energetic girls in the school stories she read usually helped, at least while she was still at home.

In the pink tiled bathroom, Lucy splashed cold water on her face. The uncomfortable shock of it on her sensitive skin was worth it for the advantage of banishing some of her lingering fatigue. She needed that shock to allow her to launch herself into the obligations of the day. Showering quickly, she cast a critical eye over her body. Had she gained weight over the summer? She did not need to give anyone reason to add fat shaming to their existing store of flaws to comment on. The potential for that to combine with the salad jokes was as obvious as it was menacing. Perhaps she ought to cut out a few treats. The thought of giving up one of the few things which made her feel more energetic and able to cope jarred her mind before plummeting like a falling lift to her stomach. Turning off the shower, she dried herself as quickly as she could, wincing as she tugged the wide toothed comb through her wet hair. Even with that sort of comb and plenty of conditioner, it hurt. She was never able to perform these tasks as quickly as other people, even when she didn't have one of her zoned-out moments in the middle of doing them. It was another mystery she could not fathom; she had no ready defence against the inevitable chivvying and criticism of her slowness. Drying her blonde hair which was beginning to show signs of darkening, she was glad that she had agreed to have it cut in a bob; she didn't care whether her style was fashionable or not but having less of it than before did help to cut down on the time it took her to get ready.

Her mother was already leaving for work ahead of the Festival crowds when Lucy came into the kitchen. She reminded her one more time that she hoped this year was going to see her get on better with other people and be more positive, and not to go around telling people she was autistic as it was bad enough the teachers having another reason to see her as different. "I am different, though", said Lucy sadly as the flat door closed, leaving her to clear away her breakfast dishes before picking up her school bag and going out to face the music.

One step at a time, Lucy bargained with herself throughout the walk to Marydean High. She could make it as far as the paving stone with a crack across the corner. Once she'd managed that, she could make it to the streetlight where the path from the flats intersected with the one crossing the park. Then she could make it to the post box next to the local shops, then the bus stop at the council service point. After that, the school gates. None of her tormentors were hanging around near the bin where the wasps gathered; that was a good start. At least there would only be a few weeks to go before the wasps were gone and the air cooled again. She took a deep breath, remembering to smile as she willed her heart to stop racing so hard; the thudding was distracting her, and she needed her wits about her. There were the familiar tiles of the main corridor. Her downcast eyes knew them all; every variation in the flecks of grey through each pale green square.

"It's so hot already! It's not even nine o'clock and my salad is wilting. Ugh, look at these limp lettuce leaves!"

Right on cue, Roseanne was brandishing her lunch box at Millie Allen and Kayla Martin, whose inane giggling ignited the familiar rage in Lucy.

"Try sticking it where the sun don't shine then, Roseanne", she thought to herself, wishing she had the courage to say it out loud. Then again, it would no doubt get her into trouble of all kinds if she did. Turning her back on the trio never felt like a safe thing to do but she had to in order to take her seat. Something lightweight, probably crumpled paper, hit the back of her head; the laughter started up yet again.

"Lucy! Luuuuu-cyyyyyyy! Not going to talk to us then? Stuck-up cow. Or are you just too stupid?"

There was no response which would stop them, including ignoring them. Wayne Benner deliberately bumped her desk as he walked past; the sudden grating sound as the heavy legs moved across the hard floor, amplified by the lack of any soft surfaces in the room caused a startle reflex she could not suppress in time. The laughter increased. Her fault! She had failed to hide it and played into their hands, exactly as her mother said!

"Look at her shaking like a leaf!"

"Limp lettuce leaf!"

Did she really have to put up with another year of this? How was the whole ridiculous limp lettuce leaf joke so important to these people when Lucy wasn't important to them? She could not believe they hadn't forgotten about it over the summer holidays, which must have been filled with the cool things they were always boasting about.

"Aren't the salad days getting a bit old now, Roseanne?"

This time, she did say it out loud. Their faces twisted into sneers of disgust as though she had said the most asinine thing imaginable; as though their immature heckling were a profound philosophical debate into which she had intruded. Roseanne contemptuously flipped her yellow hair out of her eyes ringed with fake lashes; it fell back again exactly where it had been, but her point was made. So, it appeared, life was to continue as before. Eventually the arrival of Ms Danning's English lesson provided a little respite; not from the bullies but offering the limited distraction of a subject she enjoyed.

Bringing "Jane Eyre" into this nest of vipers felt almost like sacrilege. Lucy focused determinedly on what Ms Danning was saying, trying desperately hard to concentrate. Everything she had read at home felt fuzzy and distant;

events blurred out of sequence as she fought to recall them. She had enjoyed it so much; this was "her thing", yet her mind frustratingly would not clear.

Ms Danning was talking about the infamous attic.

"So, who can tell me what is the significant turning point connected with Jane's first sight of the attic?"

Lucy's hand was already up. She could see the attic, exactly as she had visualised it as she read the story.

"She thinks she sees the ghost of a nun!"

The air seemed to leave the room. For a moment, there was perplexed silence; even Ms Danning looked blank. Even as she spoke, the horrible realisation of Lucy's mistake crashed down on her.

"Ah; you're thinking of "Villette", Lucy. That happens to..." Ms Danning tactfully suppressed the name. "That's a different novel by Charlotte Bronte. Well done for having read both of them, though."

How could she have done that? How could she possibly have gotten those two novels mixed up, especially when the Bertha Rochester plotline was so well known as to be part of popular culture? Were the lettuce jokes about to be joined by madwoman in the attic jokes? She felt profoundly thankful that Ms Danning had not said the name "Lucy Snowe". How the bullies would have loved that. Lucy Slow. Lucy Snowe Good. They'd have had a field day. What a good thing "Villette" wasn't on the reading list. She didn't even need the bullies to torment her; she was perfectly capable of doing it to herself as she continually anticipated the next blow. She deserved it! Why couldn't she stop making stupid mistakes and giving them things to use against her?

Biology was next. Still preoccupied with her unaccountable error, Lucy failed to see Jayden Phillips' foot slide out to trip her up as she made her way to her seat. She dropped her folder. More laughter, more whispering; more credence to the bullies' belief that she was useless, thanks to her own lack of vigilance. Bringing it all on herself. Mr Foley's voice barely cut through the barracking from her inner voice. He was banging on about microbial life, showing a series of images. Then insects.

A caterpillar. A pretty one with thick red and orange fur. On a lettuce leaf.

The unfairness of it all swamped Lucy. She had dodged a bullet with Ms Danning not letting on that she had muddled up a character who had her own first name, then Mr Foley had to go and project a great big vivid picture of a lettuce leaf on the screen. Predictably, a small projectile – an elastic band this time – pinged into the back of her head. Equally predictably, Mr Foley looked up to see why the image of the caterpillar was causing such amusement just in time to see Lucy turn around in frustration to growl "Pack it in!".

The three wide-eyed girls; Millie Allen, Kayla Martin and Roseanne Bell, displayed innocent shock and bewilderment at this sudden outburst of temper; there was no sign of their usual friendly smiles. Scratching his balding head, Mr Foley sighed in annoyance. Why did Lucy Penhaligon have to be so disruptive and antisocial? "Whatever your problem is, Lucy, keep it out of my classroom and let people get on with learning. Is that understood?"

All eyes were on her. Lucy had no choice but to swallow down the huge, choking mix of hurt, anger, humiliation and injustice. Yet another weapon for the bullies.

"Yes, sir."

"I can't hear you."

"Yes. Sir!"

"You need to learn some manners and respect, young lady."

Behind her, Roseanne repeated the teacher's words; triumphant, mocking, perfectly judged to be audible to Lucy but not to Mr Foley.

Home at the end of the day, Lucy was relatively safe for another few hours but by no means out of the woods. She still had to face her mother's sixth sense and a barrage of questions to which Lucy knew the truthful answers would not be welcome.

"So, how was school?"

"Fine. How was work?"

"Don't change the subject, Lucy. I can tell by your miserable face it wasn't fine. What's happened now?"

"Do you have to be so horrible about my face all the time? Half of its DNA came from you!"

"Never mind getting smart with me, madam. What problems have you managed to get into now? I want the truth."

"No you don't, Mum. But Roseanne and Millie and…"

"I'm not asking about Roseanne or Millie or half the flipping Von Trapp family. I don't want to hear about 'it's all other people's fault'. I'm asking about you."

"I can't tell the story without mentioning them! You want to know what happened; they were what happened!"

"So as usual you were the victim. Did you retaliate?"

"I told them to pack it in. They were throwing things at me."

"In the classroom?"

"Yes. Biology, And before that too."

"Did the teachers see them?"

"No, they never do."

"But no doubt they heard you lose your temper."

"Yes. Mr Foley did."

"And what did he say?"

"That I should keep my problems out of his classroom."

"Oh, Lucy. When are you going to learn? You cannot control what other people do, but you can control how you react. And you must. I'm sick to death of all this trouble. Now, I want you to peel these potatoes for me while I sort out some papers for work. And for Heaven's sake, stop sulking. You've got to start taking responsibility for your own reactions. Learn some self control. Life isn't fair. You're fourteen now, not a helpless toddler."

Her mother stormed off into the living room to organise her work. Scraping away the rough, blemished potato skins to reveal the clean whiteness underneath, Lucy wished that she could so easily remove the wrong expressions from her face along with whatever else she was presenting to the world that made her deserve such anger and hatred. She had no idea how to do what was being asked of her; no actual technique evident from her mother's insistence of what she must do. If she had one, she would already be using it. Did her mother or anybody else truly imagine she wanted any of this trouble? Morning would come around again so soon, then over and over again along the bleak road ahead. How was she supposed to keep going through this when nobody would listen or take her side?

Back at school the following day, the landmarks passed one by one, those familiar tiles counted off to the classroom door which Millie "accidentally" let go behind her to shut in Lucy's face. Lucy had to pretend to accept her fake apology; she knew she dare not risk looking like the instigator by appearing churlish, though how the teachers couldn't see through it was beyond her. Millie wasn't even trying to sound sincere. Her attempt at a noncommittal "it's OK" brought another round of giggling and whispering about how stupid she was. She remembered to watch for Jayden's outstretched foot this time. A small victory, she reminded herself; getting complacent was likely to mean being caught out by the next trap.

"Seen anything interesting in your attic lately, Lucy?", sneered the voice from behind her. "Not much chance of that, Roseanne, considering I live in a flat", she bantered back; knowing even as she said it that Roseanne and her friends would choose to believe she had taken the question literally rather than admit to themselves that she had stood up to a taunt. Sure enough, the whispers and giggles resumed. Lucy worked extra hard at tuning them out. This was all on her, after all; it was all her responsibility. She poured such vast mental energy into ignoring them, she took in little of her lessons.

At break time, Lucy endeavoured to stay out of the way but the trio of bullies seemed to be everywhere she turned. Had they cloned themselves? She simply could not get rid of them. Roseanne was drivelling on about getting various body parts waxed; an image Lucy did not particularly want in her mind, yet however subtly she moved away, they still managed to even more subtly follow her around. Kayla was saying that she could never imagine having such a thing done, especially where on the body Roseanne was talking about; for once, Lucy was of the same mind as Kayla. Millie's shift in tone to the stage whisper Lucy knew so well heralded what was coming next.

"I bet Lucy's got nothing there to wax."

"Ha! No, it's probably all plastic down there, like a Barbie doll."

"Except not pretty like a Barbie doll. It'll be all pale and pimply."

"Ugh, Millie, you're putting me off my crisps!"

Lucy tried once again to move away.

"Are you enjoying listening in, Lucy? Like fanny talk, do you? Are you a lezzie?"

"Well, Millie, you're the one who's just been speculating in some detail about my vagina, so maybe you're the lezzie; not that it should be a problem to anybody in 2019!"

"You have to admit, she's got a point there", said Sophie Scott passing by. "You three might want to think about growing up a bit. Lucy, could I borrow you for a minute to help me with some library books, please?"

Lucy was stunned into silence as she followed Sophie, one of the nicer prefects. For once, timing had worked out in her favour, though she couldn't imagine why Sophie would ask her to help especially with so little of break time remaining. They passed Mr Foley, who had seen from a distance Sophie speaking to the girls.

"More trouble, Lucy? You really are your own worst enemy aren't you. Why do you hang around them if you don't like them?"

Lucy could not pick a coherent thought let alone a sentence out of the clamour in her head right then. She was already trying to process the astonishing curve ball of Sophie unknowingly rescuing her. Now she was supposed to get her head around Mr Foley thinking she was the one hanging around her tormentors? He was quite right; why would she? The answer was simple; she wouldn't! Why couldn't he see that she was trying to get away and they were following her?

"Trouble, Mr Foley? I'm sorry, have I missed something?", Sophie was asking. "Lucy kindly agreed to help me with a task in the library. Those other girls came by and were talking amongst themselves. Lucy was minding her own business."

"Ah. Well, make sure it stays that way, Lucy", huffed Mr Foley as he walked away. What on Earth had just happened here?

The bell rang for the end of break. Sophie turned to Lucy, apologising that she had not realised the time and that Lucy should go to her next class. Stammering out her thanks, she felt tears threatening as Sophie walked away, turning back to give her a smile which Lucy could not quite read. Going to her Geography class in a daze, she was dismayed to see Mrs Maynard standing in for Mr Paterson. Oh no. Please don't let her say IT again. Please don't let her encourage that joke any more.

"Wake up, Lucy! You're in a daydream as usual!"

No no no no no...

"Wayne, tie your laces, please. We don't want you to trip over them and get a nose like a squashed tomato!"

Seriously, what was it with this woman and salad? Unexpectedly grateful to Wayne for his sloppiness diverting attention away from her, Lucy nevertheless seethed inside at the certainty that Wayne would not spend the next two years being bombarded with squashed tomato jokes. He could make a mistake and have a teasing remark made and that was that; it was over and done with. She felt... She couldn't have described how she felt. There were too many feelings and they were all too big. She must conquer them; she must take responsibility! Concentrate; get through the lesson. No mistakes; no looking vague. She must get this right.

Lunch time came. Joining the queue, Lucy soon found the trio behind her again. How did they always manage to be behind her? This time, there was a subtle increment to the usual frisson of their loathing. Lucy could sense it building like a thunderstorm in the close August air.

"She thinks she's better than us."

"Oh, she thinks she's better than everybody!"

"Hanging around with prefects now, are we? Too posh to slum it with us?"

"Ugly bitch."

"Fat prostitute."

"Prostitute? No man would go with her if she paid them!"

Roseanne poked her sharply in the back.

"Ignoring us, are you? You're nothing, remember that. You're nothing but a limp lettuce leaf! Even Mrs Maynard said that. Limp lettuce leaf! Limp lettuce leaf!"

Millie and Kayla took up the chant; Millie stepped up close and scraped the toe of her shoe down the back of Lucy's heel. Lucy whirled around; Millie blew a mocking kiss. The chant continued.

118

It hadn't happened for a long time and never at secondary school. It was coming and Lucy had no way to fight it off. She was past the point of no return as the tension, fear and chaotic mixed emotions of the day overloaded her unbearably strained autistic teenage brain. The mocking faces seemed to brighten and elongate, losing their meaning and relationship to everything around them, inverted like a photographic negative. The voices became distorted; at once distant and right inside her. She covered her ears and screamed.

Everyone turned to stare, joining in with Roseanne, Millie and Kayla's squeals of delight at this drama unfolding in front of them. This was the jackpot; this was weird Lucy on a whole new level, half the school watching in horrified primal fascination as the scene unfolded. Roseanne quickly pulled out her phone.

Lucy ran. She had no direction, no coordination. The cheering followed her; the baying of a crowd united in its urge to watch the destruction of the weak, the misfit, the outcast. To her sensitive ears it sounded like the massed roar of an entire stadium full of spectators. It echoed and painfully bounced around every hidden corner of her mind, laying waste to every comfort, every coping strategy; leaving them all crushed and splintered, meaningless. The concrete yard under her pounding feet changed to the grass of the sports field. Some instinct she could not consciously feel impelled her towards the hut where some of the sports equipment was kept. She blundered into the side of it; hands grasping for a hold, grazing against the weathered wood. She fell to her knees; curled up in the foetal position. The cheering was more distant now. There was wood and grass and quiet. She lay; she breathed; she became still. Reality began to grip her chest, her stomach, her head with icy fingers as the extent of her loss of control in front of so many people began to sink in. She wrapped her arms around her head, whimpering softly.

119

Keep still. Keep very still. Be as unobtrusive as possible and maybe the last few minutes will be erased. Maybe they won't have happened. Because they can't have happened. This can't happen. It is too big a lapse for her to ever come back from. Keep still. She must keep still and quiet. The whimpering cannot be coming from her. It is somewhere in the air.

Roseanne pressed the Stop button on her phone. This was boring, Lucy lying there making that pathetic noise. The entertaining part was over. Millie and Kayla were lagging behind her as usual; she turned to go back to the lunch queue, boredly inclining her head for them to follow. Which of course they did. Excitement over. There was fun to be had with this video, but she was hungry now.

The squealing, whooping and cheering had all stopped; it was still some time before Lucy dared move a muscle. Stiff and sore, she unfurled herself bit by bit. Her system-wide pain began to unravel itself into definable components. Her legs ached; her hands stung; her head pounded; her throat felt raw. The skin of the back and left-hand side of her neck stung with the same sensation as her hands; it took her a few moments to recognise the rubbing of her bag strap, chafing her skin from her headlong fleeing. Which everyone had seen. Everyone. She had never been able to run gracefully. What a scene; what a fool she had made of herself. Moving shakily to a sitting position, she leaned against the solid gentleness of the wooden hut. Her fingertips found its quietly reassuring, natural grain. Pressing her back against it gave her the courage to open her eyes.

There was nobody in sight. She was finished with school; how could she ever face those people again? Not only the bullies but everybody who had seen what she had allowed herself to do. She had to go. Ignoring the trembling of her legs and the stinging of her palms, she used the indentations between the planks of the hut to pull herself to her feet. It was time to be her own Bronte heroine; time to be that young woman leaving everything behind with no choice but to go her own way.

She walked, smoothing out the creases in her school skirt as best she could, across the field, across the end of the yard, through the gates. A calm purpose settled around and within her. There was nothing left to fight for except to survive; to get from A to B and figure it out when she got to B, wherever that was. The Festival tourists milled around her, flowing alongside her and onto the bus to the city centre. Their colours floated by; not touching her, not part of the moment. Mechanically, she boarded the bus; asked for Princes Street, paid her fare, took her ticket, thanked the driver. She supposed she must have smiled; nobody was telling her to.

She got off the bus. The noise of the Festival crowd swam freely in and out of her ears; colourful sound fish, fleeting and benign. Occasional shouts directed at her by people promoting their shows pierced the outer layers of her cotton wool swaddled mind with long loud swords; they glanced off the steel of her detachment, firing a spark of molten adrenalin which quickly cooled to an inconsequential glob of otherness; of elsewhere. She floated through the sliding doors of the bus station. Alarm stabbed blackly into the mother-of-pearl haze of her protected mind; she needed to engage enough to make a decision on where to go. Somewhere the colour of safe; somewhere the letters on the front of the bus fell into place like a winning combination on a fruit machine. Somewhere she could find a now in which she could keep going.

11

August 2019

If Marydean High still selected a head girl, Gabi Ramsay would have been a certainty for the honour this year. Widely respected by teachers and pupils as a responsible and caring mainstay of the school community, she had taken particular interest in pursuing initiatives tackling issues such as racism, homophobia and bullying. She spent a lot of her free time helping people online, seeking to volunteer as an anti-bullying peer support mentor and taking part in national initiatives by giving input whenever she could. Having a Polish mother had given her some experience of being bullied herself at primary school; here at secondary school she had been fortunate in finding the winning combination of a strong circle of friends and having most of her classes with the more professional, aware members of staff. Growing in confidence and respected for both her academic work and her kindness to others, Gabi had built the kind of rare reputation which takes years to craft and almost amounts to diplomatic immunity; even more rarely, she used it in a wholly altruistic way. Teachers like Mrs Maynard and Mr Foley, who were in the profession because they had wanted to stick with the familiarity of the education system and keep the holidays, quietly resented her even as they grudgingly respected her for her staunch defence of the weaker pupils who rocked the boat by needing more support. There was an aura of untouchability around Gabi Ramsay; it irked and threatened those who had reason to feel that way.

Brushing her light reddish-brown hair after a brisk lunchtime walk, she applied a discreet retouch of eyeliner, a final year privilege, to the rims of her grey eyes. She sighed at her worried reflection, exasperated by the continuing lack of progress in her efforts to set up a mentoring scheme here. The suggestion had been received with enthusiasm but when it came to making the time to work with her and put it in place, she kept coming up against a metaphorical brick wall. The conversation she had with Sophie earlier was a case in point as to why it was so desperately needed. They were both deeply concerned about Lucy Penhaligon, who they believed was being bullied by at least three people in her class. There was a rumour that Lucy was autistic; she was certainly struggling, visibly scared and unhappy. Sophie had noticed the three girls upon whom their suspicions were mostly focused, following Lucy around throughout morning break; Lucy had appeared to be trying to get away from them. When Sophie got within earshot, she had been sickened by the taunts she had overheard. She had not even wanted to repeat them to Gabi, saying simply that they were sexually belittling Lucy, clearly intending her to hear and then accusing her of eavesdropping. This was a technique they appeared to use a lot, familiar to Gabi from so much she had read. Sophie had invented the excuse of needing help with some books in the library to get Lucy away from the other girls, intending to gently question her about what was going on; before she had the chance to do so, Mr Foley had come upon them and assumed she had caught Lucy in some wrongdoing. The poor girl had been practically mute and when the bell rang, Sophie had made the judgement call not to add to her stress by asking questions or making her late for class; pretending not to have realised the time and releasing her from the supposed task.

Gabi had a study period after lunch, so she headed towards the library. As she passed through the school's main entrance area, a message was showing on the electronic notice board asking if any prefect who did not have a class to attend could please provide relief cover patrolling the science block. The science block was at the edge of the school complex, notorious for people smoking and generally getting up to mischief. Had Heather or Sophie had to go home sick, she wondered? They were rostered to do the outside duties today. Even if one of them were unavailable, she had never known a call to go out for emergency cover. She thought briefly about doubling back to report to the office confirming she was going to provide cover but some instinct she could not quite understand told her to go straight to the science block. She quickened her pace as she left the hub of the building.

"Stupid thing won't upload!"

"It might be the signal; it's rubbish round here."

"This is the one place we'll get peace to do it! If it doesn't work this time, I'll have to do it at home tonight. Awww! Another error message!"

"Come on, Roseanne, you can upload it tonight right enough; can we not watch it again instead? It's comedy gold, man!"

"Aye, all right then. I'll do it tonight; can't be bothered with this."

Roseanne, Millie and Kayla were so absorbed in watching the video playing on Roseanne's phone screen, none of them heard Gabi as she came around the science block. Looking over Roseanne's shoulder, what she saw on the screen made her want to throw up right there and then. It was a video of Lucy Penhaligon, running away with her hands over her ears as shrieking and cheering could be heard in the background. The tiny onscreen Lucy dropped to the ground, curled up in a ball. Gabi recognised the hut on the sports field as her stomach lurched again. Whatever had happened to push Lucy over the edge, and she had no doubt that what she was seeing was an autistic meltdown, these pieces of scum had filmed it and intended to post it on the Internet; in fact, only a technical glitch prevented them from already having done so.

124

"Hand over that phone immediately."

All three girls shrieked and jumped up from their huddle; Roseanne hurriedly snatched her phone away from Gabi's grasp.

"You can't do that!"

"Watch me."

Gabi had never envisaged getting physical with another pupil, especially a younger one. In this case, she was compelled to make an exception; even if it got her into trouble, she was not going to allow this devastating video to be shared. Grabbing Roseanne's arm, she deftly blocked her with her body and wrestled the phone from her grasp.

"A few of us have been keeping an eye on you three; we know you've been picking on Lucy Penhaligon and now you've taken it too far. This is going straight to Ms McAllister."

Tuning out the three bullies' frantic protests, Gabi strode back to the main building. Karen Reid, the secretary, was finishing off some filing when the prefect knocked on the window.

"Oh hey, Gabi. What can I do for you?"

"I've got a situation here, Karen. I need to see Ms McAllister urgently, please."

"Oh! I think she's still on the phone, but I'll check. Are you able to say what it's about?"

"I'm sad to say I've just caught someone with a video they filmed on their phone of somebody in their class extremely upset, screaming and running away from them, here at school."

"What? Oh, my goodness, that's terrible. Please come into the office, Gabi. I take it this is the phone with the footage on it. May I ask to whom it belongs?"

"Roseanne Bell. The footage is of Lucy Penhaligon. Somebody needs to find her and look after her."

There was a sad acknowledgement in Karen's eyes that she was not as shocked by this as she ought to have been.

A robust policy on bullying in this school was long overdue; she had seen enough of Lucy's records to be aware of the challenges she had been facing and was also familiar with Lucy's mother's insistence that the autism diagnosis was questionable and should be kept secret. That poor child. Karen cared sincerely about every one of the young people who passed through these doors and often wished that her role allowed her to do more to help the needlessly lost souls who slipped through the net of pastoral support.

Gabi handed the phone to Karen, who took it into the head's office and spoke briefly with her boss before coming back out and instructing Gabi to go and summon Roseanne, Millie and Kayla to see her. Heather McIntyre and Sophie Scott were to be discreetly instructed to search for Lucy. As Gabi returned and ushered the three crestfallen bullies into the office, closing the door behind her and heading out with Karen to help Sophie and Heather look for Lucy, something odd occurred to her.

"Karen, when I saw the alert on the notice board, I assumed Sophie or Heather must have gone home sick. They're both still here and on duty though?"

Karen looked puzzled. "What alert was that?"

"On the electronic board in the main hall. I'd come out of the bathroom and was on my way to the library to study when I saw it. Asking if any available prefect could please provide relief cover for outside patrol around the science block."

"Well, that's very strange. I certainly didn't put that message out, and I don't know of it ever having been done that way. If we needed relief cover, we'd usually check the study areas and find one of you. Ms McAllister must have done it and thank Goodness she did so that you got to those girls before they could put that awful video onto the Internet. I think there will be some progress on your anti-bullying project once we get this whole sorry business cleared up and most importantly, find Lucy."

126

Margaret McAllister's face froze in a mixture of horror, fury and shame as she watched the video on the phone, to which Roseanne had sullenly given her the unlocking code. The three girls sat gazing at the floor. Roseanne looked petulant but the underlying fear was unmistakable; Millie was snivelling, and Kayla looked as though she might faint any moment. Margaret felt no sympathy for any of them; she knew that a bully, particularly a child, was never a happy or truly strong person and that these girls needed help as well as punishment but at that moment all of her care and compassion was focused on Lucy Penhaligon.

"Explain yourself, Roseanne. Explain to me exactly what happened to bring Lucy to this state and why you felt it appropriate to film it with the intention of posting it on the Internet."

"It was just a joke. We were laughing about Mrs Maynard calling her a limp lettuce leaf and she totally flipped out. I filmed it because it was funny. Lucy's a weirdo. Nobody likes her."

Margaret set her spectacles down on her desk, regarding the cowed schoolgirl through piercing blue eyes made even more prominent by the severe cut of her silver-white hair.

"If you think that what I've seen recorded on your phone is even remotely funny, then you need help and guidance beyond what this school can give you. I don't care what your personal opinion is of Lucy; there is no justification for treating another human being this way. It has taken more than a bit of casual name calling to make Lucy become this distressed and mark my words, I am going to get to the bottom of it. Right now, my priority is to find Lucy. The three of you will remain here until I know exactly where she is and that she is safe. After that, you will leave the premises and not return for three weeks. During and after that time, whether in or out of school, you will not attempt to approach or make any kind of contact with Lucy Penhaligon. Failure to adhere to this instruction will result in more serious proceedings, and make no mistake, this is serious already. Do I make myself clear?"

The three girls nodded. Margaret sat back, impervious to their discomfort; it was becoming damningly clear to her that she and her colleagues had failed in their duty of care to Lucy. Roseanne had mentioned that Mrs Maynard had mocked Lucy in class? There was a lot to be investigated here; a lot which had apparently been happening in plain sight. The phrase "limp lettuce leaf" sparked an association in her mind; these three girls had been posting a lot on the school's social media pages about lettuce, greens, salad and anything on a similar theme. It had all looked like a laudable and pleasing attempt to share and encourage an interest in healthy eating. It had never quite fit with what she knew of the trio. Had this too been part of a relentless targeting of Lucy stemming from an unprofessional comment by one of her staff? Even though it was undoubtedly part of a bigger picture, this was deeply worrying.

Her worries were about to become even deeper.

Karen Reid knocked and entered her office, out of breath, her eyes communicating frantic concern.

"We cannot find Lucy anywhere. We have searched every room, every corner, every toilet cubicle, everywhere. Lucy Penhaligon is no longer on these premises."

Margaret closed her eyes for a moment, allowing the implications to sink in before summoning up every bit of steel and experience she possessed to take charge. Karen was regarding her with grim acceptance of the dreaded task she knew she was about to be given.

"Ms Reid, please telephone Lucy's mother."

12

August 2019

Sharon reached for her favourite yellow mug and took a quick swig of lukewarm tea, hoping that the phone would stay silent for a few more minutes so that she could finish answering the hotel's enquiry emails. At this time of year, the hours in the middle of the day were precious for keeping on top of administration in between guests checking out and new ones arriving; this year they were getting even more enquiries than usual as people struggled to find available accommodation in nearby Arbroath for the planned celebrations of the 700th anniversary of the Declaration of Arbroath in 2020. Her desk sat in a niche at the side of the reception area, its light wood and brass accessories well chosen to blend in with the nautical theme of the décor. Paintings and old photographs depicting ships, groups of fishermen and the Inverbrudock seafront gave character to the parchment coloured walls; a framed newspaper article from the 1960s with a picture of the lifeboat and its crew, lit with its own spotlight had pride of place behind the desk where Sharon worked. Across the navy-blue carpeted foyer, the main door was propped open to help the fresh air to circulate; the leaflets on the display stand next to the door fluttered gently. Background music played at an unobtrusive volume through small speakers discreetly shaded by pot plants which Sharon had watered as soon as she arrived to start her shift. She never liked to leave any unanswered emails for Ann to have to deal with, the same way she knew Ann did not like to leave any for her. The hotel staff were a small, close knit team who looked out for one another; this ethic of collaborative working and consideration filtered into the general atmosphere of welcome, goodwill and care that met every guest and was a testament to the value of independent hotels. It had contributed to the building of a loyal network of regulars; people who now felt like part of the extended family. People like Paulie Fitzpatrick.

Paulie's first stay two years earlier had been the first time Sharon encountered the title Mx in her job; she had asked how it was pronounced and what Paulie's preferred pronouns were. They had told her it was a breath of fresh air to be asked that in such a matter of fact way. Authentic inclusion was impossible to fake with any kind of tokenism if the motives were not sincere. Either "Mix" or "Mux" was fine, they had explained, though they were more than happy to be addressed as "Paulie". "I'm she / her, but happy with Sharon or Shaz", she had responded; they had exchanged the warm beginning smiles of the instant mutual rapport people encounter a handful of times in life if they are lucky. Paulie's work in tourism took them all over Scotland; their personal experiences when travelling gave them valuable insight for their work but they were clear about being off the clock when relaxing with friends they had made on their travels. They usually stayed at the Maritime three or four times a year, making the most of its convenient location and good transport links for Aberdeen, Dundee and Perth. They made a point of leaving their car at home and using public transport so that they could maximise their understanding of the tourist experience in that area too. Sharon had come to look forward immensely to their visits, sometimes getting the chance to hear a few of their stories at the quieter times; she suspected this would not be one of those times but Paulie's arrival that afternoon would still be a highlight and she was extra keen to have her work up to date so that she could give her full attention to welcoming them.

The metallic rattle of coins being counted drifted through from the bar as Jen got ready for the afternoon session; Sharon smiled to herself as she recalled an occasion when a trainee waiter had left a plate with almost £100 in tips unattended on a tray on the bar as he went to help with an order from a large group in the restaurant on an evening they were short staffed. Paulie, coming into the bar in search of an evening dram, had thoughtfully covered the plate with a metal cloche from the breakfast bar which was located at the end of the restaurant that led into the bar and was set up for the following morning's buffet service, and come to tell Sharon that they had done so. As Sharon had been taking a phone call, by the time she got to the bar the restaurant manager had mistaken the covered plate for a room service order he was to deliver and presented an astonished American tourist with a plateful of money instead of her dinner. It had taken some time for poor Don to live it down; the jokes about deep fried quid, penny Bolognese, bangers and cash and so on had outlasted the trainee's career. Although the thought of the incident always made her chuckle, Sharon's most treasured memory from that evening was of laughing with Paulie in the bar after her shift ended; they knew more about whisky than most of the staff did and she had thoroughly enjoyed the conversation they had with Jen when she offered Paulie a dram on the house to thank them for their vigilance over the unattended tips. Being unable to join them for a drink herself as she was still in uniform had not even mattered.

A middle-aged couple from London arrived to check in as Sharon finished sending her final email; a reply to a query made via a booking website. Welcoming them, she efficiently brought up their booking on her computer screen, swiped their credit card and handed them their keys. Explaining the breakfast times and advising that they book a table for dinner as the hotel was so busy, she pointed out the restaurant and bar then told the couple which direction to turn when they got out of the lift to find their room. Wishing them a pleasant stay, she watched as they took their compact cases to the lift. It always interested her to see whether guests would focus on finding their way straight to their rooms or look around, taking in the individual character of the hotel. Some people, of course, would be tired after their journey and simply want to settle in; many a time she would observe them fully taking in the details of the place in the morning when they were refreshed after a night of quality sleep. Often, they would look rejuvenated; relaxed as they had not been for some time in their busy modern lives. Sharon always felt privileged playing a small part in these interludes, so desperately needed in a society which was becoming more and more fast paced and demanding. There was a feeling in the air that humanity was coming to the point where something had to give. More and more, Sharon and her colleagues were sensing a need for a longer rest running deeply in their departing guests. Looking at the bowl of sparkly pebbles and dainty seashells which another regular guest had brought from Nairn beach, complementing her ornamental starfish on the recessed shelf to her right, she wondered whether it would ever be possible again for people to be able to be less busy and more in tune with the neglected truths of Nature.

Paulie strode through the open door, smart casual in a stylish but comfortable outfit carefully chosen for their journey. A long, fitted light biscuit-coloured cotton jacket sat loosely over terracotta coloured linen trousers and a cream shirt, their close-cropped light brown hair just brushing the collar. Lively green eyes lit up with pleasure at being back in their favourite hotel as they greeted Sharon warmly. They had been allocated their preferred room on the top floor; the booking having been made in good time before the hotel began filling up for the season. Sharon did her usual double check that no personal details were visible on her computer screen before leaving her desk and walked with Paulie to the lift. Paulie was still getting over a fear of lifts after having become trapped alone in one during a conference in Birmingham; it had become an ongoing understanding that Sharon, Ann or one of the other staff would accompany them in the lift with their luggage and in between times they could use the stairs.

The lift announced its arrival with a gentle "Ping"; the doors slid open to reveal the same plush, deep blue carpet, light walls and brass detailing as the reception area. Panels in the ceiling gave out ample light, diffused enough to be relaxing; a slight tint to the mirrors softened the overall effect while still adding to the brightness needed to make the small space more accessible to anyone with any apprehension about it. Sharon glanced at Paulie, who nodded to indicate that they were confident enough to enter the lift first. Pressing the third floor button which lit up opaque white in the meticulously polished brass panel, Sharon smiled reassuringly as the doors closed. She felt a rush of tenderness knowing this was still a difficult moment for Paulie; she could see progress in their conquering of their fear in the months since their last stay but it was an additional challenge she knew they could well have done without.

The third floor corridor was narrower than those on the floors below; magnolia walls and a light green carpet gave some illusion of space especially on a day like this when the sun beamed in through the fire escape door at the end. Pastel paintings of colourful yachts added to the efforts to lighten the space, reminding Sharon of that ancient, battered tin her mother used for tea bags. That tin looked quite as in keeping with the modern, compact kitchenette of her small new house as it had with the grander kitchen of days gone by in the family home. Carole seemed more at ease with herself these days; she seemed almost to have retired from the ongoing need to stand on ceremony which came from running such a big house and taking on the head of the family role as the eldest of three sisters. Sharon had kept as many details from her as possible about the family who had moved into their old house; they seemed to keep within the confines of the law, but their noise and intermittent heckling of Brandon were a blight on the lives of Sharon's friends who had always been the kindest of neighbours.

"Right; here you are, Room 18 all ready for you! I'll leave you to settle in."

"Thanks again, Sharon. Oh, it's so good to be back here. I had to explain about being Mx yet again at the last place I stayed, down in the Borders. 'But are you a man or a woman, really?' She didn't quite get to anatomical details, but it was looking as though that might be her next question!"

"Seriously? A member of hotel staff asked you if you're a man or a woman?"

"Yep. I answered as I always do; 'I'm non-binary. I use they / them pronouns. I'm one guest and I've booked one room. What exactly do you need me to clarify that's relevant to my stay here?'"

"Good grief. I'm so sorry you have to put up with that, Paulie. I hope she at least had the decency to be embarrassed."

"Maybe, but of course she was too professional to let it show. Not too reticent to fish for information about my private parts, because let's face it, that's what she was really asking. But too guarded to show any human feelings. I'm used to it; it annoys me more because of the people coming to terms with their identity who are a lot younger or still fragile after coming out, to themselves and other people."

"I know; I get that. You've every right to be annoyed on your own behalf too though! Nobody should be so intrusive as to ask you intimate questions like that, especially when they don't even have a personal relationship with you. Even when people do get to know you well and become part of your life, you're always entitled to your boundaries."

"Oh, I know. I just deal with it then look forward to the next time I'm going to be staying somewhere I know I won't have to expend a load of extra energy in order to do the same everyday transactions as everybody else. Oh, the funniest thing happened on the train coming here! There was a group of lads at the next table, maybe starting a stag weekend early. One of them opened his rucksack to get some cans out and a load of condoms spilled into the aisle, right in front of two elderly ladies. He was mortified, apologising profusely, scarlet in the face and one of the old ladies said 'Oh, that's quite all right, son; it's been a few years since I saw one of those and it brings back happy memories'! So he gave them each a can of Stella. They drank them too!"

"Haha, that's brilliant! You should write a book about your travels, Paulie, you honestly should!"

Sharon was still chuckling to herself as she walked back downstairs to the reception desk. As she entered the lobby, Jen rushed over from the bar.

"Sharon! Lynsey's been looking for you. She took a phone call and I gather it was someone asking specifically to speak to you. She asked me to tell you to go to her office as soon as possible." Catching sight of Sharon's expression, she hastily added; "I don't think you're in trouble or anything; she did say it was urgent though."

"Oh! I was going up in the lift with Paulie; you know they still have a fear of being in there on their own. I'd better go and see what Lynsey wants!"

"I'm sure it will be fine. Lynsey won't have a problem with you helping Paulie with their fear of lifts. She knows about it and that any of us would leave the desk for something like that."

Sharon's heart pounded with apprehension nonetheless as she went to find her boss. She had, after all, stayed away from her post for longer than necessary. Helping a guest to build up their confidence using lifts again when it was an issue by which they would be greatly disadvantaged in their job was perfectly justifiable but she would have to admit she had stayed chatting with Paulie after the lift journey was over with. The thought of having barriers put up to their growing friendship troubled her deeply; she understood the underlying need for professionalism and to treat all guests equally but it would, she knew, change the easy contentment she felt about her job and her workplace if this friendship were to be placed under a cloud. She valued her good relationship with Lynsey too; she had always been a caring, fair and appreciative manager. Trying to squash down the nervous feeling in the pit of her stomach, she knocked on the office door.

"Oh, Sharon. Please come in."

"Hi, Lynsey. Jen said you took a call for me. I'm sorry I wasn't there; Paulie Fitzpatrick had checked in and they're still too frightened to use the lift on their own, so I..."

"Hey, please don't worry about that; I appreciate how helpful you are to all our guests. That's not why I told Jen to send you to the office. I thought it best to tell you in private about the call I took."

Lynsey's hazel eyes were full of compassion as she placed a hand on her colleague's arm.

"It was your sister Louise on the phone, Sharon. I'm so sorry to have to tell you this, but your niece has gone missing from school."

Sharon collapsed into a chair, the colour draining from her face.

"Lucy? But she's vulnerable! She's only fourteen and she's autistic! What happened? Does Louise want me to call her or does she need the line kept clear?"

"Apparently there was a bullying incident and somebody filmed her running away in distress", said Lynsey, her expression heavy with anger and sympathy. "She hasn't been seen since. As you thought, your sister needs to keep the phone line clear; she had to let you know in case Lucy were to head for Inverbrudock or contact you. Louise said you and Lucy are close. Oh Sharon, I truly am so sorry and if there's anything at all we can do to support you, we will."

"Somebody FILMED her?"

"I'm afraid so. On their phone. The headmistress has confiscated it and taken steps to ensure the bullies are kept away from Lucy."

"Not before time! Why did it have to take something like this? Sorry, Lynsey; I don't mean to take it out on you but this has been a problem for a long time. One of the names the bullies keep calling her was actually started by one of the teachers!"

"Hey, don't you apologise. I was appalled by what your sister told me. What's a teacher doing calling an autistic pupil names? Any pupil come to that!"

"Oh, I wish I knew, Lynsey. Lucy was a bit slow to take something in one day; something trivial, I don't know if she even remembers what the context was but this teacher, who saw enough of the class to know Lucy was being picked on and knew about her autism diagnosis, said she was standing there like a limp lettuce leaf. In front of the whole class."

"Oh Sharon, that's appalling! The poor girl."

"So for the rest of that year, and I guess into the new school year too, it's been lettuce this, salad that. Posts on the school social media pages about healthy diet and eating your greens, all looking quite innocent but from a particular group of them who have no genuine interest whatsoever in that topic. All targeting Lucy; all making sure she can never relax for a second. I'm sad to say my sister has been in denial about Lucy's autism and has tended to push her awfully hard to fit in better and be less of a target. My cousin Bethany, the one in Perth, is autistic too; she wouldn't mind me telling you. My Aunt Sheila did the same with her. Beth has helped me understand it a bit better; she has a theory that it's about their mothers actually being so scared of what their daughters are having to go through, they look for the one aspect over which they have some control and can hope to change. So, the kids end up getting it from all sides." Sharon sighed, putting her hand to her face. "Poor Lucy. I need to get home in case she does come here. I'll need to let my mum know if Louise hasn't already, and our neighbours from the old house. Lucy hasn't been to either of our new houses; she might well go to Charlene and Brandon's. She… She loves their big ginger cat…"

Sharon's voice broke, the combination of picturing innocent Lucy happily scooping up Cheminot and suddenly realising the possibility of her encountering the loutish new tenants of their former family home proving too much on top of the distressing news. Lynsey wrapped her arms around her, reassuring her that of course she must go home. Pouring her a glass of water and handing her a tissue, she made a quick call to Jen in the bar asking her to cover Reception as Sharon had a family emergency. "Jen and I will manage between us, don't worry", she soothed her distressed colleague. "Just get yourself off home."

Taking a deep breath and wiping her eyes then drinking the proffered water, Sharon thanked her boss. Her mind wandering chaotically in several directions at once, another thought occurred to her.

"Paulie! Lynsey, could you let them know I had to leave and I'm not sure when I'll get back?"

"Of course I will. What do you want me to tell them?"

"Tell them the truth. They'll imagine all sorts otherwise. Same with Jen."

Lynsey nodded, giving Sharon's hand a comforting squeeze as she walked her back to the reception desk to collect her jacket and bag. The sunlight dazzled her as she walked out into a town which felt different from what it had been that morning. Now, it was a place to which her distressed niece may be heading; a place which held differences from what the teenager had always known. Differences which would add to her fraught state.

138

Carole had already been contacted by Louise; Charlene was as horrified, angry and concerned as Lynsey had been, asking how the school could have allowed it to come to this. Neither of them verbalised their fears about where the video footage may have ended up; the details Louise gave had been understandably sketchy as she struggled to take in what had happened to her daughter. She knew that one of the prefects had caught the bullies watching the video on the phone on which it had been filmed and that the phone had been confiscated. Nobody was saying and nobody wanted to ask whether the footage had been sent anywhere else. All they could do was wait for news. Sharon couldn't even seek solace in waiting with Charlene and Brandon or with her mother; they would each have to remain at their own home in case Lucy went there. Inverbrudock was fairly small and she had their addresses. Lucy's phone was going to voicemail; nobody even knew if she had it with her.

Sharon's second half finished cup of tea that day was turning lukewarm on her light wooden drop leaf kitchen table, the beginnings of a milky skin developing. She longed for the circumstances in which her last cup had gone cold; happily busy at work, looking forward to seeing Paulie. This one, she had made for the sake of something to do and had found herself barely able to face drinking any of it. She got up to pour it away; as she reached for the tap to rinse it away and wash the cup, her phone beeped with a text. The cup clattered forgotten into the sink.

Bethany. For once, not the name she wanted to see; the message preview soon changed her mind.

"Lucy here safe. Ran from school today. Louise aware, on way. Xx"

Sharon replied with a heart emoji then quickly texted her mother, Charlene, Jen and Lynsey: "Lucy safe. Went to Bethany in Perth! Louise on way to get her." To Jen and Lynsey's texts, she added "Someone please let Paulie know. Thanks x x

13

August 2019

Perhaps this was what the Festival crowds always felt like to Lucy. Her precious child.

The choking, claustrophobic need to get through the noise and chaos; the primal need not to have anyone get in her way and try to force her to interact; the all consuming desperation to be out of the crowds and have space to process the trauma.

Louise could normally get from her office to Marydean High in twenty minutes, give or take the usual city traffic delays. Unable to get through to any of the taxi firms, she had waited an agonising five minutes for a bus which then took another thirty to get far enough out of the city centre to even begin to pick up speed. She had wanted to scream at every tourist holding it up asking the driver questions. How could it matter which Premier Inn they wanted or what Venue 37 meant when a child had gone missing? On some level she knew this was unreasonable, yet it wasn't; it was a natural response to be feeling, given the stress of her situation.

Was this how Lucy felt? Had her daughter been trying to tell Louise something like this all the years she had thought she was merely being lazy, making excuses or blaming others for her own social and emotional mismanagement?

Was this what it took for her, Louise, to actually listen to her own child?

Was it too late?

The thought of "too late" clawed with ragged nails at the edges of her consciousness and clenched her stomach into vacuum. She fought it back down. She must step up for her daughter now; she must hold it together. Finally getting off the bus, she ran the few hundred metres to the school; breath coming in gasps, not even registering the stares of passers by; concern, fearful empathy and something like recoil in their eyes as they turned at the sight of a clearly distressed woman running into a school.

The secretary was waiting at the main entrance, her eyes fearful, her manner calm and kind. Louise allowed herself to realise she felt some admiration for Karen Reid; she was efficient and practical whilst at the same time showing herself to be highly sensitive and perceptive to the needs of the young people who often came to her initially rather than approach a guidance teacher.

"Ms Penhaligon, please come into the office." She ushered Louise inside; quietly respectful, attentive while avoiding touching her. "Take a seat, catch your breath and have some water. Ms McAllister will be with us in a moment."

Louise's head snapped upright at the mention of the headmistress' name; right then the inner office door opened and Margaret McAllister appeared.

"So how exactly have you managed to lose my daughter?"

"Ms Penhaligon, I can hardly begin to imagine what you must be going through and this will mean little to you right now but I am profoundly sorry that this has been allowed to happen. We as a school have let Lucy down badly; I offer no excuses. Now we must do what we can to work together and put this right."

"How can we? Nobody even knows where she is!"

"I have informed the police and they are constantly checking for her phone being used; right now, it is going to voicemail. I have now been updated that an officer spoke with your neighbour Mrs Robertson, who used your spare key and checked your home; Lucy is not there but your neighbour is going to stay where she can watch out for her.

Is there anywhere else you can think of that she might have gone?"

"I suppose she might go to Sharon; that's my older sister in Inverbrudock. My mother lives there too. Lucy is close to her aunt, though the family home was recently sold so she and my mother both live at new addresses where Lucy has never been."

"Would she know how to find them?"

"Possibly; she is competent with apps on her phone and she has the addresses. Inverbrudock isn't that big and it has quite a straightforward layout. My sister will be at work; she is a receptionist at one of the hotels. I will contact her. I need you to tell me what happened to my daughter today! Ms Reid said that there had been a bullying incident and one of the prefects caught her classmates with a video of it on a mobile phone showing Lucy in distress? What exactly has been done to my child and what has been done about this video?"

"I have the phone in my custody and the girls responsible were caught before they were able to share the footage with anybody else. They have been told they are suspended and they are currently being kept in one of the classrooms until their parents come to collect them. I am doing everything in my power to keep them from encountering Lucy."

"You'd better keep them from encountering me too. I have a fair idea who we're talking about here. Did they actually intend to share this video?"

"The prefect who caught them overheard one of them saying that the video wouldn't upload, so yes, I'm afraid it seems they did intend to. The prefect took the phone and brought it straight to me."

"Well, I'm glad somebody at this school did something to help my daughter. What had these girls been doing to push Lucy to the point of a meltdown? I knew there were some issues with people teasing her but I didn't think there had been violence."

142

"That is something I am going to investigate. I will be interviewing all her teachers too, past and present. It's important to realise, though, that what may seem like 'low level' bullying with little or no physical element can be every bit as damaging when it is relentless and goes on for a long time. I believe there has been a pattern of behaviour here which has been missed and this is a failing from which we need to learn. Meanwhile, we need to focus on finding Lucy. Ms Penhaligon, I know that I have no right to ask anything of you, but it is important that you do not approach any of these girls or their families. I give you my word that they will be dealt with. Right now, Lucy needs you. When we find her, and we will, she needs to know that a whole network of people is going to help her get past this and continue her education. That network needs to be strong, positive and focused on what's best for Lucy. Now, this is something we have discussed before and had differing opinions, but this needs to be said. Going forward, Ms Penhaligon, you will need to accept Lucy's autism. We all need to get to know and support the person she is, not try to change her or make her conform to a perceived ideal of what is normal."

"I just want her back, Ms McAllister. I want my wee girl!"

"I know you do, Louise. We all do."

The softening of Ms McAllister's voice and unexpected, instinctive use of her Christian name melted through Louise's defences, bringing her to the brink of tears. This time, Karen Reid placed a gently guiding hand on her back as she escorted her to the school gate.

"Now, you get yourself home and contact your mother and sister; have them contact anyone else you can think of and keep your phone free in case Lucy gets in touch. Please look after yourself, and as Ms McAllister said, we are going to work together to put this right."

Louise walked home in a daze. Fiona was in the open doorway of the flat next door, looking out as promised; wordlessly she rushed to hug Louise. She would bring some oatcakes and cheese later so that Louise would have something to pick at as and when she could; she must keep her strength up. Nodding numbly at her neighbour's thoughtfulness, social graces were beyond her right then. Everything felt woolly and alien. Putting her key in the lock on the third attempt, she felt guilt come rapier sharp as she remembered how many times she had snapped impatiently at Lucy for fumbling and being clumsy. Had that been, at least partly, a product of ongoing anxiety too?

Walking into the flat, she felt as though she were simultaneously living two lives. There was this reality where for the first time in the fourteen years of her child's life she had no idea where she was, and the other existence; the bearable one where Lucy would run to greet her, chores done, eager to please. Too eager to please. Begging to be liked. Her own daughter was constantly trying to earn her love. Checking the land line for messages dashed her hopes once again. She wandered into the kitchen, eyes automatically finding the kettle and refreshments. The version of her that was still living in the bearable existence switched it on; picked up the box of decaffeinated cappuccino sachets as the version of her frozen in this reality watched. The stuff Lucy with teenage disdain called "Anne Boleyn cappuccino"; all head, no body.

No body.

Louise sobbed.

Sharon's mobile went to voicemail; she was at work then. Louise did not keep track of her shifts. The manager at the hotel was very apologetic; Sharon was away from her desk and must be assisting a guest. Of course she would tell her what had happened as soon as possible and advise her to wait and leave Louise's phone lines available in case her niece contacted her mother. How appalling that the school let such a thing happen. Teenagers bullying a classmate and filming it was bad enough but for her to be able to leave the building distressed and nobody notice? How dreadful. In the same way as with Karen at the school and Fiona next door, the words of support reached her from a faraway place. Hearing her mother's voice was harder; telling her what had happened to her granddaughter searingly painful, cutting through the fog only to fill the space with bolts of lightning. Carole concurred that Emma should be contacted; neither of them believed that Lucy would even contemplate running off to London but then hours earlier they would not have envisaged her running off anywhere at all. In any case it was right to keep Emma informed. Carole agreed to make that call and to contact Sheila and Sandra so that Louise could keep her lines free. In the meantime, it was always worth trying Lucy's phone again.

It went to voicemail.

Staring at her stubbornly inert phone on the table in front of her, Louise watched Lucy's childhood play out in her mind's eye, unrolling and slithering onto the floor like an old cinema reel. She saw the difficult times but she also saw the times they had fun together; she saw the conversations which were intense and serious, even precocious, but memorable for the knowledge that Lucy was trusting her to share some of her world, even if merely as a visitor. She saw her compassion which could be too great for her young heart and mind to manage, leading her to cry or worry over things long after people, including Louise herself, expected her to have moved on from them. Her own heart cracked as she recalled the times when she had enough and snapped at her daughter to stop wallowing, to get over it, to stop deliberately upsetting herself to get attention. How those sudden changes in her response had distressed Lucy even more; she had never seen them coming and had taken them like physical blows. She knew that her harsh responses had been driven as much by despair at not being able to stop her daughter from suffering as by being sick of hearing about it but those sudden swings from practiced comfort to cruel rebukes must have been a huge shock to the system of an autistic child who did not always pick up on the gradual shift in her ability to feel undiluted sympathy.

The phone on the table buzzed and lit up with an incoming call. Louise jumped, adrenalin flooding through her. She opened the front cover of its pink flamingo case.

Bethany.

For Heaven's sake. Only this social misfit of a cousin would have either such hapless timing or so little common sense. Both were equally possible.

Louise had never been close to her Aunt Sheila and Uncle Gerry's strange, unhappy only child. Even as she looked at Lucy's autism in a new light, she still felt a deep-down revulsion towards Bethany's. She was a grown woman in her forties; surely she should be more integrated into the real world by now; have better instincts. This could not be Lucy's future. Never having had a relationship; calling herself asexual. Dyeing her hair blue so that people would notice that before any of the aspects of her oddness that she couldn't control. According to Mum, still holding on to some neurotic "thing" about those slender dining forks; the good ones, with which she had always been so slow to eat her Christmas dinner when the family used to get together. Absolutely ridiculous. No, this was not going to be Lucy's future. Margaret McAllister would have to like it or lump it; she was not going to indulge this whole autism thing. All right, she'd had little interaction with Bethany as an adult. She could have come around to the possibility she was doing her cousin an injustice, projecting the painfully inept child she had looked down upon onto an independent woman she didn't even properly know. Yet here she was, bumbling and blundering into a crisis, phoning her at the worst possible time. Louise remembered her enthusiastic but stilted, clearly rehearsed little speeches at those

Christmas family gatherings; no doubt she was about to be on the receiving end of another one. Pretty words. Please like me! Please notice me! It's all about me!

No. Lucy was not going to go down that road, and lonely, needy Bethany was about to be given short shrift.

"Bethany. This really isn't a good ti…"

Her cousin's voice, not heard in so long and almost unrecognised, cut in with unexpected strength and authority.

"Lucy is here."

A pause as Louise's mind flailed like a clumsy drunk on an icy pavement.

"Lucy is here in Perth with me. She is safe. Upset, but safe. Now Louise, I know you must be worried sick and all sort of things will be going through your mind right now, but I need you to listen to me. Lucy is struggling with the thought of speaking to you; she has had an exceptionally bad day and on top of that, is expecting you to be terribly angry. I am going to gently persuade her to say a few words so that you can hear for yourself that she is safe, but we need to do this calmly and at Lucy's pace. Are you with me, Louise?"

Not for the first time that day, Louise found herself wondering if the clutter of conflicted feelings blocking her ability to form a coherent response might be a taste of what another person lived with on an ongoing basis.

"Y-yes, Bethany. I am listening."

"Thank you. I know that probably wasn't easy for you to say to me. Lucy, your Mum is listening, and she will be so happy just to hear your voice. You don't need to explain anything to her right now. This is going to be done as slowly as you need. I've got the phone on speaker, so you don't need to hold it or talk right into it. I want you to describe for me what you can see right now, and your Mum will hear it and feel better for hearing your voice."

147

In an instant Louise's stored up contempt for her cousin, born of fear and ignorance, simply had no place to be. Some part of her knew that she needed to make amends; right now, all that mattered, all that could ever matter was the tiny, golden sliver of the voice she had feared she may never hear again.

"There's a window with a silver handle that has a key in it. I can see people walking along the street and there are some hills further away, across a river. And there's a Siamese cat. Not a real one, a china one. It's got bright blue eyes."

"Oh, Lucy! My darling child! I promise you, everything's going to be OK. I love you so much!"

Bethany's voice again.

"Right, I'm taking the phone off speaker now. See, Lucy? You did really well; now your Mum knows you're here and as you heard, all she cares about is that you're safe. Do you feel OK about me telling her how to get here to take you home? That's good. She's nodding, Louise. Now, do you have a pen and paper to take down my address? Will you be driving?"

"No, I gave the car up because it was costing a fortune."

"I don't drive, and Lucy will be better off travelling with someone she knows well if it has to be public transport. Are you OK to come and get her? I'm within easy walking distance of the bus and train stations."

Louise took the address and directions.

"I will let Sharon know and she can pass on the message to everyone else. You will need to let the police know if they've been involved, then get yourself up here."

"I will. Bethany…"

"It's OK, Louise. There's plenty of time to sort out everything else. The main thing is we get you and Lucy pulling together. Safe journey. It will be good to see you again."

"Yes, you too."

Ending the call, Louise grabbed her keys and rushed out of the flat. Fiona came to the door, hearing her leaving; she called out the good news.

"Oh Louise, that's wonderful! How are you getting to Perth?"

"Train, I think. It will be quicker, and I can still get her back here tonight."

"Hang on; Sam's home now. He'll give you a lift to Waverley. He said to tell you to give us a shout if you needed us to drive you anywhere. You know we'd take you right to Perth if Lucy would be OK in the car with all of us."

"Oh Fiona, would you? I think it would be no more stressful than being on public transport to be honest; it's not as though she didn't know you. Can I take a minute to text Bethany, that's my cousin who's got Lucy with her, so she can let her know what to expect?"

"Of course you can! Sam! Lucy's turned up at Louise's cousin's in Perth. Can we take her up there to get her?"

Louise heard Fiona's husband reply in the affirmative; moments later he appeared at the door, car keys in hand.

"Hey, Louise. Oh, what a relief about your poor lassie. The car's in the car park; let's go and bring her home."

"Thank you so much, both of you. Sam, I just need to text my cousin so that she can let Lucy know what and who to expect."

"Sure, we understand. You'll both have a lot to talk about, but once she's settled back in we'll all have a pizza and movie night to celebrate. Right, Fi?"

"Absolutely. You get that text sent off then we'll be on our way."

Louise felt a rush of affection for her neighbours, who had always been supportive as she raised Lucy alone. Here they were, making it clear that they would be an ongoing part of whatever she needed to do to get Lucy through this crisis. As would Bethany and the rest of the family. For the first time, Louise allowed herself to believe that the two of them did not have to do this alone. It would be tough; the bullying still needed to be addressed and that would mean painful reliving of events for Lucy as well as resistance from some people who would unavoidably still be on the scene. This was no idealised happy ending. It still worried her that Lucy would always have vulnerabilities; a big part of her still wished that her life could have been more straightforward. The important thing was her daughter was no longer facing it all alone and neither was she.

14

August 2019

Where would it be; what would be the name and shape of her new world?

Unnoticed by the crowds of people hurrying around her, Lucy thought about places she could go which were far away but where someone she knew could help her to start again.

Aunt Emma was far away in London and she sent Lucy lots of interesting things, especially about history. She didn't see her often though and Lucy knew that London would be too big, loud and dangerous. Still reeling from what had happened in school, Lucy's mental processes, her past and present were shaken and fragmented, swirled together like the bright and jagged shapes in an old-fashioned kaleidoscope. She was all the ages she had ever been, from her earliest memories upwards. Her thoughts were the primary hued, stick figured expressions of a small child with the learned reflexes of a mature teenager. Moment by moment, she was piecing together what "now" was supposed to look and feel like.

Not London. Definitely not London. Her first thought had been to go to Aunt Sharon in Inverbrudock. If a bus came in with that familiar pattern of letters, the kaleidoscope would stop whirling enough for her to get on. With a brittle flare and scatter of colours and edges, the kaleidoscope turned again. Aunt Sharon, and indeed Grandma, were not in the big house next door to the people with the friendly ginger cat any more. She had their new addresses, but they were in her phone. She did not want to switch on her phone. A jagged memory of Roseanne's gloating face rushed back into her frail mental landscape;

right before pushing it out again, she recalled a phone being held out towards her as she screamed. Held out the way people held their phones when they were taking your photo with them. Had Roseanne taken her photo? Was that moment of weakness captured, made real, recorded on screen so that she could no longer pretend it never happened?

Darkness creeping, crawling and catching at the edges of her vision again. No. Not here. She must put that thought away, nice and tidy, exactly like organising her room at home. If she kept her phone switched off, silent and sleeping, it would still never have happened and there would be no photo.

That was better. So, perhaps she could go to Charlene and Brandon. They would be able to tell her how to find Aunt Sharon; in the meantime Charlene would hug her and give her homemade cookies and let her pet the cat and it would purr, its vivid light and dark amber fur all warm and soft and silky and happy. Brandon would show her his trains and not expect her to keep talking. They would talk, but not all the time; not for so long that it made her tired and then sad about being tired. He wouldn't ask her lots of questions and make her explain. Nobody would bark "Careful!" at her every time she so much as looked at the cat. Yes, Inverbrudock would be a good shape of orange dots to drop into place on the front of a bus. She would look for that and get on.

Now the kaleidoscope was turning again, in a more soothing glide of shapes and softer colours. On the bus which had just come in, the electronic rain of light that decided its destination now soundlessly falling into place; there it was. The perfect rightness of "Perth". It was a gentle word. It had soft sounds, like a cat purring or the wind whispering through trees or a river flowing over smoothed pebbles. Picked out in lights on the front of the bus, it spoke to Lucy of safety.

The last time she had stayed at Grandma's house with her and Aunt Sharon, when her mother was away for work during one bright Easter holiday frothed with blossom, Aunt Sharon had taken her to Perth to see Aunt Bethany in the bookshop where she worked. Lucy already loved bookshops; they were quiet but in a relaxed way, not so rigidly silent that she would be told off if she spoke a fraction too loudly. They were often cool on a hot day and warm on a cold day; not one extreme to the other; simply and gently softening the air enough to take away that "too muchness". Lucy knew she wasn't allowed to be friends with Aunt Bethany on social networking sites because she was autistic too and shared a lot of stories and information about what that was like; Lucy wanted to know what it would be like when she was Aunt Bethany's age but her Mum did not want her to dwell on being autistic. She said that was a bad thing. It was permitted for her to speak to Aunt Bethany, as long as Lucy didn't go on about being autistic or say it in front of other people who didn't already know. Aunt Sharon had explained that Bethany, whom Lucy still called "auntie" even though she was a cousin not a sister and was not close to her mother, knew Louise's wishes and would not say anything that might get Lucy into trouble. Once she was older, it would be easier for her to ask Bethany the questions she wanted and deserved to. With all of that explained to her, she had relaxed and enjoyed the visit to the bookshop; afterwards the three of them had walked along beside the River Tay, crossing one bridge to visit beautiful gardens full of colour with steps to various levels then walking along and back across a different, curving silver metal bridge which ran so close to the railway line she could see the grain of the wooden sleepers from the safety of the securely fenced footpath. Brandon and Charlene, who both loved trains, had so enjoyed her describing it to them later as the cat purred sleepily in her lap. Perth was linked to all of them. Its name

153

radiated its invitation from the front of the bus and spread out in her heart, curling up warm and orange in her settling mind like Charlene's cat curling up in her lap.

That was it decided, then. Perth was her new beginning.

Placing one foot in front of the other; tremulous like Jane Eyre, determined like Catherine of Aragon; Lucy boarded the bus.

15

August 2019

Quiet midweek afternoons were the best. They allowed Bethany time to focus on a task and get significantly more done. She could sit at her favourite desk in a small room off the main shop floor and focus on administrative work; stocktaking, ordering, petty cash, so many of the tasks her colleagues tended to find boring and repetitive. Bethany felt great satisfaction in organising and keeping everything running smoothly while her colleagues spent more time with customers and answering the phone; she was entirely happy to dust and vacuum, empty the bin, clean the small staff kitchenette and toilet, anything that gave her a sense of nurturing and looking after her workplace. She was a firm believer that buildings responded to being looked after and kept clean; that it gave their atmosphere soul and texture, absorbing that care. It irked her when people assumed that she must be a dull person because of her strengths and preferences in terms of her work. She was not averse to helping a customer or taking a phone call but when she settled into a task then was constantly interrupted, or when she was trying to work in an environment with a lot of background noise, she simply became tired out. On the telephone, she struggled to make out what the caller was saying if she were not in a significantly quiet setting. Explaining repeatedly to people that it had nothing to do with her confidence or ability and will to interact with others tired her out even more than having to cope with sensory overload in the first place. She was lucky, she knew, in having found the balance she had at work; that her enjoyment of tasks others disliked shielded her from having to do so many of those which she found proportionally more difficult and taxing than they did. Bethany loved her job overall, though inevitably there were times when busy days and social or executive functioning glitches left her demoralised and unsettled.

She seemed to be tiring so much more easily these past few years. Tests had ruled out any medical cause; she was thankful for her physical health but frustrated at the lack of answers as to why she was so fatigued and why she seemed to have so little left over for anything else after work. The compact square rooms of her flat was kept tidy but would go for weeks without being dusted and the easy-care laminate floors swept; her bathroom and kitchen surfaces were kept hygienic but that was all.

As for pursuing any other interests or socialising, that had all but dried up. She was particular about accepting invitations every so often so that people would not take offence or give up on asking her, but she was getting to the stage where going out in a group or to a busy place was depleting her too thoroughly. It left her without enough time to restore her energy levels before work or whatever her next necessary commitment was. She still winced when she thought about the time she needed to use the bathroom in a restaurant, misheard the directions she was given in the noisy echoing room and went the wrong way. The jarring cacophony of all six people in the party laughing and correcting her at once had hurt her on so many levels. The noise felt as though someone had turned the inside of her head to glass then scraped polystyrene down it, but the deeper hurt had been to her sense of equality and self worth; her capacity to keep reminding herself that she was on the same level as these unimpaired people. Although the issue she had was with filtering and processing rather than actual hearing, picking things up wrongly was an embarrassing problem which was happening more and more often these days as she became increasingly fatigued. Of course no hearing test could identify this problem; when she had arranged one in her quest for understanding of her difficulties before her autism diagnosis, the normal result had once again suggested to those around her that she was lying, lazy or plain inadequate, leaving her with no defence. In addition to mishearing specific things, she would miss part of what was said because she lost concentration and zoned out. She knew it was rude and it was not something to which she could admit as it would sound as though she were bored or simply lazy. She would not even be aware that she had faded out until the awkward consequences landed on her. She truly did not want to hurt people's feelings by coming over as disinterested; the cause of her lapses was sheer exhaustion combined with sensory overload. When those lapses resulted in her response not matching what she had been asked, or in her appearing to have taken something literally or fallen for a wind-up, that would bring the discordant, ear-bleeding communal shriek of laughter once again. This was often followed by the "aaawww, aren't you just so cute, bless you" comments which withered her soul, especially when delivered with a condescending physical touch, or the dismissive scoff, toss of a head and flap of a careless hand towards her as though swatting an inconsequential fly when she expressed her feelings about it or tried to explain. It scarcely felt worth her while trying to go out socially any more, though she refused to give up altogether.

Her day in Inverness with Sharon, Charlene and Brandon had been one of those rare, standout few days which would rest poignantly in her memories; a long day when the plan worked out and she was able to sustain it. Even that had left her extra tired for the following few days and she could not account for where the time had gone when she next had a day off. With no mitigating explanation to offer to her colleagues for any drop in her productivity or increase in tired mistakes, Bethany had learned to avoid talking about her fatigue. She had disciplined herself into sacrificing most of the rest of her day to day pleasures in order to conserve her energy for her job. Thus she poured her energy into remaining emotionally invested in the place; cleaning, tidying and always looking for extra initiatives she could be taking. If she could spend hours working on something at the computer, nobody would have to know she was sometimes so exhausted she had to mentally talk herself through every step merely to cross a room; at the same time if she could occupy herself dusting every shelf in the shop, nobody would find out that her brain was so sluggish she would need a calculator for a simple sum. Bethany had become adept at manipulating her tasks to cover up whichever kind of tired she was feeling most at the time.

This idea she had for an anti-bullying event was a case in point. She had spoken with Anita about it; her manager had agreed it was a good idea, thanking Bethany for thinking of it and assuring her that she would consider it for the future. Bethany had already begun to do a bit of research, looking up display materials online and making a note of potential contacts among the local authority and third sector. Every bit of work she put in made her feel a sense of calm; a sense of doing OK, doing enough. So long as she could keep pushing through this wretched unaccountable fatigue and then doing that bit more than was asked of her, she would have fulfilled her part of the bargain and be able to allow herself some downtime.

Today, as it happened, she was spending a bit of time on the front till. Stacey had been talking about some make-up she wanted for a while; a new line which had quickly sold out. More stock was expected in that day at the department store across the street; it had not been put on the shelves yet when Stacey had checked during her early lunch break. While taking down an out of date poster from the window, Bethany had noticed someone walking past with a palette of eyeshadows in the distinctive colours and branding she had seen in Stacey's magazine sticking out of their bag. She deduced that the new stock had now been put on the shelves. When she told Stacey, offering to cover her till so that she could dash out if she wanted and count it as her afternoon break, her colleague had raised her immaculately shaped eyebrows. She didn't think, she said archly in surprise, that Bethany was interested in make-up. Patiently, Bethany had explained that she knew this was important to Stacey, therefore it was of interest to her as a colleague if she could help her to get the products she had been waiting for. Besides which, although she didn't wear it, she could still enjoy looking at the artistry of it and appreciate the colourful displays. Dana, who had been replacing books after helping a customer choose and overheard the exchange, rolled her eyes as Stacey swished out of the door. "Thank you for being so thoughtful, Bethany, in case she forgets to say it!", she had grimaced pointedly as she went to log on to the till at the other end of the currently empty shop.

Stacey breezed back in.

"Well, did you get it?"

"Yes! Thanks, Bethany!"; her scepticism forgotten, Stacey brandished the beautiful palette of deeply iridescent shades towards Bethany and Anita, who had emerged from the manager's office.

"Oh, fantastic! Let's see! Anita, she finally got that make-up; you've got to see this, it's gorgeous!"

Enjoying this moment of solidarity with the colleagues to whom she was less close, differences and social strata set aside, Bethany's attention was completely focused on the attractively packaged and artfully arranged make-up when a small voice took her by surprise.

"Auntie Betty?"

Only one person had ever gotten away with calling her "Betty" more than once, and that was many years ago; before she learned to pronounce "Bethany". Apart from occasional family gatherings and one surprise visit with Sharon around two years ago, Bethany's sole contact with her had been phone calls and letters thanking her for birthday and Christmas gifts, and sporadic text messages. For her to turn up unexpectedly on her own was astonishing enough. But "Auntie Betty", after all these years?

"Lucy?!"

The teenager in school uniform standing in front of her appeared to be in some sort of delayed shock. Her eyes were wide in her pale face and she seemed somehow younger; regressed into a past which was safer than whatever the present was holding for her. Bethany seemed locked in place, unable to translate her thought processes to action; Stacey, who had met Lucy on her previous visit, was staring openly in bewilderment. Anita quickly took charge.

"Hello, Lucy. Bethany, would you like to show Lucy where she can get a drink of water?"

"Oh! Yes, of course. Thank you, Anita. Come on, Lucy, it's through this way."

Bethany's limbs trembled as she ushered her niece through to the staff area. There was something sudden and huge pressing down upon her, calling for the kind of quick reactions she didn't naturally have. Anita had already stepped in where her own instincts ought to have gotten there first.

"Sit down; here's some water"; she deliberately kept her voice soft and low, avoiding direct eye contact. "It's safe here; you're safe. I'm going to sit here and in your own time, you can tell me anything you need to."

"I need to live here now."

"Here – you mean in Perth?"

Lucy nodded.

"Did something bad happen in Edinburgh, Lucy? It's all right if you don't feel ready to say."

"I was supposed to ignore them. Control myself. I wasn't supposed to react. At all. I did everything wrong! I

160

screamed and I ran and threw myself down and they all laughed at me!"

Those bullies! Sharon was right; this had gotten way out of hand.

"Mum said I had to take responsibility! Instead I reacted more than ever! I couldn't help it, but she says I haven't to blame other people!"

Flaming Louise! Bethany had not spoken with her cousin for a long time; she knew via Sharon that Lucy was under unreasonable pressure from her, but this was taking it too...

Louise. She presumably had no idea where Lucy was. If she had run out of school, everybody would be looking for her; the police may even be involved. Bethany needed to handle this quickly, but without risking further trauma to the fragile teenager or sending her running off again. She needed to get Lucy back to her flat, where nobody else would walk in and she could take all the time she needed.

"Lucy, you have not done anything wrong. Now, other people use this room so let's go back to my flat. There's nobody but me living there and it's just a few minutes' walk. Do you feel up to that?"

Lucy nodded again. Bethany discreetly went to speak to Anita, keeping watch the whole time in case Lucy tried to run away again. Suppressing an eye roll with some effort as Anita asked whether she would manage OK, she thanked her for allowing her to leave early and assured her that she would get in touch if she needed any emergency time off.

Lucy held on to her sleeve like a small child as they walked the short distance to Bethany's flat; evidently needing the contact but deeply conditioned not to let herself be seen holding her aunt's hand at her age. Bethany kept conversation light and fleeting, pointing out a hanging basket of deep pink and blue flowers, a seagull eating a dropped sausage roll, a car with a particularly shiny metallic finish. They walked steadily, quietly up the stairs to her second floor flat; all the time Bethany's heart pounded at the thought of the panic unfolding in Edinburgh and what Louise must be going through. Angry though she was with her cousin, she would not wish that anguish on her or anybody else.

Safely inside the flat, Bethany guided her niece to sit down, pouring her another glass of water.

"Lucy, I know what happened at school must have been so awful for you, but we need to let your Mum know you're here. She may get cross with you at times, but I promise you she wants more than anything for you to be safe."

Lucy's eyes widened.

"Please don't make me talk to her, Auntie Bethany!"

The use of her full name was a good sign; Lucy appeared to be coming out of her immediate trauma, but this still needed to be handled very delicately. She must keep the girl calm and trusting without making any promises she would not be able to keep.

"Lucy, nobody is going to make you do anything against your will. You are safe here. Nobody is going to touch you or shout at you and nobody is going to take you out of this flat without my permission. But I do need to let your Mum know that you're safe. I can make the call and put it on speakerphone so that you don't need to hold the phone or have her voice right next to your ear. I'm not going to make you talk to her directly and you don't have to talk about what happened at school right now. I only need you to say a few words so that she can hear for herself that you're here and safe. She needs to know that, and I'm going to help both of you."

If she lets me, she added silently to herself, wondering how her cousin would react to hearing her voice especially at a time like this.

With Lucy's agreement, she made the call.

As she heated some soup, another text came through from Louise, explaining that her neighbours were now

162

giving her a lift and asking her to advise Lucy of the change; that they would be going home in the car with Fiona and Sam. Bethany conveyed the information to Lucy, glad that Louise knew to give her the information in advance.

Lucy stirred her soup, her eyes following the leafy pattern around the edge of the bowl.

"I think they took my photo, Auntie Bethany."

"Who took your photo?"

"Roseanne. I saw her phone pointed at me."

Bethany's heart sank. She had experienced her own share of bullying at school but in those days, at least she had not had to contend with cameraphones and the Internet. The worst she could recall was somebody with a tape recorder pulling her hair to try to make her cry on tape and somebody else wearing mirrored sunglasses as they pushed and taunted her, so that she could see herself being the loser they said she was. All of which was bad enough to happen to a child. She prayed that the photograph would not be shared. It was another piece of bad news she would need to give Louise. If there was a photograph, it needed to be traced.

"Your head teacher is going to have to have a serious talk with Roseanne and her friends. There's a lot that's been going on that shouldn't have and although I can't tell you it will all go away, it is going to get better and you're going to be listened to more."

The entryphone buzzed and Bethany let her cousin in. The neighbours were discreetly waiting in the car.

"Lucy, are you ready? Is there anything you need me to ask your Mum to do, or not do?"

"I'm ready. Thank you, Auntie Bethany. I need her not to be angry and shout at me and to wait until all my words are out before she asks questions."

"That's more than fair, Lucy. More than fair."

163

Closing the living room door, Bethany opened the flat door as her cousin raced up the stairs. Louise was still a fine looking, well styled woman; the aloof teenager Bethany remembered was still there behind the understandably bloodshot eyes of a mother who had recently had to contemplate the possibility of losing her child. Bethany was going to have to keep her from that child for a few moments longer.

"Louise, I know you will be desperate to see Lucy and she's right in there waiting for you. For her sake, though, I need a moment of your time first."

"Bethany, you've never had a child of your own so you cannot…"

"LOUISE. Lucy needs me to tell you a couple of things, and she needs you to be calm when you see her. This is not about me. It is important for Lucy that I tell you these things. She has told me that she needs you not to be angry and shout, and to let her get all her words out before you ask her questions. That is what she has told me will help her to cope. I also need to tell you that, whatever those bullies did to bring her to this crisis, it is possible that at least one of them, Roseanne, took a photograph of her while they were bullying her."

"Oh, it's worse than that, Bethany. They filmed it."

"Oh my God. Well, Lucy doesn't know that yet. Or she's blocked it out. She said that she saw Roseanne pointing her phone at her and thought she took her photo."

"Fortunately, they were caught before they could do anything with the footage and the headmistress has the phone. Now, I am going in there to get my daughter."

"Of course. I needed to tell you that without Lucy hearing it. She needs calm."

Louise marched into the flat, calling her daughter's name. Bethany watched for long enough to see that Lucy was coping then went into her bedroom to allow them their privacy. Minutes later, two tearstained faces were thanking her and bidding her farewell. Giving Louise her landline number, Bethany made her promise to let her know how Lucy was getting on once they had taken some time to adjust, and to let her help from her own life experience of autism. Watching the car drive away, Bethany sagged against the wall; physically and emotionally exhausted. Texting Sharon to update her that Lucy and Louise were on their way home, she cleared away the soup bowls and made herself a cup of tea, which she then rushed so that she could pour herself something stronger. A small one; she was working the next day after all, and she was so tired.

So utterly tired.

Poor Lucy. Bullied and filmed in distress. Hurting so badly and feeling so unsupported she thought she needed to start again in a city she barely knew, at fourteen years old.

Bethany needed to do more. So much more. She had to make a real difference. She wished she had more energy to do something that would tangibly help. An idea and a few notes were not enough. It was time to step up. If only she wasn't so tired. See, now she was making it about herself again. She was bad. She needed to work even harder to compensate for that. She had to push herself more.

She poured away half of her drink. She hadn't even done anything significant; Anita had been the one to react when Lucy arrived in shock, while she stood there stupefied.

She needed to do better.

16

September 2019

This had always felt like a time of new beginnings; a second Spring. Bethany loved the freshness and returning colour of September; the earlier twilights, the thinning of the air and of the crowds. She had been counting the days until she could tap into the energy of the new month after the staleness she always felt by the end of August.

So far, this September had not been working out particularly well for her. A couple of painful glitches at work had floored her spirits. Every so often, the relentless chipping away of all the trivial day to day failures; forgetting to do something, mishearing and handing over the wrong amount of money, taking three attempts to pick something up; every so often, one or two of those chisel blows would take out a whole chunk of her. Two days ago she had been helping Crevan, Dana, Ash and Tommy to move some books away from where a wall was going to be repainted. The prospect of the paint smell was already unwelcome; she could already feel the sensation of it in her nose and down the back of her throat. She had known that she should make two trips as she tackled the final pile. She had simply been too tired. Picking them all up in one go felt like the less exhausting option. She had known it was a bad move even before she lifted them. Sure enough, they had teetered and fallen to the floor in an ungainly, embarrassing mess as the painters laughed at her and mockingly applauded. Then today she had the perfume controversy. It was lunchtime; she had heard a the hiss of a can of fizzy drink being opened in the staff area. Moments later, she smelled the uplifting zing of fresh cherries. "Oh, is that cherry cola?", she had asked, sniffing the air, testing her normal person workplace chat skills. Dana, completely unperturbed, had said it might be the new Wild Cherry perfume Crevan had bought her. Before she could process and think quickly enough to regroup; to be her own smooth PR rescue party, sniff Dana's extended wrist from a circumspect distance and say that no, it was a different smell she had caught, Stacey had been right in there. "Well, that was what you call a tactless remark, Bethany!", she had laughed condescendingly. Having failed to think on her feet quickly enough to be her own PR, she reverted to being her own defence lawyer, trying to explain to Stacey that a tactless remark would have been if Dana had asked "Do you like my new perfume?" and she had said "Oh, is that what it is? I thought somebody had opened a can of cherry cola". Being mistaken about the source of a scent was not being tactless. Stacey was uninterested in her need to redeem herself; no doubt she had enjoyed a mildly amusing diversion in her working day. The slightly different colleague who was such a reliable source of haplessness anecdotes having put her foot in it again was how Stacey wanted to interpret the situation. It gave her that safe feeling of being adept and whole; one with the crowd, not subject to the otherness of which everyone snugly enfolded in the mutual social wellbeing of being "in" society was secretly afraid, knowing that they were all potentially a few faux pas away from the darkness themselves. So she had done what she and others like her so often did; laughed out Bethany's name, shaken her head indulgently and turned away. Shutting her out, choosing not to hear; refusing to let her in on the big universal joke which everybody else seemed to be in on except her. While this time Bethany understood why Stacey thought the episode was funny, it bitterly echoed so many childhood occasions where she honestly had no idea why what she said was so amusing and pleas for clarification had brought that exact same response. The laugh; the shaping of her name into a tool of both dismissal and indictment; the turning away; the shutting her out from the enlightenment she so reasonably, so desperately sought.

She deserved it. She was unravelling when she most needed to be stronger. Reflecting in the merciless solitude of her flat upon these weaknesses which she could not afford because the feelings they evoked were too big for her and too small for others, she berated herself relentlessly. She was old enough now that she should be able to avoid these pitfalls; if she got caught out it was her own fault. Lucy, and others like her, were another matter. This had to be her redemption. If she was still getting into these messes at her age, still giving people ammunition to make her feel small, then she was beyond help. It didn't matter what happened to her. She must focus on these poor bullied children. It was time to get serious about this event. These humiliating misjudgements were only bearable, forgivable and something after which she was eligible for any solace if they had happened for a reason, a redemptive reason. This had to be the push she needed to stop waiting for other people and make it happen.

It was not the best time for Louise to phone her. How typical, Bethany, she chided herself; trust you to screw up on the day Louise decides to phone. This was another lesson she had learned in life, from an ongoing litany of "Trust you, Bethany; something like that could only happen to you, dear"s; it was always her own bad timing. How she was supposed to even begin to make proactive correction to that, she had no idea.

"Louise. How are you and Lucy doing?"

"She's gradually starting to open up to me a bit more. I kept her off school for a few days, but we all felt it would be better for her to start getting back to routine as soon as possible. Those girls are strictly forbidden from speaking to her or contacting her online. One of the prefects, in fact the one who caught the bullies, had been trying to get them to set up a mentoring scheme for pupils who are being bullied and it looks as though that is going to go ahead. It will all be done most discreetly; Lucy will have somebody to talk to and the school has set up youth counselling for her too. It means she has a space where she knows she will be listened to and where the whole idea is for her to talk about anything that's bothering her. Nobody's kidding themselves that there won't be any difficulties when she has to face the bullies again. At least that awful video has been deleted. They'd tried to upload it to one of the social networking sites, but it hadn't worked; some sort of outage to do with the signal, thank Heavens."

"Oh, that is a relief. It will take time for Lucy to get over this. She was so traumatised that day over having had a meltdown in front of so many people. She even called me 'Auntie Betty' when she first saw me. She was like a small child again."

"Bethany, I never did thank you properly for the help and sanctuary you gave Lucy that day. I must admit, I owe you an apology for having misjudged you. I still saw you as you were before. I had no idea how far you'd come; how well you'd overcome your own autism. I had been influenced by my own preconceived ideas of you as an adult; an older version of that autistic child, and I didn't want that for Lucy."

"Whoa. Louise, I appreciate your apology, but I need to set you straight on a couple of things here, and again I am thinking of Lucy in doing this. I AM an older version of that autistic child. Yes, I have learned things from life experience as everybody does; I have developed awareness and strategies that I didn't have as a child. That's growing up from an autistic child to an autistic adult, not overcoming autism in the sense of leaving it behind. I will always be autistic, and so will Lucy. That doesn't mean that she can't have a happy life. I have a happy life, in many ways. I have advantages and privilege that plenty of people don't, whether they're autistic or not. But I can't allow you to hold me up to Lucy as some sort of example of how to get over being autistic. You can't suddenly decide that we're friends because you think that I'm not impaired any more. That's exactly the attitude that will prevent you from supporting Lucy as she really is. The truth is, Louise, I am still impaired. I still have the physical awkwardness, the social judgement and sensory issues, the slower processing time, the executive functioning problems which make me forget things and make ridiculous mistakes. You saw me on a day when I appeared to do well. I spoke to you assertively and coherently when I phoned you because I had planned out what I was going to say, same way as I have been anticipating a conversation like this. I didn't anticipate Lucy turning up at the shop and when she did, I can hardly believe I'm telling you of all people this, but I froze. She was standing in front of me calling me by a child's nickname she hadn't used in nearly ten years, clearly in shock and looking to me as a trusted responsible adult, and I froze. It was my boss who prompted me with what to do; to take her into the staff area and give her a drink of water."

"Is that so? Oh dear, you gave me the impression of being so together when I saw you. Well, I suppose anyone personally involved would have gotten a shock when she turned up like that. Are you... Forgive me if I say the wrong thing here, but are you telling me that Lucy will also always be slow?"

"See, it's not helpful to think of it in those terms. Her brain is wired differently and that will never change. Just like any other person, there will be things she's good at and things she's not so good at. She will have good days and bad days. I'm being slightly hypocritical here because I admit I still struggle with internalised ableism; I loathe my shortcomings and all the frustrating, embarrassing glitches. I still crave approval and try to be perfect. I'm not going to give you a load of flowery rhetoric about self love. That really would be hypocritical of me. The point is you can't model one person's autism on another. You could tell me something Lucy struggled with and I could say to you, 'yes, I can see how a certain aspect of autism may have made that difficult for her; this is something that helped me, or someone else I know of.' Of course there are certain traits in common. You get to know Lucy's autism by getting to know her, not me. You already do know her autism; she is the same person she's always been."

"So what is it I need to do differently?"

"Well, you need to make sure you listen to her and believe her. Even if you don't agree with her, hear her out and accept that what she's telling you is her reality. And take her seriously. Never dismiss or laugh at her. I'm not assuming you do this, but please don't ever do that thing where she's trying to tell you or ask you something and you laugh, turn away and say her name, shaking your head. When people do that, they make us hate our identity; they make us the problem while simultaneously withholding the clarity and framework we're so urgently seeking. Laugh with her when she's laughing; I'm not saying there shouldn't be fun in your lives! But don't laugh at her. If she asks you why something is the way it is, if you don't know, be honest but remind her that you're right there with her and you'll figure it out together. She also needs to know that not every problem she encounters in life will be because of her autism. It is a part of everything, but not the cause of everything. You do need to let go of the whole narrative that autism is shameful and it's something she mustn't talk about though. I don't mean she should be telling anybody and everybody; of course there are circumstances where it's not safe or appropriate to be disclosing a vulnerability. But for instance, I understand from Sharon that you won't let her add me on social networks because I post about autism and you don't want her identifying with it?"

"She's too young for all that stuff!"

171

"How do you know? Have you even seen anything I share? She's autistic now and she needs to be learning, in a safe supportive context, what that means for her! I understand if you don't want her getting involved online with people and groups she doesn't know personally. That, I absolutely get, and I can assure you I would never add her to any groups. I don't do that anyway without asking people first and I wouldn't even ask a teenager to join anything where they would be interacting with people they didn't know. Look, I'm not saying let her add me. It's simply an example I've been made aware of, that shows you making her afraid and ashamed."

"An example involving you, of course. You're still pretty self centred, aren't you? You're what, forty-three? Forty-four?, and you're put out that a teenager hasn't added you on a social network?"

"Stop pushing me away, Louise. You know perfectly well that's not what I'm getting at. I know this is a huge adjustment for you, but Lucy needs us all to work together."

"And I suppose she'll never get married either."

"What? Where on Earth did that come from?"

"Well, you say that you still have, ah, problems like you used to and my Mum tells me that you've had to become asexual?"

"She said that? Or did she say that I am asexual, and you filled in the rest?"

"She said she told Sharon that if she didn't get a move on she'd end up like you, and Sharon said that there was a world of difference between having had a couple of relationships in the past that fizzled out and not being in any particular rush because she's happy with her life the way it is, and being asexual as you are. Oh and that Both Are Valid, of course."

"Ha! I can imagine the general gist of what Sharon would have said to such a rude remark and it would have been a lot more colourful than that. I suspect Carole gave

172

you the abridged version there! You do realise that autistic people can and do have the same range of sexual orientation as everybody else? It's perfectly possible that Lucy might get married, and have children of her own, if that turns out to be what she wants. There is no inevitability about it!"

"So your calling yourself asexual isn't because you've been unable to attract a partner because of your difficulties and you've given up?"

"No, Louise, it is not. For a start, I'm not 'calling' myself asexual. I am asexual. It does not mean that I've given up. Choosing not to pursue a sex life for whatever reason is called celibacy, not asexuality. Asexuality means that a person does not experience sexual attraction. Some are sex repulsed; some aren't bothered about it but may still have a sexual relationship because they have a partner they want to share their lives with and are happy to give them the sexual relationship they want, subject to all the usual rules of consent. The same way as someone might put up with tagging along to an activity which doesn't particularly interest them, because their partner enjoys it. They may have sex because they want to have a family. A person can be on the asexual spectrum and still occasionally experience attraction, to an exceedingly small number of people during their lifetime; those attractions can be extremely rare, but super intense. Or they may experience attraction mildly. If you want to know, in my case, I'm not repulsed by the concept of sex; I simply don't see the appeal. I can form attachments to people which are more accurately described as romantic, but they are not sexual. That attraction and the desire for that activity are not things I experience. It's nothing to do with my being autistic. Yes, I need more solitude than a lot of people do and that happens to be compatible with not wanting a sexual relationship with anybody, but it's nothing to do with autistic people inevitably failing to get partners. That's another negative assumption that Lucy doesn't need!"

173

"I see. This is an awful lot to take in."

"I know, and I think we've talked enough for one day. This is going to take time. Nobody expects you to adjust overnight. Just keep listening to Lucy and keep reassuring her."

"Yes, I agree we've talked for long enough for today. Good night, Bethany."

"Good night, Louise, and do please give my love to Lucy."

Louise hung up; Bethany, utterly drained, tried to process everything she had heard. She did not regard her asexuality as a secret, simply not relevant to anyone else and it had come as a shock to have it thrown in her face like that. Not that the assumptions were news to her. She felt another stab of shame at the memory of how she froze when Lucy first came into the shop. Louise had clearly been disgusted when she confessed that. Had she made things worse for Lucy with anything she had said on the phone? Had she talked about herself more than was appropriate? A lifetime of cliched criticism flooded in on her once more. "You're overthinking. You're making it all about you. You're self pitying. You bring it all on yourself. It's all in your head. Everyone has to walk on eggshells around you. You're so oversensitive; so difficult; so defensive. You think you're the only one with problems. You think you're special. You think you're better than everybody else." Those last two hurt the most; why couldn't people see that she was overcompensating because she thought and had so often been told the exact opposite?

It never stopped.

Bethany covered her ears with a cry of frustration. Bad, bad, bad!

She punched the cushions on the couch.

Many hours and internal replays of the conversation later, she supposed she must have slept; the alarm was ringing, and it was time to get up for work once again.

17

September 2019

Today was a better day. She was still tired and drained from the drama of Lucy's crisis the week before, but her strategies were getting her through; it also happened to be her birthday. Her colleagues had clubbed together to buy her gift vouchers which she could use at the salon she trusted for having her hair cut, and online to stock up on dye; she did the colouring herself and deep dark blue took some maintaining. She was thankful that she enjoyed the sensation of massaging and rinsing every time she recoloured her hair, which she kept a little past shoulder length in straightened layers; that soothing feeling and the end result made the smell of the product bearable. Going to her usual stylist was always a pampering treat; Bridget never commented on her home colouring or made her feel that she had to chat all the time. She cut and styled efficiently, had come to read Bethany's social energy levels reliably over the years and could gauge the right level of chat. Relaxing in the comfortable chair with the cape at exactly the right tightness around her shoulders, Bethany knew she was safe to look tired or let her attention wander without being constantly asked if she was all right. Bridget also knew to be gentle with a brush, without ever making her feel childish.

Bethany had brought cupcakes to work and accepted Ash and Tommy's invitation to play some pool in a nearby bar after they finished. The pool room was quieter than the rest of the bar; Bethany's skill varied but she made herself relax in the easy company of her colleagues, enjoying the buzz of taking her turn to go through and buy a round once both Ash and Tommy had done so twice, insisting on it for the birthday girl. They knew that although she enjoyed a bit of looking after on her birthday, it was equally important for her to keep practicing the things which made her nervous; their unquestioning acceptance and respect for her boundaries made her feel warm inside; safe and screened off from the constant critical inner voice.

After she gathered the two pint glasses, the barman abruptly grabbed her small glass of wine back, pulling it out of her hand as she attempted to draw the three drinks into a cluster she could manage. Without saying a word to her, he put it on a tray, reaching to do the same with the lads' pints which caused his hands to brush her upper chest.

"Thanks for the tray, but you could have offered instead of snatching things from me without even speaking to me."

"Well, excuse me, darling, but you looked as though you were going to drop them. I was trying to be nice."

"Trying to be nice usually involves speaking to people and asking before reaching into their personal space. You have judged me to be so clumsy I don't deserve basic courtesy. Thanks for that, bud; happy birthday to me."

"Wow. You need to sort out your attitude, princess, or you'll never get a boyfriend."

Bethany wasn't even going to begin to unpack that one. Tears stung her eyes as she took the tray back through to the pool room, the sight of her friends and the inevitable need to account for a sudden change in her mood made her even more fragile. Her attempt at a smile; at being the same celebrating birthday girl who had left the room a few minutes ago didn't quite make it.

"Are you OK, Beth?"

"I will be. Just another microaggression. Ooh, looks like you've got a plant on there with those two reds!"

Ash nodded, understanding her need to file away whatever had happened in order to salvage the evening. As a Scottish Asian and an active union rep, he was more than familiar with microaggressions and how they could relentlessly undermine people. Wishing he could take away the hurt of whatever had happened to his colleague and friend, he lined up his cue and struck the cue ball, sending one red straight towards the other and potting the one next to the pocket. Applauding, Bethany's smile was back to her mouth if not her eyes.

This was going to be the final drink; she was still working the following day. Thanking the lads for a good night out, she made her way home with mixed emotions. Oh well, that was another birthday over. She forced herself to think of the thoughtful gift her colleagues gave, and the perfectly acceptable number of cards lined up on her windowsill, including for the first time separate ones from Lucy and Louise. This was progress; building her relationship with her cousin and helping her niece was a good thing she was doing. If she could make this anti-bullying event idea come off, then her next birthday would be markedly different. She would be able to celebrate wholeheartedly; she would deserve it. She would come across better; give off a whole different vibe. People would think enough of her, including strangers on first impression, to presume competence or at least to speak to her like a valid autonomous adult and not demonise her for having boundaries.

This had to get better. She had to get better; her ability to ensure damage limitation by managing her frustrated reactions was slipping away. She did not feel that she had said anything so wrong to the barman; she had not sworn, insulted him or raised her voice beyond what was necessary for him to hear what she was saying in the by then quite busy bar. She simply hadn't swooned in humble gratitude and allowed him to claim his points for physically intervening. Now, she had the added problem of yet another enemy made whom she knew she may well not recognise if she saw them again, especially out of the context in which she had met them. She had always had trouble recognising people; even if she knew the face was familiar, she often could not place who it was or where she knew them from. This had been yet another source of frequent embarrassment, unintentional offence and mockery over the years. She had often been accused of snubbing people by passing them by at close quarters, sometimes too close for them to believe that she genuinely had not processed the visual information to register that they were there. She never intended it; she truly had not seen or recognised them and was always upset to think that she may have made someone feel shunned or unimportant. Real friends came to know not to confront her about it. In an instance like this, though, after an encounter like the one she had with the barman, her difficulty in recognising people could even be dangerous if it meant she had no way to prepare for or avoid any subsequent hostilities.

Did she really deserve the contempt he had shown in the first place? Was she such an awful person that a stranger had the right to declare her unworthy of the love he expected she must want, then further assumed she was unable to attain? Being asexual did not make that boyfriend comment any less hurtful. Had she honestly merited such a vicious personal criticism?

Surely this one couldn't be all on her. Had he offered her a tray for the drinks, in a friendly manner as though talking to an equal, she would indeed have graciously accepted. She would have been secretly glad to be spared the precarious balancing act with two full pint glasses and a wine glass which was not of a shape to stack neatly with them. Perhaps it was her fault for not having the sense to ask; for being too proud, wanting to manage the same way as Ash and Tommy already had twice each. They had bigger hands. It was all her fault. She was the problem.

No; she deserved everything she was feeling now. By next year she had to have achieved something to make up for her shortcomings.

18

October 2019

It was all beginning to come together. Every day she was at work, Bethany had been setting aside a bit of time to do some research; it had become the most cherished part of her day. She had bookmarked sources of leaflets and toolkits on bullying, read up case studies and compiled a list of the local schools and youth projects. She had drifted away from the idea of involving her colleagues at this stage; there would be plenty of time for that once she had Anita's approval for any expenses. This needed to be her doing; her contribution.

For now, it was her secret.

She could see in her mind's eye how the event would go. There would be display stands with the leaflets and copies of the handout she had compiled with websites, helplines and further reading. A couple of speakers; ideally one survivor of bullying and one teacher or youth worker. Someone could give a reading; some poetry perhaps, or even perform an original song. Her imagination soared into how many positive things could be achieved through her initiative. She pictured bullied pupils coming through the doors wide eyed and nervous, then connecting with one another and leaving with the hope and solidarity of new friendship. She imagined people passing by and walking in by chance, finding the answers they had not even realised they were looking for. She envisaged grateful parents and youth workers coming up to her with shining eyes, telling her they had been at their wits' end until she brought all these people and resources together. She foresaw the joy of a teenager or student standing up to speak in public for the first time, marking a turning point in their life. So much pain eased; even though it would be a tiny proportion of the vast ocean of all those bullied children's lonely anguish, the waves of which crashed against her soul every single day, the roar and spume calling and seeping coldly into the background to her every thought.

No, she could not risk this stalling and never getting off the ground. To keep up the momentum and pull together something she could present to Anita, she had to do this part alone. Working alone had always suited her better; it saw her at her most productive. Sharing a task took extra energy to navigate; energy which she could not spare.

She had worked an extra Saturday shift to allow Dana to go to a final fitting for her wedding dress, so she had an extra day off during the week. She called Rhona in Inverness. Better to do it from home; she could be overheard in the shop and she was still not ready to share this exciting plan with her colleagues. Rhona was impressed and excited for her; gave her the tips she asked for about budgeting, numbers and insurance. Anita was going to be so pleased that she had thought of all these factors. Busy as she was with her managerial responsibilities, Anita would be even more delighted if some speakers had already been lined up. Of course Bethany couldn't get any firm commitments until she could establish when this was going to happen; she could, however, find out when people were available thus helping to narrow down the options for a date, saving Anita even more time and effort. Sending prospective speakers her list of the titles and resources she expected to be displaying would help them to plan out their own contributions; she duly typed it up and attached it to the emails. By the next weekend, she had enough interest to put together her well developed proposal for her manager.

She had emailed the document to herself at home to print off, ceremonially with a glass of wine to celebrate the milestone. This was, after all, the last time it would all be within her control. From now she would have to wait for input and approval from others. She sat at her living room table, sipping her drink as the crisp autumn sunlight sank into its colourful frosty night pillow of sky, under blankets of dark rolling hills. It would rise in the morning in berry shimmering, leaf sparkling readiness as her own hard work came to fruition.

Morning came, as it turned out, in a disappointing blur of misty rain. Every surface seemed dragged down by the anti-climax after yesterday's beautiful evening. Bethany usually found such weather particularly exasperating as it warped her hair out of its precisely straightened lines, breaking its symmetry and catching at her peripheral vision. Today she gave both the weather and her hair the most fleeting of attention; once she left the house, all that mattered was the time she had booked in to talk with Anita. Coffee, stocktaking and dusting eased her through the treacle-slow morning, each minute dark and heavy with the approaching reality of the discussion to come. This was no longer her own private project; she could no longer follow what she had learned was the most viable strategy for getting things to work out as she needed them to. She could no longer rely exclusively upon herself and her own world view.

Anita was too still; too quiet. She had greeted Bethany warmly; when she explained to her boss why she had asked to see her, Anita had seemed a little surprised but still friendly. Now she was sitting looking back and forward through the pages Bethany had so neatly and professionally presented, her face unreadable, her body tense.

"So you've already contacted people about this?"

"Well, yes! I thought it would save time..."

"And you've told them we would be displaying specific books and resources at this event?"

"It's a plan; I was showing initiative!"

181

"Showing init… Bethany, you cannot do things like this on company time using company resources and especially represent Mackenzie Books claiming that we endorse particular titles without consulting me first! Something like this, not even I can authorise; it would have to go through Head Office! Oh, Bethany, I can see you've spent a lot of time on this and your intentions are good, but what were you thinking? Why on Earth did you contact people without even asking me first?"

"I – You said it was a good idea…"

"A good idea, yes, which I would have been willing to consider for some point in the future had you followed proper protocol and come to me with your plans! As it is, I'm sorry but this is absolutely not going to be possible. Not now, not ever! You will have to tell these people you've contacted that you made a mistake and that you did this without the knowledge and approval of your employer. There are all sorts of contractual implications around what we can promote at events. Did you discuss this with any of your colleagues?"

Bethany's world was teetering on its axis. Her feet, her stomach, her ears, her tongue all felt numb while her chest tightened unbearably and her nails dug painfully into her palms. How could this be happening? Her words tore their way through her rigid mouth as she woodenly shook her head.

"No. Well, not here; just Rhona."

"Rhona? What, in Inverness? So not only have you done this and contacted people without consulting me, you've discussed it with another branch. Bethany, this is a serious breach of protocol. Please tell me you haven't actually tried to order anything."

"No! God, no, I wouldn't have spent company money without asking you, Anita! I just needed to do something! Children are being bullied now, not at some point in the future! That was why…" Her voice began to waver. "That was why my niece was so traumatised when she came here a few weeks ago. Her classmates had bullied her to a meltdown and filmed it! I can't stand it; kids are getting hurt so badly! And now you're saying this can never happen because I messed up? Please don't make me responsible for that, Anita! Please!"

Tears were pouring down her face now. Anita sighed, burying her face in her hands.

"Look, Bethany, as I said, I know your intention was to help people, and I am sorry, deeply sorry that someone did that to your niece. But you're a responsible adult and an employee of this organisation, and you have made an unbelievably bad error of judgement. You are going to have to face up to that and live in the real world with the rest of us, where people do things the right way even though it means having to be patient, and take responsibility for their mistakes. I cannot condone what you've done, and I certainly cannot allow an unsanctioned event to go ahead just to spare your feelings."

Darkness swirled, hot and metallic as steam from an espresso shot, adrenalin flooding her system with the hurt and frustration and injustice of it all. Her emotions were so huge, they were a sensory overload in themselves. How could she be expected to handle this gracefully; to cope with this awfulness and accept it? How was she meant to arrange her face into an expression which would not draw further fire?

"JUST to spare my feelings? This is not a stupid game. Please don't pretend to care about my niece if that's how you see it. And as for living in the real world with the rest of you, I take it that's a dig at my autism. Well…"

Anita stood up from her desk, her eyes and her voice now ice cold, all sympathy gone.

"Do not play that card with me after what you've done. How dare you? Bethany, I think you'd better leave the premises right now, before you really get yourself into

183

major trouble. This is already serious misconduct. Go home, calm down and I will speak with you tomorrow in this office at nine o'clock. You would be well advised to have your union representative present for that meeting. I will arrange that. Now, leave the building. Go."

Bethany searched her fragmented mind for the instructions on how to work her legs; her vision hampered by the tears which continued to flow, she lurched towards the door. Anita had not quite finished being cruel.

"And stop crying before you walk through the shop. We have customers. Actions have consequences; take it like an adult."

That ocean tide of rage inside her from leagues of bullied children became a tsunami. Somewhere in that catastrophic surge, nine-year-old Bethany, her hair still uncontrolled and without a style of her choice watched her own pathetic, haunted face in mirrored sunglasses as the boys pushed her against the wall, fingers jabbing painfully into her chest. She tumbled over and over in the vertical sea; emerging three years old, having been painfully smacked on the bare backs of her legs, right where the skin was so sensitive. Then ordered to stop crying immediately or get the same again, harder; hurt on top of hurt. Being expected to be able to instantly stop crying in those circumstances was as feasible as King Canute trying to stop the tide. The adult in her who had these words now, to express these injustices and help these children, was herself now helpless; her foundations ripped away, drowning in her failure, her spirit angry red like the skin on those little three-year-old legs. Worthless. Nothing left to lose.

"Do you want me to leave the building immediately, or to stop crying first? Because I'm telling you now, it's one or the other. You hurt me so badly then order me to stop crying just like that? I hope somebody does to you what you've done to me. Go to Hell, Anita."

"OUT!"

If any customers saw her, she did not see them. Somehow she remembered to collect her handbag, but she did not register the shocked looks on the faces of her colleagues, nor those of passers by as she ran home sobbing. She barely even registered the traffic; it was fortunate that the two roads she had to cross were not busy. She thought that all of her tears had come out until she walked through the door of her flat, seeing the table at which she had sat the night before with her celebratory wine and the printout of her misdeeds, thinking she'd done such a good thing. She sank to the floor, sobbing.

The rest of that bottle of wine disappeared, then the remains of a bottle of vodka left over from her birthday. She normally hated getting drunk; enjoying a drink or two was one thing but she could never understand why anyone wanted to drink to the point of being sick, embarrassing themselves, losing dignity and friends or having to deal with being ill the next day. Hangovers were certainly not sensory friendly. She prided herself on making responsible choices regarding alcohol. But then, apparently she had completely and utterly failed at responsibility, or "adulting" as people liked to call it these days.

She gulped more vodka. Mixers were as redundant as she was probably about to be.

Poor Lucy. Poor all children who were going through bullying right now. She had failed them, failed them all. As if it weren't bad enough that she had failed to organise this event, she had made it so that it would never happen at all. She had made things worse; snatched a lifeline away.

The golden day in Inverness spooled through her mind on fast replay. Standing up to that menace with the clipboard; demolishing that bigoted woman who insulted Brandon on the train. (They'd applauded her! Her! What a farce.) Sitting in the bar of her favourite hotel celebrating her ideas, her plans, reflecting on the conversation with Rhona. Rhona! She would find out how disastrously wrong it had all gone! Bethany would never be able to face going into the Inverness branch again. She wouldn't be able to afford to live here any more anyway; she would have to go cap in hand back to her parents; leave this city she loved, leave her own space, go back into an atmosphere of cloying disillusionment. Her attempts to reconnect with them would come to a halt in the viscous social limbo like bullets fired into the gel they used for forensic recreations of shootings on those American detective shows. No longer within easy reach of Sharon, Charlene and Brandon; no means to get to them. No chance to build the routine to which she had so looked forward; walks along the seafront, fish suppers from Vinnie's chippy, convivial company, the music of the sea, Cheminot purring. She was tumbling from a fairground ride, lying on the base as the brightly coloured, joyous shapes flew over her head, each one striking her with a new loss, a new horror.

Louise. What was she going to tell Louise, who was finally looking to her for an example of good autism? Her cousin turned to her, difficult though it must have been after all these years and what did she go and do? Get into serious trouble at work because she failed to navigate the rules and protocols of workplace life. How was Louise supposed to feel optimistic about Lucy's future now?

What had she done?

Brought it all on herself. Again. However badly she was harmed by this; whatever the consequences, she could not access any support. It was her fault. More than ever, she was on her own. She deserved to be. She was bad.

Curled up in the corner of her living room, her bones painfully stiff, she refused them the mercy of shifting position. She drank more vodka; watched the dismal grey light drain away. Velvet night held no comfort. Eventually, hating herself even more for being too selfish to prolong her discomfort any longer, she crawled to bed.

She didn't want to sleep because she would wake up and remember. Eventually she must have dozed because she dreamed fitfully of floating over the house with the narrow forks. The sky was deep turquoise, blending effortlessly with a glassy sea and she was swimming in it, above it. A soft light shone through the skylight from the attic stairs.

19

October 2019

Stillness. Everything hurt, but she was still, and everything was quiet.

Awareness came with the chillingly soft tread and dread shadow of a returning kidnapper, mockingly throwing the pale scraps of a new day into her bedroom.

She was meant to be there at nine. Forcing herself to look at the clock, she winced as the neon digits stabbed into her line of sight, searing her with their reality. Five past seven. It didn't matter. She was going nowhere. She was staying still. She pulled the duvet around her, tight, soothing, safe. A cocoon. She was a butterfly turning back into a caterpillar.

The phone was ringing. Her land line, then her mobile. More time had passed. The sun, so unwelcome now, probed into the cream sanctuary of her bed; its long bright insistence that she get up and go on living. She wanted to be left alone; she knew she would not be.

"Bethany? Are you there?"

It was Ash; her colleague, her friend, but now first and foremost her trade union representative. She had accepted the call but could not form words.

"Bethany? I'm worried. I know what happened yesterday and firstly, I need to know you're safe. We're going to deal with this, one step at a time. I've told Anita you're ill. Can you please give me some indication that you're in a safe place right now?"

"Home."

"Home? Good! That's good, Bethany. Is anyone there with you?"

She croaked a laugh.

"Who?"

"Sorry, what was that?"

"Who'd be with me? I'm a bad person!"

"OK, Bethany, I'm coming over." There was a muffled exchange on the other end of the line; Bethany caught the words 'really concerned', 'breakdown' and 'in a bad way'. "I'll be on my own; I need you to promise me you'll let me in, OK? I need to know you're safe and if you don't let me in, we will have to have someone check on your welfare."

"Yes. I'll let you in. Nobody else."

"I promise I will come alone. Hold on, Bethany. Five minutes."

Ash had been in Bethany's flat once before, with Tommy to help her with a furniture delivery. How different a day that had been. There had been laughter and takeaway pizza. How far away both of those things seemed now. He sat at her table in a suit, ready for the meeting which she had not attended. His brown eyes were kind, but his face was grim.

"OK, so I'm not going to lie to you; we have some serious things to discuss and it's going to be a difficult conversation. Firstly, though, I need to know if you've done anything to harm yourself or if you're thinking about it."

"No. I had a lot to drink last night. Don't usually. Can't go in there. She'll kill me."

"What, Anita? She's not enjoying this any more than I am, Beth. She's read up a bit more on autism since yesterday, specifically about crises and she knows she was harsh in some of the things she said to you. She remembers Lucy turning up in shock and what a scare it gave you. She regrets telling you to stop crying; she understands why you did what you did and how upsetting it was for you to have it go so badly wrong, and she accepts that her parting shot actually hindered you from getting out of the building without causing yourself further trouble. You should have been given time to compose yourself and then Anita should have discreetly walked you to the door. But you did show an extreme reaction to her and the fact is, you breached protocol. I'm so sorry, but there's going to be a disciplinary hearing."

Bethany moaned, her body seeming to shrink into itself.

"You will be notified in writing. I will support you all the way, and we're going to talk through this; I need to understand why you went about things in the way you did. In the meantime, I would suggest that you go to your GP and get yourself signed off with stress. If you don't, it's likely that a medical suspension will be issued; that in itself is not a disciplinary measure. However, whether you're on sick leave or medically suspended, until the disciplinary is resolved you must not come to the shop and you must not have contact with any colleague apart from me. That includes people at other branches."

Bethany nodded, her throat aching; the look on Ash's face told her there was more to come.

"Officially, I am here as your union representative, not your friend. Even you and I are permitted to meet solely to discuss your case. There's something else I must make clear to you, and please believe me when I say that all of us including Anita would have avoided this if possible. I'm afraid these developments mean you cannot attend social events with work colleagues either. I'm sorry to say that includes Crevan and Dana's wedding."

Her tears now were slow and resigned, not the storm of the day before. Ash laid a hand on her shoulder as he went to get her a glass of water.

"Ash?"

Her voice was small; a lost child seeking comfort. He set the glass in front of her, letting her take her time.

"Am I going to lose everything?"

"I really shouldn't speculate; I know that uncertainty is bad for you, but I would be doing you a disservice if I said which way this would go. I do think it's unlikely to go to dismissal. You've never been in trouble before and we're going to go with all the mitigation we can. That said, there's the breach of protocol, your reaction yesterday and your not attending today's meeting without notifying us. Now, I understand a lot of that and we can build a good case around your autism making you unaware of the implications of what you were doing when you contacted external parties, plus the distress caused to you by a negative reaction you weren't in any way expecting. We will have to mention your niece coming to the shop in crisis after a bullying incident and how that has increased your focus on needing to do something to help bullied children. What I need you to help me understand is, why you had to be so secretive about it?"

"I needed it to be all mine."

"What, the credit for putting an event together?"

"No, it's not that. Well, partly, but it's more than that. I needed to have done enough for it to be real; for me to have, I don't know, paid my way. I don't mean money, I mean done something substantial!"

"So you didn't want your ideas being taken over, is that what you're saying? The reason I need to be clear on this is, your having kept it so secret makes it look as though you were aware that you were doing something wrong."

"I thought if I put in enough work, put enough flesh on the bones of it, then it wouldn't get forgotten about once it wasn't all in my hands any more. I thought if I could get it to that stage, it wouldn't fizzle out like so many other things I've tried to do. I wanted to get it past the point where I'd have to hand it over to other people and there not be enough there for them to want to take it on. I thought as long as I didn't make any actual arrangements or spend any company money, I was OK! I can't believe I've gone so wrong!"

"I get that to your mind, you were being thorough and doing your research. We can certainly make a case for your autism impairing your ability to see the more complicated pitfalls around contacting people and endorsing books and websites while you were representing the company without authorisation. Anita should have been clearer when she told you it was a good idea and encouraged your show of initiative."

"She thought I was an adult with common sense."

"Come on, Beth, hindsight is always twenty-twenty." Ash sighed, compassion filling his words. "Forgiving yourself for this is going to be a bigger battle for you than any disciplinary. Which is another reason why you should go to see your GP as soon as possible and get some support in place. Do you have people outside of work who can help you to cope with this; family or friends?"

"My cousin Sharon"; Bethany's voice broke once more as she pictured the good times and then contemplated facing her now, having to tell her what a terrible thing she had done. "She lives in Inverbrudock."

"Oh, that's not too far then; what, another five minutes or so past Arbroath?"

"That's right. I don't have so many friends here; people I say hello to but not people I could talk to about this. I don't go out often these days. My birthday was the first time I'd been out properly since July when I went to Inverness for the day with Sharon. I'm always so tired nowadays, I've nothing left over for anything else once I've done my job and the basic necessities; shopping, seeing to my meals, keeping the house reasonably clean and tidy."

"I didn't realise you were having problems with fatigue; how long has this been an issue?"

"Looking back, I can see it's been the case since my late thirties at least. I've always tired more easily than other people of my age group but it's been at the stage of limiting my work life balance since then. I've had tests and there's nothing physically wrong with me that could explain it, so I didn't see the point in boring anybody with it."

192

"Bethany, you used the phrase 'work life balance' and that is especially important. If you're having any problem with your health that's affecting you to that extent, eventually it's going to impact on your job. Besides which, we want to help you. Please don't try to struggle on alone any more. Look where it's gotten you. Will you give me your word that you'll go to see your doctor?"

"Yes, Ash. I promise. Thank you. For being a great union rep, but also for not hating me."

"Nobody hates you; I promise you that. Anita was angry but then she was upset. She certainly never hated you. She was hurt when you told her to go to Hell, though she understands your emotions were out of control. She's gutted you can't go to Crevan and Dana's wedding and she was as worried as I was when you didn't turn up this morning."

"I shouldn't have said that to her. She's my boss and it was out of order. Will you please tell her I apologise for saying that?"

"Of course I will."

"What about the others; what have they been told?"

"Well, they all know something happened yesterday; that you had a big row with Anita and left upset, but the line we give them is simply that you're signed off sick. Nobody will be told that there's a disciplinary process."

"But Dana and Crevan won't know why I'm missing their wedding!"

"I'll talk to them discreetly and tell them that you're not allowed at a work function when you're on sick leave. Don't worry; I'll make sure they know it isn't your choice."

Bethany dreaded the sound of the door closing behind Ash as he left. It meant that she was left alone with the huge, inescapable knowledge that she was going to go through a formal disciplinary hearing; she who had scrupulously followed rules her entire life. Luckily, her doctor had a cancellation that afternoon; she texted Ash to let him know she had made the appointment then slumped on the couch in an exhausted daze. Everything felt new and strange, even the familiarity of her flat and everything in it. How could this be her life? Nobody had done this to her. She had caused this. How could trying to do good turn so bad?

The doctor's surgery felt like a premonition of the harsh setting in which she imagined she would soon be pleading her case to a grim-faced panel. Bright overhead lights and that draining neutral colour which was something between brown and grey, everywhere. At least in the surgery there were a few brightly coloured posters and toys around and a couple of token pot plants to cheer the place up. The GP was sympathetic, which surprised her when she had to confess that she was there because of a bad thing she had done, not because of an illness or accident which would not have been her own fault. The appointment was nevertheless rushed and somewhat cliched; that surprised her a lot less. She was signed off for two weeks and instructed to make another appointment for then; meanwhile, she was to get some rest, make sure she ate and slept and took healthy exercise and try not to think about it all the time. As though that were even remotely an option. As for her fatigue, well, nobody was as young as they used to be, were they? Those years at medical school had clearly been well spent. Thanking the doctor politely, she made the follow-up appointment at reception then went home, updating Ash by text message once again and arranging for him to collect the sick note from her the next day. For the rest of that day, she read; watched TV; drank endless cups of tea. She slept deeply, exhausted but glad that she had not even felt tempted to drink any more alcohol. She craved cosiness; safety; some kind of purity.

Collecting her sick line the next day, Ash asked her if she had called Sharon yet. She had been unable to face it, she admitted; when she did reach out to her cousin it would be by text or online message. He impressed upon her once more how important it was for her to engage with her support network; he was sure, he insisted, that her misjudgement would not sound as bad to others as it felt to her. Especially to people who knew her well, understood her motivation and intensity and loved her for it. Bethany had her doubts, but it had to be done. She would have enough difficulty pretending to her mother on the weekly phone call that everything was fine. She couldn't contemplate keeping up the mask with Sharon too. Opening the messaging screen, her heart lurched yet again at the sight of their carefree previous messages; how many more painful reminders of the lost time of normality and freedom from this suspenseful purgatory could there be?

"Sharon, I've made a really, really bad mistake."

20

October 2019

The ominous letters always arrived on a Saturday, when support would be harder to find. Charlene had said it before about her battle to claim benefits for Brandon; Bethany had sympathised and now she had more of an idea how it felt. The stark white envelope addressed to Ms Bethany Geraldine Sawyer, with her staff number visible at the top of the clear window, glared unforgivingly real from the familiar grain of her tabletop. She knew what it contained yet the thought of opening it still sickened her. She could imagine how it felt for Brandon and the many people like him who had to open benefit decision letters not knowing what the news inside would be; whether the coming months held relief and recovery from the stress of uncertainty or a further exhausting battle. Ash had assured her that he would bring the outcome of her disciplinary in person rather than leave her to face the news alone, but here was the letter summoning her to the hearing; her transgressions listed in harsh sentences unmitigated by a sympathetic grimace or tilt of the head. Once again, she wondered how she had come to this; how she had managed to go from meticulously rule following model employee terrified of putting a foot wrong to exiled pariah a hair's breadth from the sack. The hearing date was within the two weeks she was signed off; it would take place away from the shop in a building owned by the Council where meeting rooms could be reserved. She desperately wanted to keep her job, yet how could things ever be the same again? How could she face them all, especially Anita? She could picture Stacey's knowing looks; that smug expression she had which Bethany had come to think of as her "Hapless Bethany did it again face".

She had seen it after the incident where she thought someone had opened a can of pop after Dana had tested her new perfume. She must be revelling in this. Even though the disciplinary itself would be confidential, her explosive argument with Anita had to be the talk of the shop. As if it wasn't bad enough the letter arriving on a Saturday, it was also Dana and Crevan's wedding day.

She should have been getting ready; the social anxiety and worry about coping with loud music at the reception made up for by her excitement at being part of something so happy and positive. Seeing a transgender man so proud and handsome in his suit, his lovely bride on his arm and surrounded by people enjoying celebrating a young couple in love starting their life together, had been a cherished anticipation ever since Crevan and Dana announced their engagement. True equality would come when this were no more remarkable than any other wedding but there was still something incredibly special about someone who had been through the physical and psychological journey Crevan had getting their happy ever after. Bethany would see the photos and videos, but it wouldn't be the same. Her mistakes had already cost her something she could never replace, even before any decision had been made.

Sharon had told her to come through in the afternoon; she was on an early shift at the hotel and would meet her. "Turn off your app notifications and stay off social media today", her message had advised; "It will needlessly upset you seeing all the updates from the wedding while you're not allowed to interact with them." Sharon was right; once again pain and shame lanced through her as she pictured her colleagues being told not to contact her or interact with her on social media. They would have been told it was because she was ill and needed to be kept shielded from thinking about work, but they would have put two and two together.

There was no checking in online at the station today; no string of emojis about the lovely evening she was going to have catching up with her cousin. Bethany settled into her seat on the train, once again reminding herself to keep a pleasant expression on her face. She could not afford another glitch right now; another heckle from a stranger about her needing to cheer up would not be something she was able to handle constructively. Her hyperalertness was simply too demanding on her resources; too great a proportion of her mental energy going into it. What should be an occasional level of battle readiness reserved for impending danger had always been her everyday state. It didn't help that both stress and hay fever made her eyelashes prone to falling out, sometimes leaving her eyelids almost bare and completely unprotected. She had fairly recently made the connection between that physical issue and her expression looking even more pinched and anxious because her eyes, already so sensitive, were scrunched up in discomfort. Realising this had been an eye-opener, so to speak; it gave her another crucial bit of understanding but the problem itself and the permanent state of alert remained. Aware that going too far the other way and appearing to be amused could also cause trouble, as always she had to hope that she was finding that passable middle ground and that people would be too distracted by her hair colour to pay attention to the rest of her appearance.

Sharon was waiting on the platform, her concern evident as she rushed to hug her cousin. Usually, Bethany rarely cried; aside from having been taught that it was self indulgent, the salt water stung her sensitive skin and eyes. Since everything changed at work, she seemed to be crying at the least thing; a moment of kindness was as likely to set her off as a sad thought. Sharon held her, giving her the moments of quiet adjustment she needed. A short, gentle walk later they were sitting in Sharon's small but bright, modern flat with cups of tea and ginger biscuits, perfect for dunking and giving the tea a wonderful spicy warmth.

"They won't sack you, Beth. This union rep of yours sounds excellent and they know you well enough to know you were so caught up in wanting to ease people's suffering, children's suffering. They're going to know how distressing this all is for you and that they need have no concerns about you ever risking being in this position again."

"Ash is brilliant. He knows his stuff so well. I know I'm lucky to have him on my side. I can't get my head around this; being a person who gets into serious trouble!"

"See, that's because you're not a person who gets into serious trouble. Of course this is all unfamiliar territory. This disciplinary is about what's happened, not about who you are, and it happened because of a combination of factors most of which can be explained. You were so focused on your goal, it stopped you from seeing some of the issues. That single mindedness is a part of your autism, as is being vulnerable to being caught out by the nuances of workplace etiquette. You reacted badly because you got such a shock and Anita unwittingly escalated that because she hadn't realised how big a shock it would be and didn't expect or understand your reaction. Telling you to take it like an adult was unreasonable; of course it was ridiculous to expect you to stop being upset just like that. Your doctor's note has covered you for not having been in any fit state to attend the meeting or contact your colleagues after the way you left. Making a mistake doesn't mean they don't still have a duty of care to you and you shouldn't have been left to go outside and make your own way home in that state. If you'd been hit by a car they would be in big trouble."

"That's exactly it though, Sharon; I cannot picture them having a duty of care to me. I forfeited that by doing something wrong."

"That's not how it works. Will you ever be able to allow yourself to be less than perfect? You never have been able to let yourself be fallible. You would show so much more mercy to other people who've done way worse than you have. This is your underlying lack of self worth working against you and it's something that desperately needs to be addressed. After all, what exactly is it you've done that's so morally terrible? You technically overstepped your role by losing sight of the fact you were representing your employer, because you were trying to help bullied kids. That had become an obsessive focus because of your intense concern and compassion for Lucy. Because this was all so deeply personal and your empathy is strong to the point of sometimes being unhealthy for you, you reacted with genuine distress. From that point on you were out of your depth because it led you into a situation which for you, with your need for predictability, stability and security as well as the approval of other people, is exceptionally difficult and frightening. There's no bad person in that narrative, Bethany. There's an unfortunate mistake and an environment that doesn't seem to be working out for you any more. I know you love your job, but since this happened, I've been thinking back and there's been something missing for a while, Beth. You've enjoyed aspects of it of course, but it doesn't seem to be bringing you the same fulfilment."

"The thing is, I've been finding especially these past few years that I'm tired all the time. I don't like going on about it because it's boring and miserable and I can't account for it. Oh, I've had tests for anaemia, thyroid, all the usual physical causes and everything's fine there. For which I am thankful of course, but it leaves simple laziness as an explanation. Wanting to waste all my time hiding in my own little world as my mother always said!"

"Hmm. No disrespect to Sheila, but you know how I feel about some of the rubbish you had to put up with from this family when you were going through your formative years. I know that will never fully leave you. We need to find a way for you to make peace with these ingrained thoughts. Do your colleagues know that you've been having problems with fatigue?"

"Not explicitly; most of the time I can get by at work so there's no reason to bring it up. I've told Ash now of course, and he's helped me to see that the fact it's been chipping away at the rest of my life IS relevant to work because without that balance I've become more likely to be negatively impacted at work, because I'm depleted."

"I'm so glad you've got this guy Ash; he sounds like a good friend as well as a good union rep."

"He is, though for the moment he's only my union rep. I'm allowed to have contact with him about the case and nothing else. See, this is how the world works, Shaz; bad people aren't allowed friends or any kind of solace!"

"I know it feels that way, but it honestly isn't that personal. It's just the way these processes are. Once this is all over and done with, he'll be there again as your friend."

Giving her cousin's hand a reassuring squeeze, Sharon got up to make a fresh pot of tea.

"Hold on, Beth. Before you know it, we'll be getting together in happier circumstances again. Charlene would have loved us to come over to see them; I told her we'd see how you were feeling because I know you're struggling to face people at the moment, which she completely understands. I'm proud of you making it through here; I would have come to you, but I agree it's good for you to get out of your flat for a while. But I didn't want to put too many social expectations on you today."

"Thanks. Yeah, it's better for me to get out than have someone in my flat then have to cope with the pressing silence and isolation after they go. It was awful when Ash left the other day."

"I bet it was. Remember there are a lot of people who care a lot about you and appreciate you, and that you do deserve that support."

"How's it going with those new neighbours anyway; is Brandon still getting stressed with the noise?"

Sharon rolled her eyes as she set down the tea.

"They're a pain in the backside. Loud music, the garden's a mess, they never speak to Charlene and Brandon. They're not actively harassing them beyond the occasional 'choo choo' comment but they stare ignorantly at them when they see them. Charlene has given up saying hello to them. She never even got the container back from the cookies she baked to welcome them."

"Oh, that's such a shame. They don't know how lucky they are to have people like Charlene and Brandon next door. I've never had any problems with neighbours but we've rarely gone beyond a quick hello in passing. Mind you, that suits me! I couldn't cope with this in and out of each other's houses all the time scenario that some people seem to have. A friendly smile and each knowing the other would help in an emergency is enough for me."

"Same here. I think Charlene and Brandon would happily settle for their ornaments not ending up dancing when the neighbours put music on. Brandon's trains almost get shaken off their tracks at times."

"Aawww, that must do his head in!"

"It does. We all wish that lot would move on. Oh, I meant to ask you too, if you wanted me to say anything to Louise about giving you a bit of space right now. I don't expect you'll be wanting her to know about what's happened."

"No, not really. It's such a bad example for Lucy. 'You want to feel optimistic about your adulthood as an autistic person, Lucy? Look at Aunt Bethany with her job and her own place.' Then Aunt Bethany promptly gets herself hauled up on a disciplinary!"

"I get why you wouldn't want them to know, but you do still have a job and your own place. Not that either of those things are obligatory for a worthwhile life, as you know. And one of the main things Lucy needs to avoid, as you've also said before, is believing that as an autistic person she cannot have any margin for error. I'd agree it's maybe something to tell them about afterwards rather than during, but everything can be turned into a helpful experience and you're so much stronger at that than you realise."

"Yeah, I can't think clearly about dealing with Louise right now; it's still early days, though we are making progress for Lucy's sake. If she contacts me, though, I'll know it will be focused on Lucy, and that's not a problem."

"It's so good that you're still there for them. In fact, I believe I owe you an apology. Louise did mention to me that she brought up you being asexual when she spoke to you a few weeks ago, in a way which was not particularly well informed. I know you've never seen it as a secret or a big deal and I did mention it to Mum in the context you heard about, but I hadn't realised it had gotten back to Louise. I actually went ballistic at her when she told me what she said to you, and I told Mum she shouldn't have repeated it to her without your permission."

"Oh, don't worry about that. Louise was somewhat better informed about it by the time we ended that conversation. It's probably the least of what those two have discussed about me!"

"Well, I did ask Mum if she'd disclosed anything else and there was one other thing that had cropped up. Louise knows about the narrow forks. Not that you called the house after them; I never told anyone that, but that you still remember finding them difficult."

To Sharon's relief, Bethany laughed loudly.

"I bet that's not quite how they put it either. Let me guess: 'Had A Thing' about them?"

"I rather think it was something along those lines, yes. Still, it's something else for Louise to bear in mind; a good example of manual dexterity issues. It still blows me away how many everyday things take extra energy for you, and Lucy and Brandon. Not that you can't do them; it's hard on you when it needs that constant additional effort. You're doing everything on your own too; running your own home. Frankly, it's no wonder you've run into some problems."

"That's one way of putting it. Oh, I know what you're saying about my intentions being benevolent and all that, but the fact remains I've breached workplace protocol and that is serious. I'm not going to get off scot free here. This is bad."

Sharon seemed to withdraw into herself for a moment, her expression far away.

"It's best you don't keep telling yourself that, Beth. There's nothing you can do about it right now."

There it was again; that subtle shift which Bethany was learning to recognise. The one which told her she had said something wrong, or at least unwittingly touched a raw nerve. Sometimes she had missed a cue; other times she had simply unluckily blundered into a coincidental reference to something she would have had no reason to know was a problem for the other person. In some ways that sort of misstep bothered her even more than missing a cue; bad luck was not something she could correct. She wished once again that those people who had told her over the years that the ridiculous one in a million perfect storms of hapless coincidence into which she stumbled "could only happen to you" would recognise this and not strain her already overloaded emotions with such an unhelpful, maddening remark. Whether autistic people were more prone to these mishaps, she knew logically she lacked enough impartial evidence to say, but every time she received the metaphorical pat on the head of "You Weren't To Know" she felt even more out of step with the rest of the world.

That was the "real world" in which Anita had told her she needed to learn to live. She wondered how it worked for people who had better instincts than she; who, without having to know anything which was not their business or reasonably practicable for them to know, somehow had an inbuilt steering system which would seamlessly divert them away from the blunder. Possibly they weren't even aware of it, which would explain why nobody could tell her how it worked. It was the same with timing. People didn't need to know that somebody was in the bath or had just sat down to a meal or had bad news; they simply never ended up phoning or knocking at that person's door, because this arcane, socially integrated steering system kicked in and they never got as far as intending to do so at that wrong moment. Bethany would have paid big money to have such a steering system installed; sadly, it didn't work that way. The real shame of it was that instead of her immediate response being concern for the hurt or inconvenience she had inflicted, however innocently, on the other party her first instinctive reactions when it happened were always frustration and self loathing that she had done it again. She knew this was wrong; that this was what earned her the agonising rebuke of "self centred" despite her heightened empathy and real distress at others' pain, but this was what came of her emotions being several sizes too big for her even as an adult. This was one of the realities of autism from which some people still shied away in disgust.

She loathed getting it wrong, and now she had possibly done it to Sharon after all the support her cousin had given her. She must not talk about it. Needing to be in control of what was happening to her and to understand it scientifically was such a fundamental part of her, yet she knew from experience that she had no adeptness whatsoever at telling where others drew the line between thinking and the perennial character flaw of overthinking for which people loved to pounce on her. "Got her on

Overthinking again!" How was she supposed to find answers and move forward if she wasn't allowed to think deeply without being accused of overanalysing, or talk things through without being shamed for negativity and self pity? Of course she got frustrated; so did lots of people and frustration was a natural reaction which when harnessed properly, as she tried so hard to do, galvanised people to find solutions! How were people supposed to find and mutually support others who shared their struggles if these things could not be talked about?

She suspected, while realising it would not apply in every instance, that people used the "overthinking" cutoff as a means of silencing; the same kind of technique used by those who practiced gaslighting. Knowing that the person on the receiving end of the snub had a point but not wanting to boost that person by admitting it; keeping them cowed, trivialising their thought processes, minimising their views. At the very least it was an easy way to score a few cheap points or get out of listening; overthinking was such a broad concept, a handy go-to for anyone looking to shut down a conversation. Even when it was because they didn't know what to say, it impeded the thinker from finding their own solutions. Despite autistic people having a reputation for being blunt and direct, it was equally likely that they would need to talk things through at length, going a roundabout way to work through everything they were thinking and feeling. To have dialogue constantly compressed and rushed was counterproductive. It wasn't always possible to tell the difference between oppressive motives and well meaning attempts at reassurance whenever yet another accusation of overthinking came, especially when also dealing with the frustration of having fallen into the same old trap. Even when well intentioned, what gave anyone the right to deny someone ownership of their own boundaries especially to the extent of drawing the line on their behalf as to where their thoughts should end? If anyone wanted to apply the overthinking label to their own thoughts, that was their prerogative. To apply it to someone else, though, should in her view require an ongoing consent as part of a relationship of trust. Even with someone like Sharon, whom she did trust implicitly and who had never accused her of overthinking, she dreaded putting herself in the line of fire because of the damage it would do to that trust if it did get said to her. After all, when it came to other people's responses there could never be absolute certainty. It looked as though she would have to continue her quest to figure out how to get around this lack of instinct on her own.

Life would be infinitely easier if she were a robot. Or at least had a copy of the script. She wasn't, though, and there was no script; there was only her, winging it through every interaction and now Sharon was looking at her concernedly.

"Beth?"

"Sorry. I got a bit overwhelmed there. You're right; we should change the subject. I had a vivid dream about the house the other night, the night after..." She caught herself just in time; "Whatever night it was, it doesn't matter; through the week anyway. I was floating above the house, like I was swimming in the sky. The sky was the colour of the sea. It felt so real! Beautiful. Kind of poignant, but beautiful."

"I love the way you describe things like that."

Ah, good; she appeared to have navigated back onto safe ground. She washed the teapot and cups while Sharon put away the biscuits; a bottle of wine stood chilling to accompany their fish suppers from Vinnie's. Bethany simply wanted to eat then relax on the green leather couch with their wine. She wasn't quite ready to face Brandon and Charlene; she was too fixed in her thought patterns to have come to terms yet with her feelings about having betrayed other autistic people by showing autism in a bad light through her mistakes.

"Do you mind if we do chill out here for a bit after our fish suppers? You guessed right that I don't feel up to seeing anybody else this time."

"Of course. I knew you would probably feel that way; I wanted you to know the option was there to go to Charlene and Brandon's."

"Thanks. Like you say, once this is all resolved. I must be positive. I will get through this then I'll start thinking about what else I can do to make a difference to kids like Lucy."

"You know, Beth, it's great that you're thinking positively and that you want to do something, but I have to wonder if it's really the best thing for you right now to even be thinking about planning anything big. You do know you're still making a difference to Lucy simply by being there for her and Louise? My sister may not admit it easily, but it's helped her a lot knowing she can ask you about things."

"I don't know, I mean it's great that Louise finds that helpful but it's not enough! Being there seems so, well, so inert. I need to do something more!"

Sharon stopped halfway through putting her coat on, turning to give her a searching look. Her expression was serious; she seemed to be weighing up the risks of what she was about to say. The feeling that hurt was coming descended once more.

"Bethany, are you sure this is really all about Lucy?"

"Well, not exclusively her; all the bullied kids out there!"

"Actually that's not what I meant. Yes, of course I know you want to help them; please don't think I'm doubting that for a second. I wonder, though, if there's something else going on here. Beth, please know this is coming from a place of love and concern, but is there maybe a part of you that needs the glory; that needs to prove something by doing something spectacular?"

"You think – what, you think I'm using these poor kids? Using Lucy? For personal gain?"

"No! Oh, I was afraid of this. I am not, I repeat not, suggesting that you don't genuinely want to help others. I would never, ever say that about you. I'm just not sure that it's your sole motive here. I'm not saying it's a bad thing; it's perfectly natural to want to feel rewarded for your efforts, but you've put so much pressure on yourself turning this into a crusade and I wonder if it's also about you needing feedback from other people to make up for what you don't feel about yourself."

"What exactly are you saying here, Sharon? Because I feel like I'm being kicked when I'm down."

"Oh, Bethany, no, that truly is not my intention. It's the pressure on you that I'm worried about! I do think that right now, at this point in your life, you need to put your ambition to one side and concentrate on why you need what you contribute to be so big; so visible, and what underlying need you're actually trying to meet."

"That still sounds to me like you think I'm merely pretending to care about Lucy and other children, for my own selfish ends."

"Come on, Beth, you know I would never think that. It is possible to be motivated by both care for others and self interest! The problem is when you can't see it and it leads you into harm!"

"So, help me understand this; you think that I got into serious trouble – breached workplace protocol, which is a major offence – because I wanted lots of praise? That makes no sense."

"I think that you kept your plans secret from your colleagues because you didn't want to share the credit, Beth. Which in itself would not have gotten you into trouble, but if you had let them in, it might have stopped it from getting to the point where you did the things that got you into trouble. Your colleagues being more impartial

209

might have seen more clearly where there was a potential problem with you contacting people outside the company and advised you against it; worked with you to take things forward the right way."

"Right. Because useless Bethany couldn't possibly be as smart as them."

"No! Because you were too emotionally invested to see clearly, and what I'm getting at is why!"

"Sharon, you weren't there when Lucy walked into my place of work practically in a fugue state, regressed into childhood to the point that she addressed me as 'Auntie Betty'!"

"No, I wasn't, and I am not disputing how strongly that affected you. I understand completely how that accelerated the situation; made it feel even more urgent. But Bethany, it doesn't explain why you kept your plans so secret from the others, and from what you told me in your messages through the week you were already doing that before the episode with Lucy. I'm not trying to hurt you, but this is likely to come up at your disciplinary and you're going to need to answer to people there who won't be as on your side as I am."

"I kept it secret because I couldn't afford to hand it over to people who weren't, as you said yourself, invested to the same degree I was, so that it would have fizzled out. I've told Ash that; he believed me. I'm disappointed that you don't."

"Oh, I do. I feel I should prepare you, though; they might say that Lucy turning up in the way she did should have made you want to get your colleagues involved, not continue to do things covertly. You said that Anita was truly kind and supportive that day. Oh, Bethany. You need help, honey. There is something else behind your need to do something big. Even if this idea had worked out the way you planned, once it was over and the shine had faded away, you'd still have been left with whatever that

210

something else is. We need to find out what it is, and to do that, you need to admit to yourself that it's there. It doesn't cancel out your care for others if that's what you're worried about; nothing can take that away from you. It means facing whatever else is going on with you and that's the first step to you finding peace."

"I see. So, 'Hello, my name is Bethany and I'm a praiseaholic'?"

Sharon smiled wryly.

"Many a true word spoken in jest, Beth. But I don't think it's as straightforward as that. I think there's something more fundamental, more permanent than wanting adulation that's driving this. I'm going to be a part of the help you need, but I'm not a professional and I do think that you need to talk this through with one. Autism Initiatives have a service in Perth, I believe? Charlene knows something about them; they've had a service in Edinburgh for years and they've got one based in Inverness for the Highlands too. They do a lot of good work. In fact haven't you shared a few posts from the Highland one through that self advocacy group up there that you follow? I know you've never wanted to join anything which would commit you to a programme of activities or expect you to talk about things in a group, but they don't seem to work that way. They seem to be there for people as and when they need, including one to one appointments. They're not doctors, and I think you do need some input from a medical professional right now, but they can help you to access that; back you up with an autism informed perspective."

"I know the services you mean. Maybe I will drop the Perth one an email. If they'll touch my case with a ten-foot barge pole, that is!"

"They're not there to judge! Maybe they will do a better job than I can of making you see that what you did wasn't this unforgivable act of evil you see it as."

"I don't know. I breached workplace protocols! I mean, OK, not financially or giving out confidential information, but workplace etiquette and boundaries are so rigid, it's the worst and least forgivable thing you can do short of murdering somebody. At least I merely told my boss to go to Hell. That on top of breaching protocols; I may as well have escorted her there myself!"

"Bethany! Will you please stop with the 'breaching protocols'! I know you're scared and I'm trying so hard to reassure you here, but you're deliberately working yourself up now and what you've done is honestly not the worst thing you can do in a workplace; not even close! Other people have conflicts of interest at work too, you know, and they don't necessarily have mitigating factors!"

Bethany was in that nightmare place yet again; fully aware that she was standing with her mouth hanging open, entirely unable to process or respond to the dressing down she had received out of the blue. How risibly pathetic she must look right now; how wholly in the wrong! She had lost all right to her cousin's support; another priceless ally wasted, pushed away because she didn't know how to put the brakes on when she was becoming annoying. All she could do was try to salvage a little bit of dignity; to leave quietly and calmly. Wordlessly, she went to gather her coat and bag.

"Oh Beth, I'm so sorry; I shouldn't have snapped like that. I didn't mean to. The truth is, I've got a situation at my own work at the moment but it's my problem and I haven't told you about it so it was very unfair of me to take it out on you."

So it was another 'You weren't to know' blunder. She knew that she should squash down every one of her huge feelings right there and then and put Sharon first; at least invite her to share whatever was bothering her. Resentment of this huge ask flared in her tormented soul. Why wasn't she valid enough for people to tell her these things up front before she walked into the trap? Because, of course, it wasn't always about her. Damn. She was being bad again. It was simply too big for her to fold up and put away and do the right thing. She was being tested and found wanting, again. She was supposed to feel grateful and humbled that Sharon was willing to risk upsetting her for the sake of preparing her for hard questions at the disciplinary. She was already at rock bottom with her self worth; how could she afford to be humbled even more? What might be required of her already strained mental resources in return if she incurred even more debt to the people in her life for their standing by her? Humility meant vulnerability to others and to her own emotions; although she knew that Sharon would never abuse that, her defences had to apply universally to remain strong. If she allowed any weak points, everything could come crashing through. It was all too big.

"I think I should go. I'm sorry, Sharon; I know you need and expect better of me, but I cannot cope with another curve ball right now. I cannot grovel and beg your forgiveness because yet again I've blundered into a minefield. If you want to tell me what's happening, you can message me; if you don't, that's fine too, it's your prerogative. For today, though; the day on which I received my disciplinary letter and also the day I should have been out celebrating Dana and Crevan's wedding, I think it's best I go home. I'm simply not handling this well enough to be in company."

"Beth, please don't go like this. You haven't eaten and I don't want you travelling on a Saturday night on your own in distress. You cannot keep blaming yourself for everything. I don't expect you to grovel; I was wrong to snap at you but you need to allow other people to make mistakes too without adding it to the ever growing pile of reasons to beat yourself up. You seriously need help. I know you're a perfectionist; you always have been, and you always will be, but this thing that's tormenting the life out of you goes way beyond being a perfectionist. Now, if you want to go home I will of course respect that, but please at least have a sandwich or something before you go and take some time to regroup."

"I appreciate your concern, but I honestly couldn't eat a thing. Could we just walk to the station? Please? You haven't eaten either; take that wine to Charlene's. Have your chippy with them. It's best I don't drink alcohol when I'm feeling this fragile and travelling anyway."

"If that's what you need, and good call about the drink." Sharon resumed putting on her coat, her shoulders slumped sadly. They walked slowly along the road. "I truly am so sorry, Bethany. You did not need me doing that to you. I will explain it to you, but I think you're right; this is not the time. You are in crisis and you are allowed that, same as I am allowed to make a wrong move because I've got my own problems and I'm not a saint. Can you please try to let yourself accept that nobody's in the wrong here; it was just a tough night?"

"I'll try, but there's a queue right now of things I've got to try and take in. I'm tired and there's very little try left in me; I can only deal with one mental marathon at a time. I promise you I will let you know when I'm safely home and then I will eat something light."

"Thank you. Please stay in touch. I love you, Beth."

"I love you too. Here's my train."

She was the one sober person on it; fortunately, it was not so busy that she couldn't find a seat where she felt safe and could mind her own business. Once again, she wondered how it had come to this. Taking out her phone, she had no energy left to resist the compulsion to check her social media pages. She should wait until she got home but she had acknowledged the wisdom of deciding not to drink; surely that entitled her to give in to temptation on something.

The wedding photos were unavoidable; she found that they did not upset her as she had thought they might. Still, it was better to leave those alone until she was in the safety and privacy of her own home; who knew when the emotions of the day might hit her. She checked her own page, reflexively looking at her contacts list as she often had since the trouble happened. Her colleagues would not be ordered to delete her, Ash had assured her; merely not to interact with her until told otherwise. Someone had, though; her number of contacts had gone down by one. Opening the list, she scrolled through to see whose name was missing.

Rhona. Her colleague in Inverness who had been so excited for her and helped her with her planning. The planning which she had not told Rhona she had not yet cleared with her manager. She hadn't lied about it and Rhona had not brought up the subject, but could she honestly say that she hadn't intentionally misled her? She had wanted so badly to make this happen, and now Sharon had made her face the fact that no, it wasn't exclusively about helping others. Yes, there was her own self interest too. She had needed the glory as well as to help people, and she had been deceitful to get it. Had she gotten Rhona into trouble? She had admitted to Anita that she spoke to her. They had probably questioned her. They'd have contacted Frank, the manager in Inverness; that kindly man with whom she, Sharon and Rhona had enjoyed convivial chat on that wonderful day there. The day she showed them the whisky she bought Dana and Crevan for their wedding. Frank would have called Rhona in for a meeting. More unpleasantness. They must be so angry with her. How on Earth had she come to this?

Her empty stomach rolled and clenched; she regretted not having eaten before leaving Inverbrudock. She welcomed the pain, while simultaneously longing for someone to wrap her in a duvet and tell her that it was OK; that she wasn't so wicked and twisted after all. These

215

ambivalent emotions were too powerful. She was so terribly drained. Even her eyeballs felt too heavy.

Walking through Perth Station held little comfort; she still couldn't let herself believe that it was going to be her home station for much longer. She couldn't afford to feel attached to anything here. It was late, cold and those soaring rafters echoed with the baying of Saturday night drunks. She pulled her coat tighter around her and hurried home, messaged Sharon then put a frozen meal in the microwave, checking her social networking pages on her iPad while the meal cooked.

She had never seen the autism group whose post had appeared right at the top of her feed; it hadn't been posted by anyone she knew. That was odd; it must be one of those sponsored links, though it didn't say so. The title of the article they were sharing was what instantly grabbed her attention.

Autistic Burnout.

She had heard the term before but it hadn't resonated with her; she had always assumed it applied to people who were working frenetically doing twelve plus hour days seven days a week hyperfocused on some highly technical, expert level project, or who had caring responsibilities as well as being autistic, or had lots of other disabilities. Tired as she was, from what she could see it was suggested here that burnout could be caused by simply living an everyday life but doing so under constant pressure of the type she had always felt. Like a computer trying to run two conflicting programs, she was grinding to a halt through coping alone with the general incompatibility of wider society with the autistic body and brain. Every day was a performance and every moment was fraught with tension. Exactly the kind of thing she had been thinking about on the train; the constant worry about how her facial expression looked. The accumulation of microaggressions and their effect on her self confidence, making the need to perform even more

216

acute; the pressure and self blame of glitches and misunderstandings and the added stress of how those were perceived. The patterns set in childhood and their ongoing effects; carrying that bewildered child inside her, still unable to come to terms with how she kept going wrong. Could the accumulation of all of these factors explain her growing feeling that she was in freefall, running out of time to prove herself to some unknown hierarchy as she hurtled towards an unmarked event horizon beyond which there could be no reconnection or solace? Her fatigue felt more like a craving for stillness than for extra sleep.

Devouring the article and several others to which it held links, Bethany recognised more and more that she was indeed reading about her own life. Not a tragic, disadvantaged life by any means; she was well aware that she did have and always had a lot of privileges, not least having had access to an autism diagnosis, and that others had many more reasons to feel hard done by. This was not about feeling hard done by. Just as the existence of even better and happier circumstances did not invalidate good times, neither did the existence of worse circumstances invalidate bad ones. She had all the makings of a contented, fulfilling life, but she had been battling a deep, all pervading fatigue without even truly realising it, because it had crept up on her and because she had not talked about it. These people in this article had, braving scepticism and criticism so that others like Bethany could realise that they were not alone. There was no big flashy event with guest speakers; simply people being honest about how things were for them, bravely putting those painful truths out there online and it had helped her. It had given her the help she so desperately wanted to give others, without them having to deceive anyone or break rules. Making a difference really could be that easy.

Her dinner went cold in the microwave as she read on. There was no easy way out of burnout, but people were finding ways to make peace with it; to adapt and have reasonable adjustments made. The simplest of changes to a work routine could be enough to make it feasible to still work and have a life too, whether straightaway or after a period of rest; more than a break or a holiday, and many people were not in the position to be able to. She could surely still work if she could settle and not be asked to do other tasks at a moment's notice as had been happening more and more often recently.

Was this the elusive something else which Sharon insisted was behind her obsessive drive, along with hyperempathy and the need to please? In a world where fatigue had become almost competitive and appeared to have an entry level requirement way above Bethany's levels of activity in order to be taken seriously and allowances made, had she in fact been in burnout for years and trying to bargain for permission to be tired?

21

October 2019

Watching the taillights of Bethany's train disappear, Sharon's own mind was in catch-up mode too as she processed what had happened. She had known it would be a difficult and potentially volatile conversation and she questioned the wisdom of having challenged her cousin at such an emotionally fragile time. Such things were better raised in person though. Her questioning of Bethany's full motives would have looked uncompromisingly harsh in a message without the scope for immediate clarification and the context of a warm tone, a friendly touch on the arm. It was something which had to be addressed before the disciplinary so that Bethany and her union rep could prepare better. She worried for her on the return to work which she nonetheless believed was inevitable; surely they wouldn't sack her, but those pre-emptive strikes which Bethany found so difficult and demeaning, often reacting accordingly to the detriment of her relationships, were bound to come more often now. Remembering this admittedly significant misstep, her boss and colleagues were more likely than ever now to single her out for the "don't mention"s and so on which sadly for Bethany, they now had a reason to believe she needed to be told more than others. Sharon was sure that this was a driving factor behind Bethany's frantic perfectionism; a vicious circle which made her more desperate to prove herself and therefore more liable to make mistakes which she would quite likely have avoided otherwise. It would be so much better if people would be more discreet and thoughtful in their approach. There were ways of covering eventualities without having to name and shame. Surely it was kinder for these type of warnings to be given out generally, or framed in a more positive way; for example, "This is between you and me" or "I'm only telling you this for now; it's not common knowledge yet" implied trust in the person rather than an expectation of indiscretion, while achieving the same aim of confidentiality. Even phrasing it as a request; "Please could you keep this to yourself for now". It saddened Sharon greatly that these social dilemmas leached so much of Bethany's mental energy and prevented her from seeing good in herself.

Sharon took her time walking home; she needed to clear her head before doing as Bethany had wisely suggested and taking the bottle of wine to Charlene's. Her own workplace had a more intimate, family atmosphere than Bethany's; it had a cosiness which she wished her cousin could have around her as she went about her job. It was still a workplace though, and Bethany's dilemma around protocols had brought that into sharp focus. Wincing at the memory of how she had snapped at her cousin, Sharon thought back to the day Lucy went missing.

When she knew Lucy was safe, after calming her shattered nerves with a fresh cup of tea she had hurried back to the hotel. Nobody would have expected her back that day and indeed she had already texted both Jen and Lynsey already with the good news. Afterwards, she finally admitted to herself that the real reason she returned to work was to see Paulie Fitzpatrick. She was emotional as she hugged both of her colleagues, but it was seeing Paulie that broke through her defences.

"Hey – sorry I had to dash off", she had said as she found them sitting in the bar. "My niece…" The tears had hit without warning as they held out their arms, wrapping her in a tight, comforting embrace, brushing away her profuse apologies. After having washed her face and regained her professional composure, she had still spent at least twenty minutes talking with them, filling in the background of

Lucy's bullying troubles and putting the world to rights about how bad society still was at accepting diversity. Both agreed that a lot had been achieved but there was still a long way to go. Since that evening, although she had seen Paulie infrequently throughout the rest of their stay and their next visit was not yet due, she had found herself feeling unaccountably flat when they had checked out and thinking about them more and more often as the weeks went by. She wasn't yet ready to describe it as falling in love, but there was something there which could no longer be ignored and she knew with a deep-down certainty that whatever it was, it was reciprocated. She felt a warmth to the depths of her soul; a wish to turn to Paulie above all others when she wanted to talk about personal things. There was an attraction there, without a doubt; a desire to be close without it occurring to her to categorise their body. She would love that body because it was Paulie. This, she knew beyond a shadow of doubt, was the real reason she had ended up snapping at poor Bethany even as her cousin wrestled with a frightening personal crisis, when she had kept mentioning breaching protocols at work. Although gender identity was not an issue, the fact that Paulie was one of the guests most certainly was.

She must speak in confidence with Lynsey before anything had the chance to happen with Paulie, even an honest conversation between them. How could she have challenged Bethany for her secrecy with her colleagues when she was currently guilty of the exact same thing, and in her case with no altruistic motivation? She was sure that Lynsey would have no issue with it on a personal level, but in the same way as she had emphasised about Bethany's employers, there would be boundaries to be adhered to.

"Time to practice what you preach, Sharon Penhaligon", she told herself as she walked back into her flat to collect the wine. Picking up her phone to text "heading over to you now" to Charlene, she first composed a message to

Lynsey's work phone asking to book in some time for a chat. "Everything's fine", she reassured her; "but I need to run something work related by you." The hard part was still to come but she had made the commitment and it felt right in a quietly confident, utterly definitive settling of inner peace. Trying not to think of Bethany alone in her flat, she headed to Charlene and Brandon's with a lighter step.

"I'm glad you came over; I didn't know if Bethany would be feeling up to it", smiled Charlene as she opened the door.

"It's just me, Char", Sharon told her, sadness coming over her once more at the way Bethany had left. "Beth went home. I…"

Not yet. She couldn't tell Charlene part of the story without telling the rest and it was still too soon; too new, too tentative. "She wasn't up to staying out and travelling back any later. She didn't think it would be a good idea to drink alcohol the way she was feeling, and she suggested I bring this wine round here."

"Oh, fair enough. I do feel for her, especially after all you've told me about her need to perform and be perfect. She might not think so right now given what's happened, but she's got a sensible head on her shoulders. I hope that her managers can see past this one-off misjudgement and know her well enough to accept that it was completely out of character and there were mitigating circumstances. Brandon's decided he fancies pasta tonight anyway; are you up for that? This wine will go well with it."

Charlene's home cooking held even greater appeal than Vinnie's fish suppers after such an emotionally draining day. Sharon settled into the easy contentment of helping a good friend to prepare a relaxed, informal meal; as the pasta bake cooked in the oven, Charlene went upstairs to confirm to Brandon what and who to expect at dinner time then she and Sharon sat down with a glass of wine.

"Oh well, here's to Bethany. May she soon be through here again with all of this behind her."

"Absolutely. To Bethany. Thanks, Charlene."

"How is she bearing up?"

"Pretty well in the circumstances. This union rep she has seems to be right on the ball and he's a supportive friend to her. She needs someone like that nearby. She said in one of her messages through the week that he'd told her forgiving herself for this will be a bigger battle than any disciplinary. He's right. She's going to need all of us, whatever happens at this hearing. She got the letter about it today too, and it's the day her friends at work were getting married. She couldn't go because of being off with a disciplinary pending; she's not allowed to see any of them socially."

"Oh, that's awful. Poor Bethany! It's a wonder she made it through here at all. It must have taken her some willpower to turn down a glass of this! We will need to make up for that once things have settled for her."

"We will." A blast of music through the wall made both women jump. "Oh, here we go again."

"That's ridiculously loud. How's Brandon coping with it?"

"He puts his noise cancelling headphones on, but that doesn't stop the vibration of course. The one positive thing is it never goes on for long. They seem to be having some sort of recurring problem with the electrics; trip switches cutting off whenever they're using a lot of power, but not to the extent that it should cause a trip. The landlord was asking if we've had any issues on this side."

"Let's hope it makes them want to move on. It's such a shame to see the house being treated like this. Bethany was telling me about a dream she had where she was floating over the roof, as though she were swimming in a sky with colours that blended with the sea. It was quite poignant."

"Gosh, that's actually spooky. You remember when the builders were blocking off the connecting door in the attic and they found Harriet's diary from the 1920s? Her last entry was about looking up from the attic skylight and the colours being like the sea and how she felt as though she could almost swim up into the sky."

"You're kidding! I wonder if that dream was Harriet's spirit reaching out to her then, like when she saw her in our attic that Christmas Day."

"It honestly wouldn't surprise me. There's definitely a connection there."

Brandon walked in, Cheminot at his heels. The cat chirruped a greeting which was half miaow, half purr as he jumped up onto Sharon's lap.

"Oh hey, you two! Dinner won't be long. How's your drawing coming along, Brandon?"

"Good, thanks." He held out his sketch book to reveal an impressively accurate portrait of an Inter7City refurbished 125. The high-speed train looked almost to be coming out of the page.

"That's stunning! ScotRail could use that for publicity!"

"I keep telling him that too! Right, let's get some kibble out for this ginger gannet so that we humans can get our dinner in peace. Well, relative peace anyway!"

Charlene nodded her head towards the wall from the other side of which the dull bass thump still emanated. She poured kibble into Cheminot's dish and washed her hands. The music stopped abruptly again.

The three friends enjoyed their meal, Brandon pouring himself a beer as Charlene replenished her and Sharon's wine glasses. The salty richness of ham rose to their nostrils through the popping of the cheese, perfectly golden brown as the fork broke through to the mouth coating creaminess of the sauce and fresh bite of tender broccoli; the pasta was exactly the right degree of firmness. Loading the cleared plates and cutlery into the dishwasher afterwards, Sharon thanked her friends for a lovely evening and took her leave. It was starting to rain, and she was glad to see upon checking her phone that Bethany was safely home. She looked up at her former home, wishing once again that it had gone to more respectful tenants who would be better neighbours to Charlene and Brandon. Still, she supposed, in some ways it was better than it lying cold, silent and empty. The new people were clearly making use of the whole place; as she looked up at the attic skylight, she saw that there was a light on up there.

22

October 2019

Being the lone girl in the family had its advantages; Tegan had easily bagged the big bedroom on the second floor with the ensuite bathroom, knowing that she would make more extensive use of it than her brothers. Even though her mother was constantly nagging her to clean it, her new room was by far the best thing about this new house. The boys were fighting all the time since they moved; one of them was always accusing the others of having unplugged something or moved whichever CD they had been planning to blast. Their parents were constantly short tempered because the electrics in the house were so unreliable, forever tripping so that the switches had to be reset, yet the landlord insisted there was no fault and the wiring had been thoroughly tested in the presence of both her parents. Despite arguments kicking off almost every day, nobody would ever admit to slamming the doors. Tegan herself had been accused of that up here on numerous occasions; told that nobody else had been near enough to have done it. She knew she had not; she could neither prove it nor come up with any possible theory as to who had. She was wise enough to keep to herself the footsteps she could swear she heard in the attic above her, after being ridiculed the first time she heard them. She had asked then which of her brothers had gone up there since due to the remodelling of the second floor rooms several years ago, the access to the attic stairs was in her bedroom. She supposed she must be mistaken; the footsteps must be carrying through from next door's attic. She was thankful that the sole remaining door up there was the one on the left at the top of the stairs, into their own half of what had once been the attic rooms of one large property. The original connecting door on the right having been blocked off when this half of the property was sold to their landlord after many decades of the same two families living in the two houses meant that there was one door fewer for her to keep getting accused of slamming. Maybe that weird pair of anoraks had their train set up in their side of the attic. Yet the footsteps seemed too light to be either of them, which come to think of it meant it certainly couldn't have been her brothers. No, that had to be it; the noises were all coming from next door and the footsteps sounded light because they weren't right overhead, however insistently her ears, and something more instinctive which she tried not to think about, told her otherwise.

The sound of yet another row floated up to her as she sprawled on her bed scrolling through her phone. It sounded like Daz and Gordy this time. Rolling her eyes, she paused to laugh out loud at an image of an overweight girl in a bikini. It had been posted by a friend from school; Tegan vaguely knew the girl in the picture. She was a year below them and had been known for always trying and failing to diet; now she was telling herself she was "body positive". An excuse for not trying any more, Tegan sneered to herself; sad laziness. Now, this was an area where she knew what she was doing; where she had a bit of power. Smirking to herself, she felt the little green stud of her belly bar where it nestled against her flat stomach. The scathing comment about needing a metal detector to find out whether this beached whale had one of these practically wrote itself alongside the quick photo she snapped of her own decorated belly button. How envious this girl would be when she saw it. Maybe it would give her the incentive to start trying again; maybe she was doing her a favour. Chortling triumphantly, she pressed Enter. She waited. The "Trying to upload" message came up as the little dots went round and round. How annoying. No, she did not want to try again later!, but it appeared she was not being given any choice in the matter. Stupid house! First the electrics, now the Wi-Fi. She tried switching off Wi-Fi and using her mobile data; still the comment wouldn't post. Fed up, she tossed her phone on the bed where she had been lying. She would take a shower now, then she could get up half an hour later in the morning. Yes, she had to acknowledge; having her own ensuite did have its advantages.

Coming out of the shower, Tegan dried herself off and put on her fluffy pink robe before towelling her hair. Her roots needed touching up again. She grudgingly gave the small shower cubicle a wipe down with the cleaning sponge, tossed her used towels half in and half out of the laundry basket then came through to the bedroom to use her hairdryer. Glancing at the bed, she shrieked in fright. Where had that magazine come from? When she had thrown her phone on the duvet before going into the shower there had been nothing else on there; her magazines were in a pile on the chest of drawers. Not an especially tidy pile, but stable enough that they would not have been able to slide off and even if they had, they would have landed on the floor, not the bed. It was too far away for them to have ended up there by accident. Had one of the boys sneaked in while she was in the shower? She knew deep down that they wouldn't have; they may be rough and chauvinistic, but she was still their baby sister and there was a code of protectiveness of the women in their family underneath their gruff behaviour. In any case they would never take an interest in anything in her magazines which did not have an accompanying picture of models in their underwear. They certainly wouldn't have been reading the article Tegan found herself looking at as she tentatively approached the open pages which lay over her discarded phone.

It was about fat shaming and how it had made a teenage girl severely mentally ill. At first, Tegan scoffed; wow, oversensitive or what? All she needed to do was go easy on the pies and cakes, then she wouldn't need to hate herself! As she read further, unable to tear her eyes away, she learned that there was a reason for this girl having gained weight; medication for a serious illness. She was often at the doctors or in hospital when her classmates were out enjoying themselves or in school; this was making her fall behind in her work as well as the problems she had with her health. Tegan felt sick as she read about the tortured thoughts this girl had; the desperate, harmful actions they had driven her to. She was the same age as the girl Tegan had been trying to taunt with the photo of her slim bejewelled belly and the cruel comment about the metal detector. Could that sort of thing really affect someone this badly? It was a joke, after all! It was what people did! Yet even as she thought it, she knew that wasn't true. Her comment no longer seemed funny; throwing the magazine aside, she picked up her phone to check that it had not posted while she was in the shower. It still showed the message about trying again later. Unwilling to admit to herself quite how relieved she felt, she deleted the draft, double checked that it had never posted and then deleted the photo which she had taken to add to it from her phone. She shivered as she dried her hair, despite the heat from the hairdryer and the cosiness of her robe. Suddenly discovering that she was no longer comfortable with the attitude she and many of her friends had adopted was an unsettling feeling; she felt somehow disconnected from a complacent smugness which had become a habit.

She paused; the hairdryer held still in the middle of a sweep down the length of her hair as something else occurred to her. The helplessness she felt when she knew she hadn't slammed the door but had no defence against her accusers; was this how people like the girl in the article felt because of the kind of things she and her friends did and said? The unease about the footsteps she kept thinking she heard, unable to talk about it to anyone because she had been so disbelieved and laughed at; was this how it felt to be one of those people she and the rest of the so-called "normal" crowd felt so powerful putting down?

Tegan yelped as the heat of the hairdryer concentrated on one point registered in her consciousness; she quickly moved it away, its mechanical whine still loud next to her ears. She knew that she wanted to talk to her friends about this; at least Hayley, who had known her for the longest. Would they laugh at her? Would she become the outsider; on the receiving end of the casual ostracism they had been dishing out? Was she brave enough to take the risk? Once she had finished drying her hair, she would read that article properly. It might help her to decide what to do.

Meanwhile, up in the silent, empty attic directly above her, the door softly closed.

23

October 2019

The Autism Initiatives one stop shop in Perth had an instant calming effect as Bethany walked through the door. The light grey building came to an elegant rounded point at the narrow intersection of two streets; inside, a wide seating alcove made the most of the bay window as an open staircase curved upwards. She had struggled to make that step into the unknown, cutting off phone calls before even dialling the number and staring for half an hour at a blank email to which she couldn't even ascribe a subject line, before giving up and going for a walk. When she passed the building and recognised it, remembering from what she had seen that it was open for appointments that day, she decided on a whim to take a look to gain a bit more of a mental backdrop to help her with that initial email. These were not the kind of circumstances in which she felt confident introducing herself to new people. She would merely say that she was autistic and looking to find out what was available.

The approachable, welcoming man who answered the door instantly put her at ease. He was one of these people with whom she could imagine herself chatting about anything, instinctively knowing that she would not be judged. He introduced himself as Matt; he didn't work there, he explained, but at the Edinburgh service and he was there for a meeting. However long he had been in Scotland, he had not lost his South London accent, nor evidently his allegiances; breaking through her nervousness he asked her if she were by any chance a Chelsea supporter because of her blue hair. Laughing, Bethany pointed out that the Perth team St Johnstone also played in blue before finding herself explaining all about the line of defence her unusual hair colour created for her when she felt uncomfortably visible due to her autistic traits. Matt listened receptively, nodding but allowing her all the time she needed to get out what she wanted to say. When she finished with "Besides which, I think the colour totally rocks", he roared with approving laughter. "I've got a mate up in the Highlands I reckon you'd get on well with", he smiled, before going on to explain that he was the manager of the three Autism Initiatives one stop shops in Scotland and some of the people from the Highland one were on their way for the meeting. If a senior manager were this down to Earth and open minded, Bethany reasoned, then surely these people would not flinch at the thought of helping her to state her case at work if need be. Taking a deep breath, she blurted out that she had gotten into some trouble at work and had a disciplinary coming up. She added that both her union rep and her cousin who was her closest support believed that her autism was a contributing factor and that she had recently been led to research autistic burnout which she felt was also involved. As she hoped, Matt was completely unfazed. He asked her if she knew when the hearing was going to be; when she told him the date, he apologised that it was unlikely anyone would be free at short notice to go with her but he assured her that if she needed to appeal, they would support her. In the meantime, he advised her to book an appointment with the team based here and get herself registered so that at least she would feel less isolated at a difficult time. Bethany thanked Matt profusely, feeling extremely fortunate to have met him; he had exactly the right balance of listening, humour and gravitas to make her feel comfortable, heard and supported without sacrificing any of her autonomy. She hoped that her dealings with the one stop shop would bring her into contact with some of the autistic people in the Highlands too; from what she had seen online, they too had a strong and warm community vibe without any need to conform or commit to anything beyond what each individual needed and wanted from the service. The Highlands held such appeal for autistic people with the slower pace of life and less population density but with that idyll came geographical isolation, fewer funded services and more stressful, expensive travel to access them. That spoke of crucial need even without the difficulties of trying to fit autism accessibility into already overstretched mainstream services, so Bethany could see how vitally important such a service as the one stop shop would be to the Highlands. Few people could be naïve enough nowadays to imagine that living in a beautiful place meant that life was easy; she could well imagine what a lifeline the Highland one stop shop must be to autistic people up there. They were coping with the same difficulties as anyone trying to get by in a society not compatible with their neurology, often in more conventional and socially structured communities which intentionally or otherwise marginalised them.

She needed more conversations like the one she had engaged in with Matt; where she could talk through all the things which, if properly addressed before now, might have kept her out of trouble. She had sat up late, well into the early hours of Sunday researching autistic burnout; microwaved cottage pie gone cold was unlikely to make it onto her list of favourite meals any time soon but it had been worth it for the relief she found in avidly reading article after article by autistic people who had been through what she was finally recognising in herself. The biggest revelation had been that it did not necessarily take years of recognised hardship to reach burnout; the ongoing everyday slog of camouflage and hypervigilance could do it. Children could experience it, Lucy more than likely among them. If she had still been in with a chance of arranging that anti-bullying event, this would have been yet another strand to it; yet more understanding to be shared!

As she sat in her living room in the extra still quiet of the night, her eyes dry and aching, her muscles stiff with lack of movement and the combined chill of the dead hours and the body at its lowest ebb, for the first time she had truly absorbed what Sharon said about it being possible to have both self interest and care for others. She knew with the stark clarity which came when one was too cold, stiff, tired and emotionally wrung out to have any room left for obligatory caveats and niceties that yes, she absolutely could and did care about the unseen struggles of others while simultaneously seeking the vindication she craved to allow her to cope with her own. Of course it was possible to have both of those motives!

She had gone to bed eventually, waking late on Sunday feeling wiped out yet somehow washed clean. She had several messages from Sharon asking how she was, passing on regards from Charlene and Brandon not forgetting purrs and head bumps from Cheminot, and updating her on the noisy neighbours. She had replied briefly about having had a revelation, sending Sharon links to some of the articles she had read, then made herself brunch and strong coffee. Allowing her mind and body to unhurriedly enjoy the restorative effect of the much-needed nourishment in complete stillness and quiet, the only sounds being occasional traffic and distant voices outside, felt like the beginnings of deep relaxation. Sharon's response shimmered with empathy and enthusiasm; she wholeheartedly agreed and was relieved to have informed backing to her conviction that there was something more behind Bethany's transgression at work. They both agreed that there was infinitely more to be learned; that there must be so many discoveries yet to be made about the complex ramifications of autism. The existence of the one stop shops was vital both for steering the wider world towards these discoveries and for helping autistic people to cope in the meantime. Bethany had promised her cousin once again that she would connect with the one in Perth. The rest of Sunday had been profoundly restful; Bethany spent most of the day simply being in the moment, not needing to prepare for another Monday at work yet, free to stop and breathe and recover.

Returning home after her productive visit to the one stop shop, Bethany updated Sharon and Ash, bringing the latter up to speed about her burnout theory with the links she had sent to Sharon. Ash added weight to the conviction she now shared with her cousin, promising that they would be able to strengthen her case even further by building this in. Both were enthusiastic about her having connected with Matt and Autism Initiatives. The unexpected time to breathe allowed Bethany to develop her theories even further; putting the present time with its available knowledge into the context of the past and the future. She speculated about the possibility of hitherto unknown causal connections being discovered between the autistic brain and the functioning of the body's electrical and magnetic fields. A recurrent issue she had noticed throughout her life was the tendency for buttons and touch screens not to respond well to her. So many times she had been jovially called weak, left mute with impotent rage as people brushed her aside and successfully gained a response from lift buttons, key fob entry systems and suchlike, impatiently accusing her of not having performed the simplest of procedures correctly. How could anyone manage not to press a lift button hard enough or accurately swipe a key fob over a clearly marked panel? This added to the occasions which did not involve anybody else but were still infuriating because they shouldn't happen; the times she had to press the remote control buttons multiple times before getting a response even with a brand new battery, the times when her phone keypad failed to register until she tapped for the second or third time. She had nothing to offer in the way of explanation; repeated contempt and derision shored up

235

pitted and rusted self loathing with rigid scaffolding, preventing what might otherwise have been a natural process of erosion allowing something better to be restored on the well hidden foundations. Perhaps the day was coming when a pragmatic scientific explanation would bring the same society-wide validation which nowadays prevented epileptic and schizophrenic people from facing the ducking stool, though the disability benefit assessment procedures in this day and age proved that there was still a long way to go. Both Ash and Sharon received her theories with interest, appreciating their plausibility and her vision; whether or not there was any truth in them, her enquiring mind and focus on the bigger picture were a prime example of what was needed for humanity to progress. How fortunate it was that the one stop shops were there to facilitate the necessary intersection of study and lived experience.

After a few days of absolute downtime, Bethany found herself craving walks by the River Tay in the deepening afternoon dusk. Lucy had reminisced about her earlier visit with Sharon as she waited for Louise to collect her on that terrible day; how they had walked along the broad esplanade pausing to read the displays about the history of the area before crossing the main bridge and taking in the serenity of the Rodney Gardens and sculpture trail, returning to the city centre via the enchanting Tay Viaduct. This long, gracefully curving structure carried the Aberdeen to Glasgow line and passed over Moncreiffe Island which surprisingly housed a golf course. Bethany loved to walk this route, popular and well lit enough to be safe, as the streetlights were coming on. There was something primal about the gentle handover of dusk; the light falling softly and fearlessly from the sky. It seemed to hold the assurance that it was safe to glow once more from the artificial yet equally fundamental network of filaments which held its power in safe keeping throughout the night.

This completely different yet similarly important continuity allowed that inherent need for illumination to be sustained until it was time to return the torch to Nature with the quietly assured bloom of each new morning. Once she got out of this limbo, Bethany determined to build this walk into her new routine. Not every day; once all her commitments were restored, that would be an unsustainable target and cause stress instead of relieving it. She must not make too many plans; as Sharon had so wisely said, this was a time to focus on the moment, clearing the way for a reimagined and realigned future.

24

November 2019

Buildings definitely retained traces of feelings and emotions which were experienced within them intensely enough or for a long enough period. Bethany wondered how many times this stark, formal room had been used for meetings of the type she was about to endure. She could feel the walls humming with the apprehension of others who had come and gone. Ash sat beside her in the waiting area, serious and professional in his suit while his eyes held unmistakable kindness and compassion. He had been able to give her one bit of good news the day before as they prepared; they had gotten an unexpected lucky break. The regional manager to whom the hearing would usually have been allocated, Bruce Farquhar, was known to be particularly strict; he abhorred displays of emotion and took a hard line with anything which pushed the boundaries of corporate etiquette. Ash had previously warned Bethany to prepare for a gruelling meeting. A glitch in the online system had wrongly shown him to be on leave and the allocation had passed to Nicola Alford from Aberdeen. By the time the error was discovered, Nicola and her PA's travel arrangements had been made and it had been decided to leave it as it was. Bethany's insides nevertheless churned with fear as they sat on the uncomfortable red plastic chairs which were the sole concession to colour in this ominous grey chamber.

A woman in a dark blue skirt and light blue blouse, a lanyard around her neck showing her to work in the building glanced at them as she passed. "She must be wondering what I've done", murmured Bethany.

"She might think I'm the one who's done something!", smiled Ash reassuringly. "Anyway, this building isn't only used for disciplinaries. She might think we're a couple planning to get married! Not that anybody would have the ceremony itself in this place."

Bethany snorted with laughter despite the grave situation. "Well, judging by how terrified I know I must look, that would make you Henry VIII!"

She smiled to herself as Ash laughed heartily, remembering Louise's most recent email wherein she had been talking about Lucy's interest in that period of Tudor history. Louise was gradually warming to her and coming around to the realisation that Lucy's autism was not an illness or a shameful secret; that there were aspects of it which would prove positive once Lucy had the right support in place. She still would not have dreamed of telling Louise about her current situation. Aside from fearing her lingering judgement, she legitimately did not want to make her afraid for Lucy's future all over again. It was still too early in that whole dynamic for her to destabilise it with a bombshell like this.

The lady in the blue outfit came out of a door at the end of the short corridor. "The room is ready for you now and I've just had a call to say that your colleagues are on their way. Would you like to come through?"

No, thought Bethany; I would like to be almost anywhere else on the planet including quicksand, crocodile infested swamps and active volcanoes. "Thank you", she smiled politely; after all, this lady was merely a bystander whom she envied for not being involved beyond the administration of booking the room.

The glass of water which Ash had poured for her was already slick with sweat from her hands when the door opened and Anita walked in accompanied by an approachable-looking woman with short chestnut hair framing a kind face. Behind them holding a brown folder

239

was another younger woman with black hair and what Bethany surmised was workplace friendly toned-down Goth make-up; Bethany and the young woman exchanged discreet nods of fellow unconventional style recognition. After a carefully neutral hello, Anita introduced the two women as Nicola Alford and her PA, Sarah North, who was there to take the notes. Nicola opened the meeting.

"Thank you all for coming and I know none of us, especially Bethany, would have wanted to be here today in these circumstances. Bethany, I have been advised that you are autistic and that you are currently signed off due to mental distress. I also understand that you are a sole householder and that your continuing employment enables you to stay in Perth where you are closer to your support network than you would be if you had to return to your family home. Ashraf has informed me that you have also registered at an autism support service in Perth which would not be available in your home town. My role here today is to make sure that we as your employer minimise any further distress to you, as much as it is to address the allegations against you. For all these reasons, I am taking the unusual step of removing dismissal as an option right away."

Bethany gasped, turning to look at Ash who was nodding and smiling; his relief restrained but tangible. As her emotions rushed over her like a released elastic band pinging back, the memory popped incongruously into her mind that Ash had said Nicola and Sarah were coming by train; a sudden lump rose in her throat as she pictured them travelling over the viaduct where she had been enjoying her peaceful evening walks. Taking in all the faces around the table, even Anita's, she saw unexpected kindness.

"Bethany, I'm sure you will want this meeting to be over with as soon as possible but if you do need to take a break, please let us know. Now, we were going to be considering some remarks which you made to Anita on the day you revealed your plans to her; I understand that an apology has already been tendered via your union representative and I accept that your response was caused by intense emotional shock and distress. Anita and I are both happy to consider that aspect as having been resolved outside of the disciplinary process. I am also satisfied with the evidence which explains your having missed the meeting you were asked to attend; Ashraf's account of your mental state when he came to your home on that day as well as your having since provided a medical certificate from your GP. You have complied fully with all other requests, to the extent of forgoing attending the wedding of two of your colleagues which I understand meant a lot to you. Therefore, today we are only going to be looking at your breach of company protocols by contacting outside agencies without authorisation and by endorsing particular products on behalf of the company within those unauthorised communications."

Adrenalin flooded Bethany's system once again; even with Nicola's mercy up to this point, it all sounded so bad.

"We also need to address the fact that you involved a colleague at another branch, Rhona Flanagan, without telling her that you had not sought authorisation for what you were doing."

So Rhona had been dragged into the investigation. There was no doubt in her mind now that her former friend had deleted her by choice and had reason to hate her. The initial relief dissipated as a sick feeling settled in Bethany's stomach. Ash stepped in, his voice quietly authoritative.

"If I may interject here, Nicola, we put it that the fact Bethany sought advice from Ms Flanagan whom she knew was involved in organising similar events at her own branch demonstrates that she was making attempts to do things the correct way. In Bethany's mind, this was all research and planning; she believed that so long as she did not make any commitments or spend any company money, she was not doing anything wrong. When she spoke with Anita initially about wanting to arrange an anti-bullying event, Anita had commended her for showing initiative; Bethany's autistic focus and literal interpretation caused her to perceive that as consent to do the research she was undertaking. Bethany accepts that she should not have contacted outside agencies or endorsed products without specific authorisation to do so. However, I must remind the meeting that a short time before the misconduct took place, her niece had arrived in the shop in a state of distress having run away as a direct result of prolonged bullying at school. There is no doubt that this affected Bethany's judgement and prevented her from being objective; there was no deliberate attempt or intention to deceive or compromise Ms Flanagan."

"Thank you, Ashraf; I appreciate that, and I wish to reassure you that Ms Flanagan was never accused of any wrongdoing. Bethany, I have indeed been made aware of what had happened with your niece and I am truly sorry that you both had to deal with that crisis. There has never been any question in anyone's mind that your intention was always to do good and to help vulnerable people. However, as you know, there are certain protocols which we cannot allow our employees to circumvent. I am confident that you have learned from your mistake and that you will not repeat it. I must ask you, though, to clarify your reasons for keeping your plans so secret from your colleagues until such a late stage."

Bethany looked at Ash, who nodded. She cleared her throat and sipped more water.

"I was afraid that if I didn't hold on to full ownership of what I was doing, it would fizzle out. I didn't think it would be as important to other people as it was to me and I was afraid that unless I did as much of the work in advance as I possibly could, it would never happen. Of course now it's never going to happen in any form, because I messed up, and so because of me some poor child like Lucy – that's my niece – might never get the help and hope they would have otherwise!"

"Now, let's take a moment here; Bethany, that is an excessively big responsibility to place upon yourself. Have you been told that no anti-bullying event will ever take place here because of what you did?"

"Well, Anita did say that she had been prepared to consider it and now she wasn't. She said, 'Not now; not ever'."

"Anita, is that true?"

"I did say that this unsanctioned event could never go ahead, and yes, I said that I had been prepared to consider the idea up to then but it would never happen now. Looking back, I can see how I may have given the impression that I was ruling out any future anti-bullying event in order to punish Bethany. That was not my intention. I simply needed to make sure that this unauthorised planning was going to stop before it became any more serious a breach. I did think it was a good idea when you first suggested it, Bethany, and I realise now that I should have been clearer about what could and couldn't be done and made a plan with you at the start instead of leaving it so open to interpretation. Believe it or not, I was disappointed about the way things turned out. My hands were tied."

"Thank you, Anita; I appreciate you clarifying that. I am extremely concerned that Bethany, an autistic employee, was sent home alone in distress with a belief that she had prevented children like her niece from getting help. Did anyone check on her welfare?"

"Ashraf did as soon as Bethany failed to turn up for the meeting. The staff were aware that there had been a confrontation between Bethany and me; I forbade them from speculating or from contacting her and arranged to meet with Ashraf, who was not in the shop when the incident happened, at eight thirty the following morning before Bethany was instructed to be there at nine. I was concerned with confidentiality and with possibly compromising any investigation."

"I see. Bethany's safety should have been your first concern, Anita. It gravely worries me that no contact was made until the next morning. There are lessons to be learned here in dealing with distressed employees, regardless of them having done something wrong. Going forward, I am going to recommend autism training and mental health first aid training throughout our management structure. Although I must agree that all parties contacted by Bethany need to be advised that this was unauthorised and that this event will not be able to go ahead, I see no reason to place a ban on such an event, properly arranged, in the future. To my mind, such a ban would be inappropriate, unnecessary and quite frankly an act of psychological cruelty to Bethany given her personal experiences and enhanced empathy. This has been a salutary lesson and a humiliating experience for you, Bethany; not least because we are going to have to make that approach to the people you contacted. Is there anything further you would like to add before I make my recommendations?"

"I would like to apologise once again for my rudeness to Anita and for embarrassing the company. I would also like to add that some reading I have been doing during my time off has led me to believe I may have been in autistic burnout for some time without realising it. With my union representative's agreement, I would like to put that forward as further mitigation, please. I have been struggling with excess fatigue for several years, with medical tests ruling out any physical cause. There are other things like increased sensitivity to noise, making silly mistakes and forgetting things more, taking longer to do things, all of which can be signs of burnout. With hindsight I have realised that I was trying so hard to do something big so that I could feel I had contributed enough to society to be able to allow myself the rest and easing off which my mind and body have been trying to tell me I need. I admit that I did not disclose any of this at work, so I couldn't expect any allowances to be made. I couldn't back it up with any justification, so I didn't think there was any point. I've often been called lazy or a daydreamer, things like that, when I was actually tired and trying to keep up in my head. I haven't been doing well socially; I say the wrong things, pick things up wrongly. I don't fit in and I hardly ever go to anything social because I'm too tired, or because I know that if I do go, I will be too exhausted to do my job properly the next day. I'm sorry, Anita; you're my manager and you shouldn't be finding out about it like this. I always thought I was a bad person and not trying hard enough."

"Oh, Bethany. I honestly had no idea, and Nicola please be assured that Bethany is a valued member of my team who is in fact known for her thoughtfulness and caring attitude to her colleagues as well as her commitment to the job. I should have picked up on at least some of this, enough to realise you were struggling and check in with you."

"Thank you for that. I will share with you that I have some knowledge of autistic burnout through someone close to me and although it would be unethical of me to attempt to confirm it to you, the things you have described give me cause to strongly recommend that you explore this with the autism support service you have joined. When does your medical certificate run out, Bethany?"

"Tomorrow. I have a follow-up appointment with my GP."

"Good. I would suggest that you get another certificate and we can look at an eventual phased return for you, with reasonable adjustments put in place. Now, as you know I will have to consult with my guidance before making a final decision, but I am confident that I will be recommending a written warning. Which would be an unpleasant but necessary formality; I have every faith that you will not do

245

anything like this again. Would you like me to give the decision directly to you, or to Ashraf?"

"To Ash, please. We were hoping it could be done that way."

"Right, that will be arranged. Now, you take it easy for the rest of the day. This has been a traumatic thing for you to have to go through; we're all, and this includes yourself, going to be involved in taking better care of you from now on."

"Thank you so much, Ms Alford. You have been so kind."

"Oh, it's Nicola, please, and you are welcome."

The air had seldom felt so fresh as it did in the moment when Bethany walked out of that dreary building into the sunlight. The hardest part was over; Ash told her how well she had done and counselled her wisely to go home and to spend the rest of the day doing gentle, enjoyable and undemanding activities. Using her jigsaw app and a word game one with beautiful scenic backgrounds on her iPad had always brought her relaxation and pleasure; in between those she read and listened to some of her natural sounds CDs. Despite her expectations of being relentlessly awake until the decision came, she slept.

25

November 2019

It was a warning. Ash texted with the good news as Bethany was leaving for her doctor's appointment. Nicola Alford had been as good as her word and rushed the decision through as quickly as she possibly could. Bethany did not consider herself religious, but she did believe that some sort of good force was out there; she offered up thanks to whatever twist of fate had intervened to put Nicola in charge of her hearing. She had no doubt in her mind that had it been Bruce Farquhar, it would have been a vastly different meeting and quite possibly a different outcome. Ash had insisted that they would have been in an exceedingly difficult position had they dismissed her, once they had checked her work email log and satisfied themselves that no confidential information had been given out. She tried not to think about the message which would be going out to the people with whom she had made contact, telling them about her awful mistake. Ash and Sharon were both right; she needed to put this behind her now. Her doctor shared her relief and agreed to sign her off for another month; with the recognition of her burnout came a subtle physical change as she allowed her body and mind to acknowledge their fatigue. She was surprised by the euphoria she felt; how could it feel this good to give in to being tired all the time? How could it make her step lighter even as she allowed it to feel heavier? Perhaps it was not a case of giving in to anything but of adapting to what was already there; jettisoning some of the excess baggage.

Ash met her for a coffee after work and collected her doctor's note. There was genuine joy in his eyes as he told her how absolutely relieved all her colleagues were to hear that she would be back with them, hopefully before too long. "I didn't want to make you too emotional by telling you this while you were still waiting to hear what would happen", he said, "but Dana and Crevan asked me to let you know that they will be saving their bottle of whisky until you are available to share a dram with them once they get back from honeymoon." Yet again Bethany found her eyes misting over. She had thoroughly enjoyed the tasting sample she was given when she bought the bottle in Inverness; although she still preferred wine, she could see herself learning to better appreciate this national drink in all its complexity. After all, she did not see alcohol as a means of getting drunk; good quality malt whisky was to be savoured, not wasted on blurred faculties and this was in keeping with how she liked to enjoy a drink. How special it was that Dana and Crevan wanted to share a dram with her. A huge rush of affection for all her colleagues, including Anita and even Stacey, spread through her with a warmth reminiscent of that golden inner glow in the convivial shop in Inverness.

As expected, Sharon resisted saying "I told you so". She skipped all that and went straight to "Get yourself on a train and get through to Inverbrudock; we've got some celebrating to do!" The details were finalised and tomorrow she would be doing precisely that. Bethany used an app on her phone to order a pizza to collect; there was nothing quite like the sensory hit of spicy pepperoni, perfectly blended and textured cheese, and darkly sweet tomato puree to fill and settle her stomach which no longer needed to clench with fear. While her pizza was being prepared, she walked alongside the Tay and across the curving viaduct, her footsteps on its metal walkway resonating with the chime of optimism returning to her soul.

That night, she slept soundly; cradled in that deep relaxation which came from releasing fear and tension the magnitude of which was not fully apparent until after the event. If she dreamed, she had no memory of it when she awoke into a crystal bright November morning.

Staying in the other half of the house with the narrow forks was going to feel interesting, that was for certain. Charlene, she was assured, was excited at the opportunity to host an overnight guest whom she knew was a happy and bolstering presence in Brandon's life as well as an increasingly cherished friend to her. Sharon's message had gone on to say that Charlene's one concern was whether there would be more noise from next door; Bethany suspected that they would be too busy catching up, celebrating and looking forward to be too disadvantaged by any unwanted sound effects. She packed her overnight bag, wrapping her nightshirt and a change of clothes around the special bottle of wine from Exel Wines and high quality olive oil from Provender Brown which she had been out earlier to pick up as thankyou gifts for Charlene inviting her to stay at such short notice. Toiletries and her phone charger completed the necessities for her night away. Satisfied that she had everything she needed and was leaving her flat secure, she messaged Sharon to tell her which train she expected to be catching and the time she would arrive in Inverbrudock. This time, she would be checking in on her social networking pages and the happy emojis would be flowing from the keypad.

With her ticket safely tucked into her phone case, Bethany walked out of the station booking office as people were arriving off a train from Inverness. She still had lots of time until her train to Inverbrudock, so she stood back to allow them to pass through the concourse area before making her way through to the other side of the station. The jolt of familiarity came too late for her to avoid being seen; of course, not having been at work she had no way of knowing that Rhona was going to be in Perth.

"Bethany! Hi. Look, I have to get to…"

"Rhona, I understand; I know this is awkward for you too, but I've had the, ah, meeting now and I want to apologise to you. I involved you in something which was my own personal ambition, for a variety of reasons, and I should have told you that I hadn't had it approved yet. I am so sorry for any trouble I have caused you."

"I appreciate you saying that, Bethany; I hope that things work out for you. I admit I was disappointed to learn that you hadn't gone through the proper channels, but I do understand why you asked for my advice."

"Thank you, Rhona. I realise that I could have put you in a difficult position. I don't know what else to say except that I truly am sorry. I got completely carried away with the need to do something about bullying because a few weeks after I saw you when I was in Inverness with Sharon that day, my niece turned up at the shop in a really bad way. Lucy is autistic too and she has been severely bullied; on the day she came here, she had been goaded to the point of a meltdown which had been filmed on somebody's phone. That wasn't your problem, though; I shouldn't have risked getting you into trouble."

"Oh Bethany, that's awful; I am sorry to hear that, and I understand better now why you did it. How old is Lucy; is she all right now?"

"She's fourteen. She's getting there, gradually. Her mother is Sharon's sister; she and I never got on but we are pulling together now to help her to accept Lucy's autism and to be on her side for who she actually is, not for the daughter Louise wanted her to be."

"I'm glad; I honestly am. The thing is, my dad was seriously ill in hospital when Anita called about the issue and when Frank asked me to come to the office, I thought he was going to give me bad news. Which wasn't your problem, just as your family situation wasn't my problem."

"Oh Rhona, I'm so... I don't even know what to say. I can't imagine how distressing that must have been for you. No wonder you... Your dad, is he..."

"He's over the worst. Thank you. Look, I need to go now otherwise I'll be late. I might see you in the shop after my meeting."

"I'm actually signed off now; apparently I've got a potential case of autistic burnout and I'm working through that, figuring out how I'm going to deal with it going forward. I'm on my way to meet up with Sharon in Inverbrudock. A bit of a quiet celebration of still having a job."

"Oh! I see. Well, take care of yourself, Bethany."

"You too, Rhona."

As she watched her colleague walk away, Bethany knew in her heart that there would be no renewed contact request on social media. She and Rhona would speak at work; they would be cordial and sincerely wish one another well, but their personal friendship would not pass this test. It was not meant to continue into this new stage of her life; with sad but newly feasible acceptance, she let it go. Once more she found herself processing an intersection of bad timing and Weren't To Know; the familiar surge of shame and overwhelming anxiety slowed into a calmer, more structured and logical response.

She recognised that she was feeling resentment at having been caught out in hapless timing again despite trying so hard to be a positive in others' lives; she recognised that she genuinely cared about the distress which had been caused to Rhona, however unwittingly, by her unwise choices. She understood that both distinct streams of emotion were real, and both were valid; neither cancelled out the other. She understood that their conflated existence along with their intensity had a disproportionate but nonetheless real effect on her, caused by her neurology which was not of her choosing, though how she used this understanding was something in which she did have a choice.

She understood that every situation which had an effect on her was thus by definition partly about her; that acknowledging and processing it did not mean she deserved to be charged with making it ALL about her. She wasn't even claiming a fifty-fifty split; even if it was a tiny bit about her, she still had the right to deal with that, with support if needed. As did every other person; she was not applying the principle exclusively to herself. Society so often polarised things in the exact way it was so fond of accusing autistic people of "always" doing!

She understood that this may be the beginning of healing.

26

November 2019

Sun glinted on the Aberdeen train as it pulled into Platform 2 and Bethany recognised the pointed nose and long white carriages of an Inter7City; the newly refurbished 125 trains about which Brandon and Charlene got so excited. Pulling out her phone to take some photographs for them as it glided to a halt, she couldn't help being reminded of a blue point Siamese cat. Its silhouetted landmarks from the seven Scottish cities darkened the engines and a small part of each sleek silvery carriage in deepening blue grey, reminiscent of the shading and markings on that breed. All it needed was the bright blue eyes. Bethany had to resist the urge to pet it as she stood well back waiting for it to stop and the new push button doors to be activated. There was unquestionably something special about these trains and this new phase in their working life carried a pervasive sense of a new beginning at a stage where one would not have been expected. Perhaps if she could come to terms with her burnout and adapt her life accordingly, she too could have a new start and learn to enjoy her trips out with less, or more manageable, anxiety. Having no anxious feelings at all was not a reasonable or practicable goal; she would be happy to have what anxiety was there equalled or superseded by more pleasant feelings at least some of the time.

"You got a refurb!"; Sharon had clearly been spending more time around Charlene and Brandon too as she practically danced on the platform at Inverbrudock. She had become even closer to them since her mother's house was sold and, like Bethany, was enjoying sharing the things which brought them such enthusiasm. Hugging her cousin tightly, Bethany felt the tension and upset of their last meeting drain away.

"Come on; let's go to the pub."

The Fulmar's Nest was quiet on a midweek afternoon; they easily found a table overlooking the sea. Greeting Helen behind the bar who was lovingly polishing the nautical themed brass fittings so like those in the hotel, Sharon introduced Bethany who felt the usual warm glow when Helen said she had heard a lot about her. Except that it was not quite the same; for once it lacked the stubbornly intrusive edge of "uh oh, what exactly have they heard?" Under no illusion that those thoughts would never come back, she found herself able to simply enjoy this break. Even if she never felt so anxiously on display again, though, the blue hair was staying. Calling out thanks to Helen and clinking her wine glass against her cousin's, some habits still died hard.

"Of course, I'm not going to be checking us in on social media in a pub or posting anything about having a drink. My work would understand me going to see my cousin who is my main support, but partying on sick leave wouldn't look great! See, I'm doing it again; getting in there proving that I've thought of it before anybody can give me a pre-emptive warning. I should know you better than that, shouldn't I?!"

"Oh, don't worry about that. Nobody expects you to change overnight and there's nothing wrong with thinking out loud! There are years of reasons for everything you feel and all these defences you've built, Beth. If you need to say that, just say it. It's honest conversation and it's a valid point; where's the harm?"

"You have no idea what a breath of fresh air that is. As is this beautiful view!"

The sea was relatively calm today, no more than a faint frosting of white tips on the barely perceptible waves. Far out, a tanker glowed brick red in the low afternoon sun.

"I saw Rhona at the station. She was down for another meeting. I don't want to go on about the whole work saga, not today, but I got to explain to her about Lucy and she got to explain to me that when she was called into the office to be asked about my having phoned her, she thought she was going to get bad news because her dad was in hospital. That and not realising that I had other motives besides personal ambition was why she unfriended me, I gather. I didn't ask her directly; it seemed a bit childish. Anyway, she accepted my apology for involving her and she showed concern for Lucy so that was fair enough. I don't think it will ever be the same though. Sometimes you know that a friendship has run its course and that was more closure than a lot of people get."

"You have come a long way, Beth. I was annoyed that Rhona hadn't stood by you when you said in one of your messages that she'd deleted you, I must admit, though like yourself I did wonder whether she had been told to if she was involved in the investigation itself. As you say, though, it's time for celebrating. Though I do have one thing to confess to you which is tied in to the whole workplace protocols issue. When I most unfairly jumped down your throat for talking about breaching them, it was because I hadn't been honest with Lynsey about something and I was being a bit hypocritical talking about you being secretive. The thing is, I'm fairly sure that I'm heading towards having something going with one of our regular guests. Their name is Paulie; they're non-binary. Oh, it feels so good to say that out loud! About something possibly developing between us, that is. The non-binary identity is important, but incidental to how I feel; they are Paulie. They / them pronouns are simply part of introducing them."

"Oh, Shaz! That's such wonderful news! If anyone deserves happiness, it's you!"

"Thank you; that means so much. You're the first person I've told apart from Lynsey. I owe it to you in a way, because I couldn't keep on hiding it from her once I'd had such a go at you for being secretive at work when you had your own valid reasons for it the same as I did. Anyway, Lynsey wasn't the least bit bothered. She said that while it might be an issue if we worked for one of the big chains, she knows me well enough to know that I would always be professional at work, that I would never take financial advantage of the hotel by giving anything away without permission and that I would never favour one guest to the detriment of another. The fact I'd been upfront with her before anything could happen was important to her, though she did also laugh and say that it was pretty obvious there was a spark between us!"

"That honestly is so lovely, Shaz. Lynsey sounds like the coolest boss. Anita's actually all right too; the way she was at the meeting proved that she will be there for me or anybody else when it counts. She'd had no idea that I'd been having problems with fatigue. I did apologise to her for that being the time and place she found out about it; it wasn't the best scenario to drop that on her, in front of a regional manager who was already less than impressed by my having been allowed to leave in distress and nobody check on me until the next morning."

"I have to say, Beth, I'm less inclined to forgive Anita for that than you are. Anything could have happened to you the state you were in that night from what you told me afterwards. If she does right by you from now on, though, that's something."

"We always do forgive people who hurt us more easily than we forgive those who hurt our loved ones."

"Exactly. That's my phone ringing, just a second. Oh, it's Sandra."

Aunt Sandra! Bethany had not heard their aunt's voice for a long time, though they were in touch on social media and she was always interested to hear how George and Joseph were getting on. Memories of them as happy, giggling boys at Christmas always made her smile and took some of the edge off her strained recollections of the house with the narrow forks. Whatever Sandra had called Sharon about, it was clearly good news.

"Bethany's here! Yes, it's quiet in here right now; the signal's good in here. Would you like a quick word, Beth?"

Bethany appreciated Sharon's consideration of the environment; accommodating her struggle to process what was being said on the phone if there was background noise. Mobile phones could be especially difficult. The pub was still quiet; the hum of the fruit machine in the corner and the distant cries of the seagulls were not going to stand in the way of a chance for her to talk with her favourite aunt.

"Hey, Sandra!"

"Bethany! It's so lovely to hear your voice! I saw your post about being on your way to Inverbrudock so I'm glad I caught you both together where you're able to speak. I was calling to say that Joseph and Barry got their application approved to adopt so they're going to have a wee boy."

"Oh, Sandra, that's wonderful news! I'm so happy for all of them. He'll be a lucky boy to have them as his dads. I will congratulate them myself when they announce it of course; until then, it's so good to hear it from you and to be able to congratulate you and Dave on becoming grandparents again."

"Thank you so much, Bethany. Are you keeping well yourself?"

"Yes, thanks; I'm doing away and enjoying a bit of quality time with Sharon, and Charlene and Brandon of course." Now was not the time to tell Sandra any more detail than that.

"Oh yes, I remember them being next door to Carole. Have they still got that big friendly cat?"

"Cheminot? Oh yes, he's thriving. I'm staying over tonight so I expect he'll come and sleep on my bed. I hope so anyway! He's such a sweetie. How are George and Jessie and Hannah?"

"Oh, they're all grand. Hannah is turning into quite a cook. She loves trying new recipes and thinking of creative twists to them; impressive for a twelve-year-old."

"She'd get on well with Charlene then! I'll hand you back to Sharon now and let you catch up with her; it's been lovely hearing your voice. Love to Dave too!"

"And to you. He's come in now in fact. Dave! I'm on the phone to Sharon about Joseph and Barry's news and Bethany's with her! She says hello."

Bethany could hear her uncle's enthusiastic reaction; she glowed inside to think of the warm extended family into which Joseph and Barry's son was being brought to enjoy a loved and cherished childhood. Handing the phone back to Sharon, she raised her glass to the North Sea as the late afternoon colours danced on the surface of her wine and began to transform the sky.

Finishing their drinks, the two of them said goodbye to Helen and set out on the short walk to Charlene and Brandon's. Both were more than ready for a good meal from Vinnie's chip shop; the plan was that they would go to the house, Charlene would show Bethany her room and she could put her overnight bag in there then they would walk along the promenade to get their food. It was already getting dark and the cold bite of approaching winter was a growing hint in the still gentle night air of late autumn.

They heard the commotion before they even saw the van outside next door. The Slaughter brothers arguing was nothing new, but this seemed to be more serious than usual and the main cause of disagreement appeared to be them blaming each other for not loading up the van quickly enough. As they got closer, the two women realised that Charlene was outside watching them too.

"Come ON, Gordy! I'm telling you; we're not spending another night in this house. It's possessed or something!"

258

"Shut up, Stu; you sound like a scared wee lassie!"

"Boys, that's enough! Get the suite into the van; that will do for tonight and we'll come back for the rest in the daylight. I must admit I'm not happy to be here another minute after dark. I never thought I'd say this but there's definitely something in that house that doesn't want us there."

Charlene's voice called across:

"What's happened? Tegan, are you OK?"

"She's fine. Mind your own business. We're moving out. This house is…"

"Daz! Don't go around saying it to the neighbours; you'll get us locked up!"

"Right, whatever's gone wrong in the house, when I see a teenage girl crying and being hustled out of her home I want to know if she needs help."

"Look, we're going and that's that. You'd be in a state too if you had doors slamming and taps turning themselves on and off right in front of you spraying you with cold water. Not to mention trip switches going off every time you tried to listen to a bit of music."

Charlene, Sharon and Bethany all smiled wryly at Mrs Slaughter's understatement of "listen to a bit of music".

"Good luck living next door to that. The landlord's going to need to arrange an exorcism or something. I never believed in it before but there's something going on in there."

The thought occurred to Bethany that his landlord insurance was unlikely to cover the cost of an exorcism; for the time being, she kept the thought to herself. Judging the volume of her voice was always hit and miss; no adult in their forties should still need to be shushed. With the circumspect self protection which would always be in her, she held her peace and watched.

Tegan's wavering voice called out to Charlene: "I'm sorry for laughing at your brother for liking trains when we

259

moved here." Before Charlene could respond, two of the boys – it was impossible to tell which ones in the chaos – steered their sister gently but firmly away. The van doors were slammed shut and it screeched off, followed by the Slaughters' car which rounded off the surreal scene with a textbook comedy backfire. What would happen next, Bethany wondered in astonishment and still not out loud; somebody run out to hit them over their heads with a frying pan and slip on a banana skin?

Charlene broke the shocked silence: "So did that really happen? We didn't all imagine it; they're going?"

The three of them looked at one another. This time Bethany did voice the thought that had struck her; in fact, had struck them all.

"Harriet?"

The same instinct made all of them look up. A light remained on in the attic.

"I'll try to catch them tomorrow and make sure they switch that off if they do come back for the rest of their things"; Charlene attempted to restore some feeling of normality as they went inside. Cheminot brushed against Bethany's ankles and followed as Charlene showed her the cosy spare room on the first floor where she would be sleeping. A well worn but still sturdy light purple candlewick bedspread covered the single bed; a modern but classically styled pine chest of drawers complemented it well. A lamp with an opaque off-white shade over a round copper coloured touch base sat on top of the small nightstand which matched the chest of drawers. It had everything she needed for a comfortable night's rest. Her gifts of wine and olive oil were received with appreciation of her thoughtful choice; there was little else to unpack, which was a good thing since everyone was now more than ready for something to eat.

Brandon and Charlene's orders noted, Sharon and Bethany took the familiar walk along to Vinnie's chippy while their friends got the table ready and put the plates to warm. Vinnie recognised Bethany for her friendly smile as well as her hair; as always, an extra bit of fish was included for Cheminot. "He's such a soft touch when it comes to cats, it's a wonder he sells enough fish to people to turn a profit", mused Sharon affectionately as they walked back to the Sutherlands' home.

"Hey, Shaz, look; the light's off now in the attic of your old house!"

"Well, so it is. Isn't that interesting?"

"Yes, isn't it just."

The meal and wine, which was soon followed by the bottles both Sharon and Charlene had provided, lent the evening the gentle opalescent sheen of a celebration long awaited but given a softer tone by the need for processing and sleep. Brandon remarked admiringly on Bethany's luck in having gotten an Inter7City train for her journey; it was still a matter of chance when and where they appeared in the schedules as the refurbishment programme continued. He was looking forward, albeit with mixed emotions, to seeing the new Azuma trains passing by on the LNER services to Aberdeen later in the month having seen them on test runs; the Highland Chieftain to Inverness would also become an Azuma soon after that. The loss of the 125s from the long distance services would be poignant and they were all thankful to see them continue in Scotland with the Inter7City project. Sharon was working a late shift the next day; not having the day off after an evening get-together with wine seemed not to faze her in the slightest. After their conversation in the pub, Bethany had an inkling as to why that might be. She felt a strong sense of things coming full circle, falling at last into their rightful pattern. Settling into her comfortable bed, she had no more than a few moments to register the soft thud of Cheminot jumping up beside her and stroke his silky fur before his purring sent her off to sleep.

In the morning, sunlight sparkled on a greenish silver sea. Charlene looked up from her cooking as Bethany and Cheminot padded in; both hungry, one with distinctly better table manners than the other. Brandon was already up, finishing his orange juice as he played a game on his phone. Over breakfast, the main topic of conversation was what was going to happen next door. Would the Slaughters definitely take the rest of their things and go, and who would move in next? The relief at the departure was already tinged with the dread return of uncertainty; Bethany felt it deeply for her friends. Charlene had confided in her over several messages, not wanting to lean on Sharon since it was her family household who had unavoidably initiated that uncertainty by selling up and Charlene didn't want her to feel bad. Besides, there was no substitute for the input of another autistic person to help her to understand and support her brother. She had described watching helplessly as Brandon became more withdrawn and subdued; his sleep badly disrupted by the anxiety about who was going to move in, then by the noisy habits of the Slaughters. The two halves of this house so desperately needed to be in harmony again.

27

November 2019

Lizzie O'Sullivan sighed as she drank the last of her lukewarm tea and sat back in her chair in the cramped utility room she used as a home office. There was a certain desperation now to her searches through the house rental listings every day. They were almost halfway through November now; the chances of finding anywhere in time to be in before Christmas were not looking good. With Michael due to retire in January, all they wanted was to find a bigger place outside of a city environment; still within reach of Glasgow for visiting their friends, but somewhere quieter where they would have the space to let Niamh and Jordan move in permanently. They would be so much better off with the support of the whole family available. Michael's retirement bonus plus Lizzie's home based work would allow them to pay a deposit and rent until this house was sold; perhaps if they found the right place, a landlord may even be open to them buying them out some time in the future. Jordan's autism and dyslexia were causing him such stress, the sensory overload of living in a busy town in Fife where he had to spend time in various after school clubs until Niamh could get home from her job in Dundee was becoming unsustainable. Even if they moved somewhere which would mean a change of schools, hard as that would be, the benefits of Lizzie and Michael being there for both of them full time would be incalculable. She had been focusing her search on the East Coast of Fife and as far up as Stonehaven; again nothing suitable was showing up there in those areas today. Deflated, she resigned herself to looking further afield once more in the slim hope that something would show up in another area which was so perfect it would make Niamh consider the added upheaval of having to change jobs worth it. Lizzie decided that a fresh cup of tea would bolster her morale; trying not to think about how long it could take before they found something suitable, she went to put the kettle on.

Sitting down again with her tea, she decided that next she would click on the listings for the Borders. As she moved the mouse to do so, the computer screen did one of those annoying jumps they do every so often, causing her to click on the area where she had already looked. Shaking her head in frustration, she was about to return to the main menu when her hand stopped in mid-air. There was a property there which had not been listed when she was last in that screen. It must have been uploaded in those few minutes she had been away making her cup of tea; she certainly would have noticed it if it had been there earlier.

Inverbrudock. She had heard of the town but didn't know a lot about it; looking at the map she saw that it was a short way north of Arbroath, well within commuting distance for Niamh. The property was on the seafront and appeared to be semidetached; half of what looked as though it may have been one big house originally. Five bedrooms plus fully floored and insulated attic space. Five bedrooms was more than they needed but they could afford the rent and it would mean that Ian, Maureen and their families could visit, helping even more with relationship building for Jordan. Maureen in particular being able to visit more often would be a huge bonus; Niamh missed her sister terribly and Inverbrudock was nearer to where she lived than Niamh's current home in Fife was. Lizzie noted that access to the attic stairway was from one of the bedrooms on the second floor; her imagination began to take flight as she pictured Jordan having a sensory area up there. In a house like this, especially if they had good neighbours, perhaps he could once again become the happy boy who had always enjoyed fishing with his grandfather and helping her in the kitchen.

The landlord was offering entry by mid December. Michael had leave to use up and could commute from there for a few weeks; Inverbrudock was on the Glasgow to Aberdeen railway line with a good frequent service. They could be in by Christmas.

Finding out more about the town could wait; Lizzie had learned in life that there was a lot to be said from going with her gut instincts. She shuddered to think that if it hadn't been for her computer screen jumping and making her click where she hadn't intended to, she would not have been looking at that area again until the following day, by which time how likely was it that a property like this would still have been available? It had been agreed that she should go ahead and arrange a viewing as soon as possible rather than risk missing out by waiting to consult the family if a good enough property came up; this one definitely qualified.

Setting aside her well earned cup of tea, Lizzie picked up the phone.

Epilogue

December 2019

Light flowed in gently transitioning waves of colour around the branches of the Christmas tree and the warm smell of gingerbread wafted from a candle in a jar, safely set back on a high shelf. The family laughed and joked as they carried plates and serving dishes through to place on the table, which was covered with a gold edged cream easy wipe cloth. Newly opened presents and the last remaining partly unpacked boxes from the move dotted the edges of the big room, creating a feeling of unhurried, happy chaos. Ten-year-old Jordan sat at the table; his favourite soft toy dog close by on a bean bag; safe from any spillage but within reach for him to pet it. Plenty of room had been allowed when setting his place so that he could have a couple of his stim toys on the table beside him to offset the differentness of the festive meal. A box of crackers sat unopened, ready for the others to enjoy later when he was away having some cherished downtime in his sensory room, three floors away from the unpredictable loud noises of the crackers being pulled. His cousin Jack had promised to save him a party hat and a prize.

The house was right again; its energy vibrated on the rare, hidden frequency of a lasting and stabilised peace. Watching, the part of her which had never been able to rest began to dissipate, seamlessly and painlessly, into the flow of all lives.

Her energy would endure, shaped and strengthened by the needs she had found and flowed into on a whole subatomic level for which living humans had no words yet in order to intervene. She would continue in the structure of the empathy, sense of justice and fierce urge to protect the vulnerable which had absorbed and made good use of that energy ever since it was fully harnessed by the lonely unease of a six-year-old out of her depth in this house.

People had generally heard about those aspects of what they called paranormal activity which more directly affected physical things, such as when she raised the floorboard so that the builder would find her diary to carry her story to her family, and stopping all of the loud noises in the house which so upset her great-great-nephew. As the need for change in the house grew, so did her manifestations. Frightening, without ever harming, the teenage girl had been a necessary by-product of that; the girl's energy had been on the cusp, still capable of being pulled towards better frequencies. Those aspects of intervention which had become possible with the technology of the new millennium were perhaps not so well known, yet. Stopping the video of the tormented teenager's meltdown from uploading; making an electronic alert appear to send the prefect with the brightly lit caring aura to where she would bring justice upon those who had deliberately inflicted harm. Reaching into the beating heart of computer algorithms to make the right information appear to the lost, disconnected woman that six-year-old who had struggled in the house with the narrow forks had become, so that she would realise what was happening to her. Manipulating systems so that the compassionate lady who would understand and give the right outcome was put in control of her disciplinary hearing. Making sure that the right new family came to this house.

The attic room which had been her sanctuary had become one again. The kind man who had bought the house to rent out had arranged for an electrician to put in sockets so that colour changing lamps and starscape projectors could light the sloping ceiling with soothing colours. Plump cushions were scattered across the floor, giving the boy a soft place in which to curl up or stretch out; looking up at the sky as she had almost a century ago. She could move on now; she would always be connected, but she was free.

She was wearing her beloved red coat again! She was back in the form she occupied in those days before she passed; exactly as she had been for that moment when the visiting cousin came to this room. The boy looked up and smiled with unquestioning acceptance.

"Hi! I live here now. My name is Jordan O'Sullivan. What's yours?"

"Hello! My name is Harriet Sutherland. You may call me Hattie."

"Did you live here before?"

"Yes. I lived here in my time, and now it is your time. I came to wish you a Merry Christmas and tell you that you will be safe here. You're going to feel better. I had to come and tell you that; it is time for me to move on now."

"Oh, OK. Thank you. It was nice to meet you, Hattie."

He waved casually, quite as though he were seeing off a schoolfriend at the front gate. His light projectors captured his attention once more. She floated gently out of his thoughts.

The ice particles in the midwinter sky aligned into tiny latticed prisms, catching and holding the light as it fell in curtains of deep turquoise, then teal, then blue. Orange shimmered below her at the horizon as she swam upwards; the glass of the skylight giving no more resistance than the air into which she merged. The glittering crystals caught her up into the endless sweeping colours of infinity.

Author's Notes

The idea for this story initially came to me when I was visiting my parents, who are nothing like Bethany's family, over Christmas 2018. They have a good set of dinner cutlery with narrow three-pronged forks which only gets used at Christmas. Although eating with them was not a big problem for me and I was always doing so in our own family home with only my parents and one set of grandparents, it came to my mind quite how difficult it could potentially be for an autistic child in circumstances more like those which I created for Bethany. I had a sudden vivid image of the already frequently misunderstood and scared child nervously asking her mother if they were going to the house with the narrow forks again and so the first part of the story was born.

The closure which Sharon, the childhood ally I wished I had, facilitates for Bethany with regard to that part of the story was already in my mind when I shared a special train journey home with my dear friends Lyndon (Dins) and Kathleen, on whom Brandon and Charlene are based. Cheminot the cat is a complete invention; he simply strolled into my imagination with his tail up and twitching, already purring and bringing the warmth a ginger cat brings to any story. Kathleen's warmly evocative post on a social media site about their plans being settled; that they would get some chips in Perth before joining the Highland Chieftain train to Inverness, then the joyous journey the three of us spent together, resonated with the feelgood easy-going vibe I had in mind for this wonderfully contrasting episode in the adult Bethany's return to the house. I am forever grateful for Dins and Kathleen being part of my life; we are family.

For some time, that closure was the end of the story as it existed in my mind. Once I began to get serious about writing it to publish, I knew that it had to become something longer and more layered. Harriet came about because I love a ghost story especially involving hidden stairs and attics, but also because I wanted to include a reminder that autism has always been around, including in girls and thus in the women those girls would grow up to be. The paranormal activities I ascribe to Harriet's spirit are wish fulfilment; interventions we could all do with at times in a world which can be so difficult to navigate. I leave it to you, the reader, to make your own choices as to whether they are a bit of fantasy for which you need to suspend disbelief, or whether they are in fact entirely plausible. I know which I believe; all opinions are valid!

Time passed; commitments and fatigue did their combined thing and it was my privilege of being in a suitable situation during the Covid19 lockdown of 2020 which eventually made it possible for me to knuckle down and get this written. I had originally intended to set the house of the title in Arbroath; I knew I wanted it to be somewhere on the East Coast between Dundee and Aberdeen and my first proper visit to Arbroath in December 2019 settled that. Of course the lockdown, while providing the time and space I needed to get writing, also precluded any further travel for research into my setting so I created Inverbrudock; a small, completely fictitious town to the north of Arbroath. All businesses there are entirely made up and not based on any real establishment. Bethany's employer is also entirely fictitious and no connection to any real bookshop chain or its staff disciplinary procedures should be inferred. Marydean is a fictitious area of Edinburgh and the school attended by Lucy is not based on any real school. Other businesses mentioned in Perth and Inverness are real.

The Autism Initiatives one stop shops in Inverness for the Highlands, Perth, and Edinburgh are of course entirely real and the reason for my writing. They provide invaluable, autism aware and accepting support in a wide variety of life situations as well as offering groups and drop-ins. These are the settings in which the shattered pieces are put back together when real life plays out without the intervention of a benign spirit like Harriet: when the meltdown video or cruel post gets onto the Internet; when the bullies are never caught in the act; when the tough, inflexible manager chairs the disciplinary hearing; when the noisy, intimidating neighbours do not move on. Like Bethany, any autistic adult is welcome to register for their services and use them as and when needed with no expectation of committing to any activities which are not what they are looking for.

http://highlandoss.org.uk/

http://perthoss.org.uk/

http://www.number6.org.uk/

Autism Rights Group Highland (ARGH) is also entirely real and does highly regarded, strong and helpful work in group advocacy. It is entirely made up of autistic people.

http://www.arghighland.co.uk/

The books by Keelan LaForge which Bethany recommends to her colleague Rhona have proved invaluable to me as they made me realise as nothing else ever had that I had become severely psychologically abusive to myself, reminiscent of how her protagonist's partner gradually drags her down. These books show the processes involved so clearly and illustrate what sort of thing we all need to be looking for if we are concerned about anyone, including about ourselves. Keelan's work can be found at the following link:

https://www.amazon.co.uk/His-Mighty-Hand-3-Book/dp/B07MNT56FW/ref=sr_1_10?dchild=1&keywords=Keelan+LaForge&qid=1588523444&sr=8-10

I have used some dramatic licence to give both Bethany and Lucy the ability to come up with witty comebacks and erudite explanations instantly in response to challenging situations. The reality is often quite different for autistic people under stress, resulting in greater misunderstanding and even violence. We are more likely to freeze or blurt out something which sounds inappropriate, rude or aggressive. The voice I have given to my characters is that which I wish I were able to summon up on the spot; its use here is intended to help the reader to better understand where another person might be coming from should they see us in such a situation in real life. During and after an incident on her birthday, Bethany gives some pointers on how best to offer help if you believe it is needed. For a more comprehensive and constructive insight into this, encompassing other disabilities which attract the same kind of unwanted intervention, please check out the Twitter campaign #JustAskDontGrab (note no apostrophe as hashtags do not accept punctuation), created by Dr Amy Kavanagh; a visually impaired autistic woman. Amy's blog Cane Adventures is a useful resource for first-hand accounts of accessibility issues:

https://caneadventures.blog/

A lot of information is available online about autistic burnout, written for and by autistic people. These are two examples:

An Autistic Burnout: Kieran Rose; theautisticadvocate.com, 21st May 2018 (Warning: Includes descriptions of suicidal thoughts)

https://www.google.com/url?sa=t&source=web&cd=5&ved=2ahUKEwi9_ozXi5jpAhXEWhUIHQYaBjoQFjAEegQIARAB&url=https%3A%2F%2Ftheautisticadvocate.com%2F2018%2F05%2Fan-autistic-burnout%2F&usg=AOvVaw1RzuMj15vRwnpvEtVv7n76

Interview with Dora Raymaker by Fergus Murray; Thinking Person's Guide to Autism, 29th August 2019

http://www.thinkingautismguide.com/2019/08/autistic-burnout-interview-with.html

Dr Emily Lovegrove is an autistic woman based in Wales who has long experience of developing anti-bullying strategies with autistic people in mind. Her book published in May 2020, "Autism, Bullying and Me" is written primarily for people around Lucy's age. Her website, thebullyingdoctor.com has more information:

https://www.google.com/url?sa=t&source=web&cd=&ved=2ahUKEwj4pPqt0sTpAhUzShUIHR31DiAQFjAFegQIAhAB&url=http%3A%2F%2Fwww.thebullyingdoctor.com%2F&usg=AOvVaw07YgUQOrA1I-N251jRcOgT

For general advice and resources on bullying:

Scotland: RespectMe.org.uk

https://www.google.com/url?sa=t&source=web&cd=1&ved=2ahUKEwi-oYbL65fpAhXRN8AKHc6-

C_sQFjAAegQIAxAB&url=https%3A%2F%2Frespectme
.org.uk%2F&usg=AOvVaw1p7RvabXCEFUc3JxjyaYZN

Northern Ireland: Anti-Bullying Forum

https://www.ncb.org.uk/northern-ireland/evidence-and-impact/northern-ireland-anti-bullying-forum

England and Wales: Anti-Bullying Alliance

https://www.anti-bullyingalliance.org.uk/

I wrote Paulie as non-binary with no indication of whether they present as male or female in order to demonstrate that identity is whole and valid without having to specify male or female at all, but it is important to note that some non-binary people present as more overtly one gender than the other, or entirely one gender. Some use gender specific pronouns; some prefer they / them; some use more than one set of pronouns and others use rarer non gender specific pronouns. The important thing is to ask and respect the answer. For support or more information on how to be an ally to the LGBTQIA+ community:

www.lgbt.foundation

Transgender and non-binary page, LGBT Foundation:

https://www.google.com/url?sa=t&source=web&cd=&ved=2ahUKEwjUrNXwrtvpAhXAVBUIHdmVA80QFjAj egQICRAB&url=https%3A%2F%2Flgbt.foundation%2F who-we-help%2Ftrans-people%2Fnon-binary&usg=AOvVaw2YIA70GdWo2xpeDO8w1aXU

Asexuality:

https://www.asexuality.org/

I am thankful to you for reading this book but there are many non-white creatives out there who do not have the unearned privilege I do. No words of mine can or should tell their stories. Racism is still a major issue in our society and it intersects, often brutally, with other types of prejudice such as ableism and homophobia. I urge you to learn from campaigns such as #BlackLivesMatter and seek out sources of the work of black, brown and indigenous artists, such as:

UK: Blacknet:

https://www.blacknet.co.uk/

USA: Black Creatives Directory:

www.distinctlydc.com

All endorsements are my own, made as a private individual. All links are active at the time of publication.

Blessed Be,

Kat Highland

Printed in Great Britain
by Amazon